M≥

D0913284

APR 0 3 2024

Tanar clamped an arm around the Korsar's head and turning
swiftly, hurled the man heavily to the ground.

TANAR
of PELLUCIDAR

By
EDGAR RICE BURROUGHS

Introduction to the Bison Books Edition by
PAUL COOK

Frontispiece by
PAUL F. BERDANIER

UNIVERSITY OF NEBRASKA PRESS
LINCOLN AND LONDON

FIC SF BURROUGHS
Tanar of Pellucidar /
35000094464681
MAIN

Introduction to the Bison Books Edition © 2006 by the
Board of Regents of the University of Nebraska
All rights reserved
Manufactured in the United States of America
⊗

First Nebraska paperback printing: 2006

Library of Congress Cataloging-in-Publication Data
Burroughs, Edgar Rice, 1875–1950.
Tanar of Pellucidar / Edgar Rice Burroughs; introduction
to the Bison Books edition by Paul Cook; frontispiece by
Paul F. Berdanier.—Bison Books ed.
p. cm.—(Bison frontiers of imagination)
ISBN-13: 978-0-8032-6257-7 (pbk.: alk. paper)
ISBN-10: 0-8032-6257-4 (pbk.: alk. paper)
1. Earth—Core—Fiction. I. Title. II. Series.
PS3503.U687T2 2006
813'.52—dc22   2006009256

This Bison Books edition follows the original in beginning the
prologue on arabic page 11; no material has been omitted.

Introduction to the Bison Books Edition

PAUL COOK

By the time Edgar Rice Burroughs (1875–1950) published *Tanar of Pellucidar* in 1929, he was already well established as one of America's most beloved writers of popular fiction. His career as an author began in 1911 after a series of failed business ventures compelled him to turn to his first love, writing. Burroughs first found success when he sold *Under the Moons of Mars* (later entitled *A Princess of Mars* for book publication in 1917) to *All-Story* in 1912, in which he introduced the first of his major heroes, John Carter. Tarzan, perhaps Burroughs's greatest character, also made his initial appearance in 1912, in *Tarzan of the Apes*.

For about two decades Burroughs managed to write four to five books a year, most serialized in pulp fiction magazines such as *All Around*, *All-Story Magazine*, *All-Story Cavalier*, *The Blue Book Magazine*, and *New Story* to name just a few. To the chagrin of his editors—but not his legion of readers worldwide—Burroughs was interested in a variety of fantastic landscapes and gallant heroes, and he jumped about in his storytelling, first writing about Mars, then about Tarzan and Africa, then going back to Mars, then Africa again, and so on. He published all of his novels in serial format first, and such was their success that they almost immediately came out in book form. A. C. McClurg Publishing would publish most of Burroughs's books from 1912 (*Tarzan of the Apes*) to 1929 (*The Monster Men*). Burroughs's work also found quick success in foreign markets and in translation. His popularity was further boosted by the invention of cinema. Among the earliest full-length movies ever made was the silent *Tarzan of the Apes* in 1918, starring Elmo Lincoln. (There would be forty-eight Tarzan movies in all and a 1970s television series starring Ron Ely, who would go on to play Doc Savage, another pulp-era hero.)

Burroughs wrote stories in his Tarzan and Mars series exclusively from 1912 to 1921, when, after writing the stand-alone novel *The Mucker* (a contemporary picaresque tale about a scoundrel who leaves America on a murder rap only to fight an isolated community of Japanese samurai on a Pacific island), he began his third great series, the Pellucidar stories. The first tale was *At the Earth's Core*, followed by *Pellucidar* in 1923. *Tanar of Pellucidar* was published in 1929 and was Burroughs's thirty-third book overall. It was, as was the case with just about every other Burroughs book, an instant hit with his readers. The Pellucidar series continued with a Tarzan novel, *Tarzan at the Earth's Core*, in 1930, and then with *Back to the Stone Age* in 1935 and *Land of Terror* in 1939. The series concluded with *Savage Pellucidar* in 1944 when Burroughs was sixty-nine and a war correspondent living in Hawaii.

One outstanding feature of all of Burroughs's series is that each of the novels in them can really stand alone. Few have cliff-hanging endings that absolutely *require* the reader to buy the next book to see what happens. This is particularly true of the Pellucidar novels. Each book is essentially complete, with the main plot elements wrapped up nicely (although every now and then there appear a few minor loose ends that eventually need to be dealt with).

The Pellucidar series begins with *At the Earth's Core* wherein David Innes and Abner Perry take a giant borer down through the earth's crust to see what they can see. When they discover that their incredible machine cannot turn around and return them to the surface, they continue, breaking through at a depth of five hundred miles into Pellucidar, a world within our world, on the inside of a hollow shell with a perpetually glowing central sun. Pellucidar is, for the most part, a late Pleistocene world replete with saber-toothed tiger–like *tarags*, wooly mammoths called *tandors*, bears called *ryths*, massive crocodile-like creatures known as *labyrinthodons*, a few nasty *hyaenodons*, and atavistic ape-men. The regular humans of Pellucidar are ruled by a repugnant race of reptilian creatures called Mahars until these creatures are later subdued by Innes and Perry.

Early in *At the Earth's Core* Innes falls in love with the primitive but entrancing Dian the Beautiful, who is promptly abducted. Innes goes after her, and the chase is on. This is indeed the template for quite a number of Burroughs's novels (particularly after 1930 when his writing seems to lose some of its joie de vivre), which are filled with all manner of kidnappings, pursuits, daring rescues, and breathless escapes. Through it all, whether on the Moon or Mars, in the future or distant past, or inside the earth or on its surface, we get to see the strange imaginary lands and near-mythic heroes and heroines Burroughs has created.

Stories of a hollow Earth were not new to literature. Tales of heroes venturing into the underworld in search of truth or the meaning of life (or even of a beloved, as in Orpheus and Eurydice or Dante Alighieri) are as old as humankind. Such a tale is called a *katabasis* and the Pellucidar series is one. The Pellucidar stories, however, owe less to Gilgamesh and Odysseus than to the works of Edgar Allan Poe (*Hans Pfaal* and the short story "Ms. Found in a Bottle") and Jules Verne (particularly *Journey to the Center of the Earth*). While these books detail journeys in underground labyrinths, the first hollow Earth story was written by Ludvig Baron von Holberg in 1742. It was a social satire called *Journey to the World Under-Ground*. Later on, the hollow Earth story gets embellished by a hole either at the North or the South Pole (or both) that leads directly to the inner Earth. (A side note: Tarzan travels by zeppelin to Pellucidar in *Tarzan at the Earth's Core* by entering into a hole in the ocean at the North Pole.)

The narrative formula that Burroughs uses for *Tanar of Pel-*

lucidar is similar to that of many of his other books; only the framing device is different. The novel begins with young Jason Gridley, who has invented a special kind of radio that picks up Abner Perry's signals from Pellucidar. This storytelling conceit is soon dropped, and the story becomes the tale related by Perry over the Gridley device. Burroughs then assumes a standard third-person limited omniscient narration with multiple changes in point of view throughout the novel. This narrative strategy of verisimilitude is a hold over from the days when authors felt that their novels had to be framed in some credible way in order for their readers to believe what they had to say (even if it was all made up). *Moll Flanders*, by Daniel Defoe and published in 1722, is told in a diary format, and Samuel Richardson's *Pamela* (1740) is a compilation of letters (about six hundred pages' worth).

Tanar of Pellucidar is about Tanar the Fleet One, son of Ghak, who is dispatched with ten thousand warriors to protect the Empire (founded by David Innes) from the descendants of Spanish Corsairs (now called Korsars), who long ago wandered down into Pellucidar via the hole in the ocean at the North Pole. Tanar and his army are provided with guns and explosives developed by the technology Innes and Perry brought with them from the topside world, but Tanar is captured by the Korsars, who are led by a garrulous black-bearded pirate called the Cid. Innes mounts an expedition to rescue Tanar but is, in turn, also captured. The novel becomes a wild tale of love (Tanar falls for the Cid's beautiful daughter, Stellara) and heroic combat, with most of the loose ends tied up by the end.

Many critics have suggested that by the time Burroughs had gotten around to writing his third Pellucidar book he was relying on timeworn narrative clichés of capture, rescue, and escape to such a degree that most of the inventiveness of the earlier books was missing. What *Tanar of Pellucidar* does have is some of Burroughs's best physical writing. Burroughs's style owes a great deal to the languorous prose of late Victorian writers, particularly Robert Louis Stevenson and Rudyard Kipling. He also owes something to Henry James in his use of long, complex sentences and Jack London for his compact narrative detail. The punchy, crisp narrative line common to pulp fiction of the Great Depression (particularly the Doc Savage novels and the stories of Dashiell Hammett) had yet to evolve. What we get instead in Burroughs is the elegant compound sentence filled with color and a dynamic motion that propels the reader ever-onward.

Here, for example, is the opening to chapter 5 of *Tanar of Pellucidar*:

> So filled with fear was Stellara's tone that Tanar felt the hair rise upon his scalp as he wheeled about to face the thing that had so filled the girl with horror, but even had he had time to conjure in his imagination a picture worthy of her fright, he could not have imagined a more fearsome or repulsive thing than that which was advancing upon them.

While this sentence is designed to tell us something of Tanar's mental processes in a moment of danger, there doesn't seem to be much padding of sheer data merely to fill out the narrative. Burroughs didn't need to pad anything. For example, take this sentence from chapter 4:

> Just beyond the barrier loomed two gigantic mammoths—huge tandors, towering sixteen feet or more in height—their wicked eyes red with hate and rage; their great tusks gleaming in the sunlight; their long, powerful trunks seeking to drag down the barrier from the sharpened stakes of which their flesh recoiled.

Again, the reader is swayed, not only by Burroughs's elegant prose and description, but also by the grace and exactness of his word choice.

Despite its welter of de rigueur captures and escapes, *Tanar of Pellucidar* nonetheless speeds right along. It is a good model of Burroughs's sense of wonder and his skill at cranking out a good yarn. Many critics consider Burroughs's next novel in the Pellucidar series, *Tarzan at the Earth's Core* (serialized in 1929, published in book form in 1930), to be an excellent addition to both the Tarzan and Pellucidar series. After *Tarzan at the Earth's Core*, however, the Pellucidar series begins to wane in inventiveness and energy, and some of the stories do seem padded (particularly *Savage Pellucidar*). Burroughs, though, wrote many other novels, including the Venus series, as well as several moderately successful stand-alone novels.

Burroughs's legacy rests on four of the finest series in both science fiction and fantasy. He was writing at a time when modern science fiction had yet to fully mature, but his lasting contribution to the field was his profound sense of wonder and adroit storytelling. Edgar Rice Burroughs's reputation as one of the most popular writers of the twentieth century remains strong, even if his brand of science fiction now reads more like fantasy. It's still fun.

A NOTE ON SOURCES

I would like to recommend three books that might help readers explore Edgar Rice Burroughs further. The first is Richard A. Lupoff's *Edgar Rice Burroughs: Master of Adventure* (Canaveral Press, 1965). The hardbound version (reprinted by the University of Nebraska Press, 2005) has a wonderful index; the original paperback version (Ace Books, 1965) has no index at all. The second book is an excellent and very concise sourcebook by Erling B. Holtsmark called *Edgar Rice Burroughs* (Twayne Publishers, 1986). Finally, for the so-called pulp-era (which is generally said to begin with the appearance of *Tarzan of the Apes* in *All-Story* in October 1912) is *The Adventure House Guide to the Pulps* (Adventure House, 2000).

To
JOAN BURROUGHS PIERCE II

CONTENTS

TANAR
OF
PELLUCIDAR

PROLOGUE

JASON GRIDLEY is a radio bug. Had he not been, this story never would have been written.

Jason is twenty-three and scandalously good looking—too good looking to be a bug of any sort. As a matter of fact, he does not seem buggish at all—just a normal, sane, young American, who knows a great deal about many things in addition to radio; aeronautics, for example, and golf, and tennis, and polo.

But this is not Jason's story—he is only an incident—an important incident in my life that made this story possible, and so, with a few more words of explanation, we shall leave Jason to his tubes and waves and amplifiers, concerning which he knows everything and I nothing.

Jason is an orphan with an income, and after he graduated from Stanford, he came down and bought a couple of acres at Tarzana, and that is how and when I met him.

While he was building he made my office his headquarters and was often in my study and afterward I returned the compliment by visiting him in his new "lab," as he calls it—a quite large room at the rear of his home, a quiet, restful room in a quiet, restful house of the Spanish-American farm type—or we rode together in the Santa Monica Mountains in the cool air of early morning.

11

Jason is experimenting with some new principle of radio concerning which the less I say the better it will be for my reputation, since I know nothing whatsoever about it and am likely never to.

Perhaps I am too old, perhaps I am too dumb, perhaps I am just not interested—I prefer to ascribe my abysmal and persistent ignorance of all things pertaining to radio to the last state; that of disinterestedness; it salves my pride.

I do know this, however, because Jason has told me, that the idea he is playing with suggests an entirely new and unsuspected—well, let us call it wave.

He says the idea was suggested to him by the vagaries of static and in groping around in search of some device to eliminate this he discovered in the ether an undercurrent that operated according to no previously known scientific laws.

At his Tarzana home he has erected a station and a few miles away, at the back of my ranch, another. Between these stations we talk to one another through some strange, ethereal medium that seems to pass through all other waves and all other stations, unsuspected and entirely harmless—so harmless is it that it has not the slightest effect upon Jason's regular set, standing in the same room and receiving over the same aerial.

But this, which is not very interesting to any one except Jason, is all by the way of getting to the beginning of the amazing narrative of the adventures of Tanar of Pellucidar.

Jason and I were sitting in his "lab" one evening discussing, as we often did, innumerable subjects, from "cabbages to kings," and coming back, as Jason usually did, to the Gridley wave, which is what we have named it.

Much of the time Jason kept on his ear phones, than which there is no greater discourager of conversation. But this does not irk me as much as most of the conversations one has to listen to through life. I like long silences and my own thoughts.

Presently, Jason removed the headpiece. "It is enough to drive a fellow to drink!" he exclaimed.

"What?" I asked.

"I am getting that same stuff again," he said. "I can hear voices, very faintly, but, unmistakably, human voices. They are speaking a language unknown to man. It is maddening."

"Mars, perhaps," I suggested, "or Venus."

He knitted his brows and then suddenly smiled one of his quick smiles. "Or Pellucidar."

I shrugged.

"Do you know, Admiral," he said (he calls me Admiral because of a yachting cap I wear at the beach), "that when I was a kid I used to believe every word of those crazy stories of yours about Mars and Pellucidar. The inner world at the earth's core was as real to me as the High Sierras, the San Joaquin Valley, or the Golden Gate, and I felt that I knew the twin cities of Helium better than I did Los Angeles.

"I saw nothing improbable at all in that trip of David Innes and old man Perry through the earth's crust to Pellucidar. Yes, sir, that was all gospel to me when I was a kid."

"And now you are twenty-three and know that it can't be true," I said, with a smile.

"You are not trying to tell me it is true, are you?" he demanded, laughing.

"I never have told any one that it is true," I replied; "I let people think what they think, but I reserve the right to do likewise."

"Why, you know perfectly well that it would be impossible for that iron mole of Perry's to have penetrated five hundred miles of the earth's crust, you know there is no inner world peopled by strange reptiles and men of the stone age, you know there is no Emperor of Pellucidar." Jason was becoming excited, but his sense of humor came to our rescue and he laughed.

"I like to believe that there is a Dian the Beautiful," I said.

"Yes," he agreed, "but I am sorry you killed off Hooja the Sly One. He was a corking villain."

"There are always plenty of villains," I reminded him.

"They help the girls to keep their 'figgers' and their school girl complexions," he said.

"How?" I asked.

"The exercise they get from being pursued."

"You are making fun of me," I reproached him, "but remember, please, that I am but a simple historian. If damsels flee and villains pursue I must truthfully record the fact."

"Baloney!" he exclaimed in the pure university English of America.

Jason replaced his headpiece and I returned to the perusal of the narrative of an ancient liar, who should have made a fortune out of the credulity of book readers, but seems not to have. Thus we sat for some time.

Presently Jason removed his ear phones and turned toward me. "I was getting music," he said; "strange, weird music, and then suddenly there came loud shouts and it seemed that I could hear blows struck and there were screams and the sound of shots."

"Perry, you know, was experimenting with gunpowder down there below, in Pellucidar," I reminded Jason, with a grin; but he was inclined to be serious and did not respond in kind.

"You know, of course," he said, "that there really has been a theory of an inner world for many years."

"Yes," I replied, "I have read works expounding and defending such a theory."

"It supposes polar openings leading into the interior of the earth," said Jason.

"And it is substantiated by many seemingly irrefutable scientific facts," I reminded him—"open polar sea, warmer water farthest north, tropical vegetation floating southward from the polar regions, the northern lights, the magnetic pole, the persistent stories of the Eskimos that they are descended from a race that came from a warm country far to the north."

"I'd like to make a try for one of the polar openings," mused Jason as he replaced the ear phones.

Again there was a long silence, broken at last by a sharp exclamation from Jason. He pushed an extra headpiece toward me.

"Listen!" he exclaimed.

As I adjusted the ear phones I heard that which we had never before received on the Gridley wave —code! No wonder that Jason Gridley was excited, since there was no station on earth, other than his own, attuned to the Gridley wave.

Code! What could it mean? I was torn by conflicting emotions—to tear off the ear phones and discuss this amazing thing with Jason, and to keep them on and listen.

I am not what one might call an expert in the intricacies of code, but I had no difficulty in understanding the simple signal of two letters, repeated in groups of three, with a pause after each group: "D.I., D.I., D.I.," pause; "D.I., D.I., D.I.," pause.

I glanced up at Jason. His eyes, filled with puzzled questioning, met mine, as though to ask, what does it mean?

The signals ceased and Jason touched his own key, sending his initials, "J.G., J.G., J.G." in the same grouping that we had received the D.I. signal. Almost instantly he was interrupted—you could feel the excitement of the sender.

"D.I., D.I., D.I., Pellucidar," rattled against our ear-drums like machine gun fire. Jason and I sat in dumb amazement, staring at one another.

"It is a hoax!" I exclaimed, and Jason, reading my lips, shook his head.

"How can it be a hoax?" he asked. "There is no other station on earth equipped to send or to receive over the Gridley wave, so there can be no means of perpetrating such a hoax."

Our mysterious station was on the air again:

"If you get this, repeat my signal," and he signed off with "D.I., D.I., D.I."

"That would be David Innes," mused Jason.

"Emperor of Pellucidar," I added.

Jason sent the message, "D.I., D.I., D.I.," followed by, "what station is this," and "who is sending?"

"This is the Imperial Observatory at Greenwich, Pellucidar; Abner Perry sending. Who are you?"

"This is the private experimental laboratory of Jason Gridley, Tarzana, California; Gridley sending," replied Jason.

"I want to get into communication with Edgar Rice Burroughs; do you know him?"

"He is sitting here, listening in with me," replied Jason.

"Thank God, if that is true, but how am I to know that it is true?" demanded Perry.

I hastily scribbled a note to Jason: "Ask him if he recalls the fire in his first gunpowder factory and that the building would have been destroyed had they not extinguished the fire by shoveling his gunpowder onto it?"

Jason grinned as he read the note, and sent it.

"It was unkind of David to tell of that," came back the reply, "but now I know that Burroughs is indeed there, as only he could have known of that incident. I have a long message for him. Are you ready?"

"Yes," replied Jason.

"Then stand by."

And this is the message that Abner Perry sent from the bowels of the earth; from The Empire of Pellucidar.

INTRODUCTION

IT MUST be some fifteen years since David Innes and I broke through the inner surface of the earth's crust and emerged into savage Pellucidar, but when a stationary sun hangs eternally at high noon and there is no restless moon and there are no stars, time is measureless and so it may have been a hundred years ago or one. Who knows?

Of course, since David returned to earth and brought back many of the blessings of civilization we have had the means to measure time, but the people did not like it. They found that it put restrictions and limitations upon them that they never had felt before and they came to hate it and ignore it until David, in the goodness of his heart, issued an edict abolishing time in Pellucidar.

It seemed a backward step to me, but I am resigned now, and, perhaps, happier, for when all is said and done, time is a hard master, as you of the outer world, who are slaves of the sun, would be forced to admit were you to give the matter thought.

Here, in Pellucidar, we eat when we are hungry, we sleep when we are tired, we set out upon journeys when we leave and we arrive at our destinations when we get there; nor are we old because the earth has circled the sun seventy times since our birth, for we do not know that this has occurred.

Perhaps I have been here fifteen years, but what matter. When I came I knew nothing of radio— my researches and studies were along other lines— but when David came back from the outer world he brought many scientific works and from these I learned all that I know of radio, which has been enough to permit me to erect two successful stations; one here at Greenwich and one at the capital of The Empire of Pellucidar.

But, try as I would, I never could get anything from the outer world, and after a while I gave up trying, convinced that the earth's crust was impervious to radio.

In fact we used our stations but seldom, for, after all, Pellucidar is only commencing to emerge from the stone age, and in the economy of the stone age there seems to be no crying need for radio.

But sometimes I played with it and upon several occasions I thought that I heard voices and other sounds that were not of Pellucidar. They were too faint to be more than vague suggestions of intriguing possibilities, but yet they did suggest something most alluring, and so I set myself to making changes and adjustments until this wonderful thing that has happened but now was made possible.

And my delight in being able to talk with you is second only to my relief in being able to appeal to you for help. David is in trouble. He is a captive in the north, or what he and I call north, for there are no points of compass known to Pellucidarians.

I have heard from him, however. He has sent me a message and in it he suggests a startling theory that would make aid from the outer crust possible if—but first let me tell you the whole story; the story of the disaster that befell David Innes and what led up to it and then you will be in a better position to judge as to the practicability of sending succor to David from the outer crust.

The whole thing dates from our victories over the Mahars, the once dominant race of Pellucidar. When, with our well organized armies, equipped with firearms and other weapons unknown to the Mahars or their gorilla-like mercenaries, the Sagoths, we defeated the reptilian monsters and drove their slimy hordes from the confines of The Empire, the human race of the inner world for the first time in its history took its rightful place among the orders of creation.

But our victories laid the foundation for the disaster that has overwhelmed us.

For a while there was no Mahar within the boundaries of any of the kingdoms that constitute The Empire of Pellucidar; but presently we had word of them here and there—small parties living upon the shores of sea or lake far from the haunts of man.

They gave us no trouble—their old power had crumbled beyond recall; their Sagoths were now numbered among the regiments of The Empire; the Mahars had no longer the means to harm us; yet we did not want them among us. They are eaters of human flesh and we had no assurance that lone hunters would be safe from their voracious appetites.

We wanted them to be gone and so David sent a force against them, but with orders to treat with

them first and attempt to persuade them to leave
The Empire peacefully rather than embroil themselves in another war that might mean total exter-
mination.

Sagoths accompanied the expedition, for they
alone of all the creatures of Pellucidar can con-
verse in the sixth sense, fourth dimension language
of the Mahars.

The story that the expedition brought back was
rather pitiful and aroused David's sympathies, as
stories of persecution and unhappiness always do.

After the Mahars had been driven from The
Empire they had sought a haven where they might
live in peace. They assured us that they had accepted the inevitable in a spirit of philosophy and
entertained no thoughts of renewing their warfare
against the human race or in any way attempting to
win back their lost ascendancy.

Far away upon the shores of a mighty ocean,
where there were no signs of man, they settled in
peace, but their peace was not for long.

A great ship came, reminding the Mahars of the
first ships they had seen—the ships that David and
I had built—the first ships, as far as we knew, that
ever had sailed the silent seas of Pellucidar.

Naturally it was a surprise to us to learn that
there was a race within the inner world sufficiently
far advanced to be able to build ships, but there
was another surprise in store for us. The Mahars
assured us that these people possessed firearms and
that because of their ships and their firearms they
were fully as formidable as we and they were much

more ferocious; killing for the pure sport of slaughter.

After the first ship had sailed away the Mahars thought they might be allowed to live in peace, but this dream was short lived, as presently the first ship returned and with it were many others manned by thousands of bloodthirsty enemies against whose weapons the great reptiles had little or no defense.

Seeking only escape from man, the Mahars left their new home and moved back a short distance toward The Empire, but now their enemies seemed bent only upon persecution; they hunted them, and when they found them the Mahars were again forced to fall back before the ferocity of their continued attacks.

Eventually they took refuge within the boundaries of The Empire, and scarcely had David's expedition to them returned with its report when we had definite proof of the veracity of their tale through messages from our northernmost frontier bearing stories of invasion by a strange, savage race of white men.

Frantic was the message from Goork, King of Thuria, whose far-flung frontier stretches beyond the Land of Awful Shadow.

Some of his hunters had been surprised and all but a few killed or captured by the invaders.

He had sent warriors, then, against them, but these, too, had met a like fate, being greatly outnumbered, and so he sent a runner to David begging the Emperor to rush troops to his aid.

Scarcely had the first runner arrived when another came, bearing tidings of the capture and sack of the principal town of the Kingdom of Thuria; and then a third arrived from the commander of the invaders demanding that David come with tribute or they would destroy his country and slay the prisoners they held as hostages.

In reply David dispatched Tanar, son of Ghak, to demand the release of all prisoners and the departure of the invaders.

Immediately runners were sent to the nearest kingdoms of The Empire and ere Tanar had reached the Land of Awful Shadow, ten thousand warriors were marching along the same trail to enforce the demands of the Emperor and drive the savage foe from Pellucidar.

As David approached the Land of Awful Shadow that lies beneath Pellucidar's mysterious satellite, a great column of smoke was observable in the horizonless distance ahead.

It was not necessary to urge the tireless warriors to greater speed, for all who saw guessed that the invaders had taken another village and put it to the torch.

And then came the refugees—women and children only—and behind them a thin line of warriors striving to hold back swarthy, bearded strangers, armed with strange weapons that resembled ancient harquebuses with bell-shaped muzzles—huge, unwieldy things that belched smoke and flame and stones and bits of metal.

That the Pellucidarians, outnumbered ten to one, were able to hold back their savage foes at all was due to the more modern firearms that David and I had taught them to make and use.

Perhaps half the warriors of Thuria were armed with these and they were all that saved them from absolute rout, and, perhaps, total annihilation.

Loud were the shouts of joy when the first of the refugees discovered and recognized the force that had come to their delivery.

Goork and his people had been wavering in allegiance to The Empire, as were several other distant kingdoms, but I believe that this practical demonstration of the value of the Federation ended their doubts forever and left the people of the Land of Awful Shadow and their king the most loyal subjects that David possessed.

The effect upon the enemy of the appearance of ten thousand well-armed warriors was quickly apparent. They halted, and, as we advanced, they withdrew, but though they retreated they gave us a good fight.

David learned from Goork that Tanar had been retained as a hostage, but though he made several attempts to open negotiations with the enemy for the purpose of exchanging some prisoners that had fallen into our hands, for Tanar and other Pellucidarians, he never was able to do so.

Our forces drove the invaders far beyond the limits of The Empire to the shores of a distant sea, where, with difficulty and the loss of many men, they at last succeeded in embarking their depleted forces on ships that were as archaic in design as were their ancient harquebuses.

These ships rose to exaggerated heights at stern and bow, the sterns being built up in several stories, or housed decks, one atop another. There was much carving in seemingly intricate designs everywhere above the water line and each ship carried at her prow a figurehead painted, like the balance of the ship, in gaudy colors—usually a life size or a heroic figure of a naked woman or a mermaid.

The men themselves were equally bizarre and colorful, wearing gay cloths about their heads, wide sashes of bright colors and huge boots with flapping tops—those that were not half naked and barefoot.

Besides their harquebuses they carried huge pistols and knives stuck in their belts and at their hips were cutlasses. Altogether, with their bushy whiskers and fierce faces, they were at once a bad looking and a picturesque lot.

From some of the last prisoners he took during the fighting at the seashore, David learned that Tanar was still alive and that the chief of the invaders had determined to take him home with him in the hope that he could learn from Tanar the secrets of our superior weapons and gunpowder, for, notwithstanding my first failures, I had, and not without some pride, finally achieved a gunpowder that would not only burn, but that would ignite with such force as to be quite satisfactory. I am now perfecting a noiseless, smokeless powder, though honesty compels me to confess that my first experiments have not been entirely what I had hoped they might be, the first batch detonated having nearly broken my ear-drums and so filled my eyes with smoke that I thought I had been blinded.

When David saw the enemy ships sailing away with Tanar he was sick with grief, for Tanar always has been an especial favorite of the Emperor and his gracious Empress, Dian the Beautiful. He was like a son to them.

We had no ships upon this sea and David could not follow with his army; neither, being David, could he abandon the son of his best friend to a savage enemy before he had exhausted every resource at his command in an effort toward rescue.

In addition to the prisoners that had fallen into his hands David had captured one of the small boats that the enemy had used in embarking his forces, and this it was that suggested to David the mad scheme upon which he embarked.

The boat was about sixteen feet long and was equipped with both oars and a sail. It was broad of beam and had every appearance of being staunch and seaworthy, though pitifully small in which to face the dangers of an unknown sea, peopled, as are all the waters of Pellucidar, with huge monsters possessing short tempers and long appetites.

Standing upon the shore, gazing after the diminishing outlines of the departing ships, David reached his decision. Surrounding him were the captains and the kings of the Federated Kingdoms of Pellucidar and behind these ten thousand warriors, leaning upon their arms. To one side the sullen prisoners, heavily guarded, gazed after their departing comrades, with what sensations of hopelessness and envy one may guess.

David turned toward his people. "Those departing ships have borne away Tanar, the son of Ghak, and perhaps a score more of the young men of Pellucidar. It is beyond reason to expect that the enemy ever will bring our comrades back to us, but it is easy to imagine the treatment they will receive at the hands of this savage, bloodthirsty race.

"We may not abandon them while a single avenue of pursuit remains open to us. Here is that avenue." He waved his hand across the broad ocean. "And here the means of traversing it." He pointed to the small boat.

"It would carry scarce twenty men," cried one, who stood near the Emperor.

"It need carry but three," replied David, "for it will sail to rescue, not by force, but by strategy; or perhaps only to locate the stronghold of the enemy, that we may return and lead a sufficient force upon it to overwhelm it."

"I shall go," concluded the Emperor. "Who will accompany me?"

Instantly every man within hearing of his voice, saving the prisoners only, flashed a weapon above his head and pressed forward to offer his services. David smiled.

"I knew as much," he said, "but I cannot take you all. I shall need only one and that shall be Ja of Anoroc, the greatest sailor of Pellucidar."

A great shout arose, for Ja, the King of Anoroc, who is also the chief officer of the navy of Pellucidar, is vastly popular throughout The Empire, and, though all were disappointed in not being chosen, yet they appreciated the wisdom of David's selection.

"But two is too small a number to hope for success," argued Ghak, "and I, the father of Tanar, should be permitted to accompany you."

"Numbers, such as we might crowd in that little boat, would avail us nothing," replied David, "so why risk a single additional life? If twenty could pass through the unknown dangers that lie ahead of us, two may do the same, while with fewer men we can carry a far greater supply of food and water against the unguessed extent of the great sea that we face and the periods of calm and the long search."

"But two are too few to man the boat," expostulated another, "and Ghak is right—the father of Tanar should be among his rescuers."

"Ghak is needed by The Empire," replied David. "He must remain to command the armies for the Empress until I return, but there shall be a third who will embark with us."

"Who?" demanded Ghak.

"One of the prisoners," replied David. "For his freedom we should readily find one willing to guide us to the country of the enemy."

Nor was this difficult since every prisoner volunteered when the proposal was submitted to them.

David chose a young fellow who said his name was Fitt and who seemed to possess a more open and honest countenance than any of his companions.

And then came the provisioning of the boat. Bladders were filled with fresh water, and quantities of corn and dried fish and jerked meat, as well as vegetables and fruits, were packed into other bladders, and all were stored in the boat until it seemed that she might carry no more. For three men the supplies might have been adequate for a year's voyage upon the outer crust, where time enters into all calculations.

The prisoner, Fitt, who was to accompany David and Ja, assured David that one fourth the quantity of supplies would be ample and that there were points along the route they might take where their water supply could be replenished and where game abounded, as well as native fruits, nuts and vegetables, but David would not cut down by a single ounce the supplies that he had decided upon.

As the three were about to embark David had a last word with Ghak.

"You have seen the size and the armament of the enemy ships, Ghak," he said. "My last injunction to you is to build at once a fleet that can cope successfully with these great ships of the enemy and while the fleet is building—and it must be built upon the shores of this sea—send expeditions forth to search for a waterway from this ocean to our own. Can you find it, all of our ships can be utilized and the building of the greater navy accelerated by utilizing the shipyards of Anoroc.

"When you have completed and manned fifty ships set forth to our rescue if we have not returned by then. Do not destroy these prisoners, but preserve them well for they alone can guide you to their country."

And then David I, Emperor of Pellucidar, and Ja, King of Anoroc, with the prisoner, Fitt, boarded the tiny boat; friendly hands pushed them out upon the long, oily swells of a Pellucidarian sea; ten thousand throats cheered them upon their way and ten thousand pairs of eyes watched them until they had melted into the mist of the upcurving, horizonless distance of a Pellucidarian seascape.

David had departed upon a vain but glorious adventure, and, in the distant capital of The Empire, Dian the Beautiful would be weeping.

TANAR OF PELLUCIDAR

Chapter One

STELLARA

THE great ship trembled to the recoil of the cannon; the rattle of musketry. The roar of the guns aboard her sister ships and the roar of her own were deafening. Below decks the air was acrid with the fumes of burnt powder.

Tanar of Pellucidar, chained below with other prisoners, heard these sounds and smelled the smoke. He heard the rattle of the anchor chain; he felt the straining of the mast to which his shackles were bent and the altered motion of the hull told him that the ship was under way.

Presently the firing ceased and the regular rising and falling of the ship betokened that it was on its course. In the darkness of the hold Tanar could see nothing. Sometimes the prisoners spoke to one another, but their thoughts were not happy ones, and so, for the most part, they remained silent— waiting. For what?

They grew very hungry and very thirsty. By this they knew that the ship was far at sea. They knew nothing of time. They only knew that they were hungry and thirsty and that the ship should be far at sea—far out upon an unknown sea, setting its course for an unknown port.

Presently a hatch was raised and men came with food and water—poor, rough food and water that smelled badly and tasted worse; but it was water and they were thirsty.

One of the men said: "Where is he who is called Tanar?"

"I am Tanar," replied the son of Ghak.

"You are wanted on deck," said the man, and with a huge key he unlocked the massive, hand-wrought lock that held Tanar chained to the mast. "Follow me!"

The bright light of Pellucidar's perpetual day blinded the Sarian as he clambered to the deck from the dark hole in which he had been confined and it was a full minute before his eyes could endure the light, but his guard hustled him roughly along and Tanar was already stumbling up the long stairs leading to the high deck at the ship's stern before he regained the use of his eyes.

As he mounted the highest deck he saw the chiefs of the Korsar horde assembled and with them were two women. One appeared elderly and ill favored, but the other was young and beautiful, but for neither did Tanar have any eyes—he was interested only in the enemy men, for these he could fight, these he might kill, which was the sole interest that an enemy could hold for Tanar, the Sarian, and being what he was Tanar could not fight women, not even enemy women; but he could ignore them, and did.

He was led before a huge fellow whose bushy whiskers almost hid his face—a great, blustering fellow with a scarlet scarf bound about his head. But for an embroidered, sleeveless jacket, open at the front, the man was naked above the waist, about which was wound another gaudy sash into which were stuck two pistols and as many long knives, while at his side dangled a cutlass, the hilt of which was richly ornamented with inlays of pearl and semi-precious stones.

A mighty man was The Cid, chief of the Korsars —a burly, blustering, bully of a man, whose position among the rough and quarrelsome Korsars might be maintained only by such as he.

Surrounding him upon the high poop of his ship was a company of beefy ruffians of similar mold, while far below, in the waist of the vessel, a throng of lesser cutthroats, the common sailors, escaped from the dangers and demands of an arduous campaign, relaxed according to their various whims.

Stark brutes were most of these, naked but for shorts and the inevitable gaudy sashes and head cloths—an unlovely company, yet picturesque.

At The Cid's side stood a younger man who well could boast as hideous a countenance as any sun ever shone upon, for across a face that might have taxed even a mother's love, ran a repulsive scar from above the left eye to below the right hand corner of the mouth, cleaving the nose with a deep, red gash. The left eye was lidless and gazed perpetually upward and outward, as a dead eye might, while the upper lip was permanently drawn upward at the right side in a sardonic sneer that exposed a single fang-like tooth. No, Bohar the Bloody was not beautiful.

Before these two, The Cid and The Bloody One, Tanar was roughly dragged.

"They call you Tanar?" bellowed The Cid.

Tanar nodded.

"And you are the son of a king!" and he laughed loudly. "With a ship's company I could destroy your father's entire kingdom and make a slave of him, as I have of his son."

"You had many ships' companies," replied Tanar; "but I did not see any of them destroying the kingdom of Sari. The army that chased them into the ocean was commanded by my father, under the Emperor."

The Cid scowled. "I have made men walk the plank for less than that," he growled.

"I do not know what you mean," said Tanar.

"You shall," barked The Cid; "and then, by the beard of the sea god, you'll keep a civil tongue in your head. Hey!" he shouted to one of his officers, "have a prisoner fetched and the plank run out. We'll show this son of a king who The Cid is and that he is among real men now."

"Why fetch another?" demanded Bohar the Bloody. "This fellow can walk and learn his lesson at the same time."

"But he could not profit by it," replied The Cid.

"Since when did The Cid become a dry nurse to an enemy?" demanded Bohar, with a sneer.

Without a word The Cid wheeled and swung an ugly blow to Bohar's chin, and as the man went down the chief whipped a great pistol from his sash and stood over him, the muzzle pointed at Bohar's head.

"Perhaps that will knock your crooked face straight or bump some brains into your thick head," roared The Cid.

Bohar lay on his back glaring up at his chief.

"Who is your master?" demanded The Cid.

"You are," growled Bohar.

"Then get up and keep a civil tongue in your head," ordered The Cid.

As Bohar arose he turned a scowling face upon Tanar. It was as though his one good eye had gathered all the hate and rage and venom in the wicked heart of the man and was concentrating them upon the Sarian, the indirect cause of his humiliation, and from that instant Tanar knew that Bohar the Bloody hated him with a personal hatred distinct from any natural antipathy that he might have felt for an alien and an enemy.

On the lower deck men were eagerly running a long plank out over the starboard rail and making the inboard end fast to cleats with stout lines.

From an opened hatch others were dragging a strapping prisoner from the kingdom of Thuria, who had been captured in the early fighting in the Land of Awful Shadow.

The primitive warrior held his head high and showed no terror in the presence of his rough captors. Tanar, looking down upon him from the upper deck, was proud of this fellow man of the Empire. The Cid was watching, too.

"That tribe needs taming," he said.

The younger of the two women, both of whom had stepped to the edge of the deck and were looking down upon the scene in the waist, turned to The Cid.

"They seem brave men; all of them," she said. "It is a pity to kill one needlessly."

"Poof! girl," exclaimed The Cid. "What do you know of such things? It is the blood of your mother that speaks. By the beards of the gods, I would that you had more of your father's blood in your veins."

"It is brave blood, the blood of my mother," replied the girl, "for it does not fear to be itself before all men. The blood of my father dares not reveal its good to the eyes of men because it fears ridicule. It boasts of its courage to hide its cowardice."

The Cid swore a mighty oath. "You take advantage of our relationship, Stellara," he said, "but do not forget that there is a limit beyond which even you may not go with The Cid, who brooks no insults."

The girl laughed. "Reserve that talk for those who fear you," she said.

During this conversation, Tanar, who was standing near, had an opportunity to observe the girl more closely and was prompted to do so by the nature of her remarks and the quiet courage of her demeanor. For the first time he noticed her hair, which was like gold in warm sunlight, and because the women of his own country were nearly all dark haired the color of her hair impressed him. He thought it very lovely and when he looked more closely at her features he realized that they, too, were lovely, with a sunny, golden loveliness that seemed to reflect like qualities of heart and character. There was a certain feminine softness about her that was sometimes lacking in the sturdy, self-reliant, primitive women of his own race. It was not in any sense a weakness, however, as was evidenced by her fearless attitude toward The Cid and by the light of courage that shone from her brave eyes. Intelligent eyes they were, too—brave, intelligent and beautiful.

But there Tanar's interest ceased and he was repulsed by the thought that this woman belonged to the uncouth bully, who ruled with an iron hand the whiskered brutes of the great fleet, for The Cid's reference to their relationship left no doubt in the mind of the Sarian that the woman was his mate.

And now the attention of all was focused on the actors in the tragedy below. Men had bound the wrists of the prisoner together behind his back and placed a blindfold across his eyes.

"Watch below, son of a king," said The Cid to Tanar, "and you will know what it means to walk the plank."

"I am watching," said Tanar, "and I see that it takes many of your people to make one of mine do this thing, whatever it may be."

The girl laughed, but The Cid scowled more deeply, while Bohar cast a venomous glance at Tanar.

Now men with drawn knives and sharp pikes lined the plank on either side of the ship's rail and others lifted the prisoner to the inboard end so that he faced the opposite end of the plank that protruded far out over the sea, where great monsters of the deep cut the waves with giant backs as they paralleled the ship's course—giant saurians, long extinct upon the outer crust.

Prodding the defenseless man with knife and pike they goaded him forward along the narrow plank to the accompaniment of loud oaths and vulgar jests and hoarse laughter.

Erect and proud, the Thurian marched fearlessly to his doom. He made no complaint and when he reached the outer end of the plank and his foot found no new place beyond he made no outcry. Just for an instant he drew back his foot and hesitated and then, silently, he leaped far out, and, turning, dove head foremost into the sea.

Tanar turned his eyes away and it chanced that he turned them in the direction of the girl. To his surprise he saw that she, too, had refused to look at the last moment and in her face, turned toward his, he saw an expression of suffering.

Could it be that this woman of The Cid's brutal race felt sympathy and sorrow for a suffering enemy?

Tanar doubted it. More likely that something she had eaten that day had disagreed with her.

"Now," cried The Cid, "you have seen a man walk the plank and know what I may do with you, if I choose."

Tanar shrugged. "I hope I may be as indifferent to my fate as was my comrade," he said, "for you certainly got little enough sport out of him."

"If I turn you over to Bohar we shall have sport," replied The Cid. "He has other means of enlivening a dull day that far surpass the tame exercise on the plank."

The girl turned angrily upon The Cid. "You shall not do that!" she cried. "You promised me that you would not torture any prisoners while I was with the fleet."

"If he behaves I shall not," said The Cid, "but if he does not I shall turn him over to Bohar the Bloody. Do not forget that I am Chief of Korsar and that even you may be punished if you interfere."

Again the girl laughed. "You can frighten the others, Chief of Korsar," she said, "but not me."

"If she were mine," muttered Bohar threateningly, but the girl interrupted him.

"I am not, nor ever shall be," she said.

"Do not be too sure of that," growled The Cid. "I can give you to whom I please; let the matter drop." He turned to the Sarian prisoner. "What is your name, son of a king?" he asked.

"Tanar.".

"Listen well, Tanar," said The Cid impressively. "Our prisoners do not live beyond the time that they be of service to us. Some of you will be kept to exhibit to the people of Korsar, after which they will be of little use to me, but you can purchase life and, perhaps, freedom."

"How?" demanded Tanar.

"Your people were armed with weapons far better than ours," explained The Cid; "your powder was more powerful and more dependable. Half the time ours fails to ignite at the first attempt."

"That must be embarrassing," remarked Tanar.

"It is fatal," said The Cid.

"But what has it to do with me?" asked the prisoner.

"If you will teach us how to make better weapons and such powder as your people have you shall be spared and shall have your freedom."

Tanar made no reply—he was thinking—thinking of the supremacy that their superior weapons gave his people—thinking of the fate that lay in store for him and for those poor devils in the dark, foul hole below deck.

"Well?" demanded The Cid.

"Will you spare the others, too?" he asked.

"Why should I?"

"I shall need their help," said Tanar. "I do not know all that is necessary to make the weapons and the powder."

As a matter of fact he knew nothing about the manufacture of either, but he saw here a chance to save his fellow prisoners, or at least to delay their destruction and gain time in which they might find means to escape, nor did he hesitate to deceive The Cid, for is not all fair in war?

"Very well," said the Korsar chief; "if you and they give me no trouble you shall all live—provided you teach us how to make weapons and powder like your own."

"We cannot live in the filthy hole in which we are penned," retorted the Sarian; "neither can we live without food. Soon we shall all sicken and die. We are people of the open air—we cannot be smothered in dark holes filled with vermin and be starved, and live."

"You shall not be returned to the hole," said The Cid. "There is no danger that you will escape."

"And the others?" demanded Tanar.

"They remain where they are!"

"They will all die, and without them I cannot make powder," Tanar reminded him.

The Cid scowled. "You would have my ship overrun with enemies," he growled.

"They are unarmed."

"Then they certainly would be killed," said The Cid. "No one would survive long among that pack an' he were not armed"; he waved a hand contemptuously toward the half naked throng below.

"Then leave the hatches off and give them decent air and more and better food."

"I'll do it," said The Cid. "Bohar, have the forward hatches removed, place a guard there with orders to kill any prisoner who attempts to come on deck and any of our men who attempts to go below; see, too, that the prisoners get the same rations as our own men."

It was with a feeling of relief that amounted almost to happiness that Tanar saw Bohar depart to carry out the orders of The Cid, for he knew well that his people could not long survive the hideous and unaccustomed confinement and the vile food that had been his lot and theirs since they had been brought aboard the Korsar ship.

Presently The Cid went to his cabin and Tanar, left to his own devices, walked to the stern and leaning on the rail gazed into the hazy upcurving distance where lay the land of the Sarians, his land, beyond the haze.

Far astern a small boat rose and fell with the great, long billows. Fierce denizens of the deep constantly threatened it, storms menaced it, but on it forged in the wake of the great fleet—a frail and tiny thing made strong and powerful by the wills of three men.

But this Tanar did not see, for the mist hid it. He would have been heartened to know that his Emperor was risking his life to save him.

As he gazed and dreamed he became conscious of a presence near him, but he did not turn, for who was there upon that ship who might have access to this upper deck, whom he might care to see or speak with?

Presently he heard a voice at his elbow, a low, golden voice that brought him around facing its owner. It was the girl.

"You are looking back toward your own country?" she said.

"Yes."

"You will never see it again," she said, a note of sadness in her voice, as though she understood his feelings and sympathized.

"Perhaps not, but why should you care? I am an enemy."

"I do not know why I should care," replied the girl. "What is your name?"

"Tanar."

"Is that all?"

"I am called Tanar the Fleet One."

"Why?"

"Because in all Sari none can outdistance me."

"Sari—is that the name of your country?"

"Yes."

"What is it like?"

"It is a high plateau among the mountains. It is a very lovely country, with leaping rivers and great trees. It is filled with game. We hunt the great ryth there and the tarag for meat and for sport and there are countless lesser animals that give us food and clothing."

"Have you no enemies? You are not a warlike people as are the Korsars."

"We defeated the warlike Korsars," he reminded her.

"I would not speak of that too often," she said. "The tempers of the Korsars are short and they love to kill."

"Why do you not kill me then?" he demanded. "You have a knife and a pistol in your sash, like the others."

The girl only smiled.

"Perhaps you are not a Korsar," he exclaimed. "You were captured as I was and are a prisoner."

"I am no prisoner," she replied.

"But you are not a Korsar," he insisted.

"Ask The Cid—he will doubtless cutlass you for your impertinence; but why do you think I am not a Korsar?"

"You are too beautiful and too fine," he replied. "You have shown sympathy and that is a finer sentiment far beyond their mental capability. They are——"

"Be carerul, enemy; perhaps I am a Korsar!"

"I do not believe it," said Tanar.

"Then keep your beliefs to yourself, prisoner," retorted the girl in a haughty tone.

"What is this?" demanded a rough voice behind Tanar. "What has this thing said to you, Stellara?"

Tanar wheeled to face Bohar the Bloody.

"I questioned that she was of the same race as you," snapped Tanar before the girl could reply. "It is inconceivable that one so beautiful could be tainted by the blood of Korsar."

His face flaming with rage, Bohar laid a hand upon one of his knives and stepped truculently toward the Sarian. "It is death to insult the daughter of The Cid," he cried, whipping the knife from his sash and striking a wicked blow at Tanar.

The Sarian, light of foot, trained from childhood in the defensive as well as offensive use of edged weapons, stepped quickly to one side and then as quickly in again and once more Bohar the Bloody sprawled upon the deck to a well delivered blow.

Bohar was fairly foaming at the mouth with rage as he jerked his heavy pistol from his gaudy sash and aiming it at Tanar's chest from where he lay upon the deck, pulled the trigger. At the same instant the girl sprang forward as though to prevent the slaying of the prisoner.

It all happened so quickly that Tanar scarcely knew the sequence of events, but what he did know was that the powder failed to ignite, and then he laughed.

"You had better wait until I have taught you how

to make powder that will burn before you try to murder me, Bohar," he said.

The Bloody One scrambled to his feet and Tanar stood ready to receive the expected charge, but the girl stepped between them with an imperious gesture.

"Enough of this!" she cried. "It is The Cid's wish that this man live. Would you like to have The Cid know that you tried to pistol him, Bohar?"

The Bloody One stood glaring at Tanar for several seconds, then he wheeled and strode away without a word.

"It would seem that Bohar does not like me," said Tanar, smiling.

"He dislikes nearly every one," said Stellara, "but he hates you—now."

"Because I knocked him down, I suppose. I cannot blame him."

"That is not the real reason," said the girl.

"What is, then?"

She hesitated and then she laughed. "He is jealous. Bohar wants me for his mate."

"But why should he be jealous of me?"

Stellara looked Tanar up and down and then she laughed again. "I do not know," she said. "You are not much of a man beside our huge Korsars— with your beardless face and your small waist. It would take two of you to make one of them."

To Tanar her tone implied thinly veiled contempt and it piqued him, but why it should he did not know and that annoyed him, too. What was she but the savage daughter of a savage, boorish Korsar?

When he had first learned from Bohar's lips that she was the daughter and not the mate of The Cid he had felt an unaccountable relief, half unconsciously and without at all attempting to analyze his reaction.

Perhaps it was the girl's beauty that had made such a relationship with The Cid seem repulsive, perhaps it was her lesser ruthlessness, which seemed superlative gentleness by contrast with the brutality of Bohar and The Cid, but now she seemed capable of a refined cruelty, which was, after all, what he might have expected to find in one form or another in the daughter of the Chief of the Korsars.

As one will, when piqued, and just at random, Tanar loosed a bolt in the hope that it might annoy her. "Bohar knows you better than I," he said; "perhaps he knew that he had cause for jealousy."

"Perhaps," she replied, enigmatically, "but no one will ever know, for Bohar will kill you—I know *him* well enough to know that."

Chapter Two

DISASTER

UPON the timeless seas of Pellucidar a voyage may last for an hour or a year—that depends not upon its duration, but upon the important occurrences which mark its course.

Curving upward along the inside of the arc of a great circle the Korsar fleet ploughed the restless sea. Favorable winds carried the ships onward. The noonday sun hung perpetually at zenith. Men ate when they were hungry, slept when they were tired, or slept against the time when sleep might be denied them, for the people of Pellucidar seem endowed with a faculty that permits them to store sleep, as it were, in times of ease, against the more strenuous periods of hunting and warfare when there is no opportunity for sleep. Similarly, they eat with unbelievable irregularity.

Tanar had slept and eaten several times since his encounter with Bohar, whom he had seen upon various occasions since without an actual meeting. The Bloody One seemed to be biding his time.

Stellara had kept to her cabin with the old woman, who Tanar surmised was her mother. He wondered if Stellara would look like the mother or The Cid when she was older, and he shuddered when he considered either eventuality.

As he stood thus musing, Tanar's attention was attracted by the actions of the men on the lower deck. He saw them looking across the port bow and upward and, following the direction of their eyes with his, he saw the rare phenomenon of a cloud in the brilliant sky.

Some one must have notified The Cid at about the same time, for he came from his cabin and looked long and searchingly at the heavens.

In his loud voice The Cid bellowed commands and his wild crew scrambled to their stations like monkeys, swarming aloft or standing by on deck ready to do his bidding.

Down came the great sails and reefed were the lesser ones, and throughout the fleet, scattered over the surface of the shining sea, the example of the Commander was followed.

The cloud was increasing in size and coming rapidly nearer. No longer was it the small white cloud that had first attracted their attention, but a great, bulging, ominous, black mass that frowned down upon the ocean, turning it a sullen gray where the shadow lay.

The wind that had been blowing gently ceased suddenly. The ship fell off and rolled in the trough of the sea. The silence that followed cast a spell of terror over the ship's company.

Tanar, watching, saw the change. If these rough seafaring men blenched before the threat of the great cloud the danger must be great indeed.

The Sarians were mountain people. Tanar knew little of the sea, but if Tanar feared anything on

Pellucidar it was the sea. The sight, therefore, of these savage Korsar sailors cringing in terror was far from reassuring.

Some one had come to the rail and was standing at his side.

"When that has passed," said a voice, "there will be fewer ships in the fleet of Korsar and fewer men to go home to their women."

He turned and saw Stellara looking upward at the cloud.

"You do not seem afraid," he said.

"Nor you," replied the girl. "We seem the only people aboard who are not afraid."

"Look down at the prisoners," he told her. "They show no fear."

"Why?" she asked.

"They are Pellucidarians," he replied, proudly.

"We are all of Pellucidar," she reminded him.

"I refer to The Empire," he said.

"Why are you not afraid?" she asked. "Are you so much braver than the Korsars?" There was no sarcasm in her tone.

"I am very much afraid," replied Tanar. "Mine are mountain people—we know little of the sea or its ways."

"But you show no fear," insisted Stellara.

"That is the result of heredity and training," he replied.

"The Korsars show their fear," she mused. She spoke as one who was of different blood. "They boast much of their bravery," she continued as though speaking to herself, "but when the sky frowns they show fear." There seemed a little note of contempt in her voice. "See!" she cried. "It is coming!"

The cloud was tearing toward them now and beneath it the sea was lashed to fury. Shreds of cloud whirled and twisted at the edges of the great cloud mass. Shreds of spume whirled and twisted above the angry waves. And then the storm struck the ship, laying it over on its side.

What ensued was appalling to a mountaineer, unaccustomed to the sea—the chaos of watery mountains, tumbling, rolling, lashing at the wallowing ship; the shrieking wind; the driving, blinding spume; the terror-stricken crew, cowed, no longer swaggering bullies.

Reeling, staggering, clutching at the rail Bohar the Bloody passed Tanar where he clung with one arm about a stanchion and the other holding Stellara, who would have been hurled to the deck but for the quick action of the Sarian.

The face of Bohar was an ashen mask against which the red gash of his ugly scar stood out in startling contrast. He looked at Tanar and Stellara, but he passed them by, mumbling to himself.

Beyond them was The Cid, screaming orders that no one could hear. Toward him Bohar made his way. Above the storm Tanar heard The Bloody One screaming at his chief.

"Save me! Save me!" he cried. "The boats— lower the boats! The ship is lost."

It was apparent, even to a landsman, that no small boat could live in such a sea even if one could have been lowered. The Cid paid no attention to his lieutenant, but clung where he was, bawling commands.

A mighty sea rose suddenly above the bow; it hung there for an instant and then rolled in upon the lower deck—tons of crushing, pitiless, insensate sea—rolled in upon the huddled, screaming seamen. Naught but the high prow and the lofty poop showed above the angry waves—just for an instant the great ship strained and shuddered, battling for life.

"It is the end!" cried Stellara.

Bohar screamed like a dumb brute in the agony of death. The Cid knelt on the deck, his face buried in his arms. Tanar stood watching, fascinated by the terrifying might of the elements. He saw man shrink to puny insignificance before a gust of wind, and a slow smile crossed his face.

The wave receded and the ship, floundering, staggered upward, groaning. The smile left Tanar's lips as his eyes gazed down upon the lower deck. It was almost empty now. A few broken forms lay huddled in the scuppers; a dozen men, clinging here and there, showed signs of life. The others, all but those who had reached safety below deck, were gone.

The girl clung tightly to the man. "I did not think she could live through that," she said.

"Nor I," said Tanar.

"But you were not afraid," she said. "You seemed the only one who was not afraid."

"Of what use was Bohar's screaming?" he asked. "Did it save him?"

"Then you were afraid, but you hid it?"

He shrugged. "Perhaps," he said. "I do not know what you mean by fear. I did not want to die, if that is what you mean."

"Here comes another!" cried Stellara, shuddering, and pressing closer to him.

Tanar's arm tightened about the slim figure of the girl. It was an unconscious gesture of the protective instinct of the male.

"Do not be afraid," he said.

"I am not—now," she replied.

At the instant that the mighty comber engulfed the ship the angry hurricane struck suddenly with renewed fury—struck at a new angle—and the masts, already straining even to the minimum of canvas that had been necessary to give the ship headway and keep its nose into the storm, snapped like dry bones and crashed by the board in a tangle of cordage. The ship's head fell away and she rolled in the trough of the great seas, a hopeless derelict.

Above the screaming of the wind rose Bohar's screams. "The boats! The boats!" he repeated like a trained parrot gone mad from terror.

As though sated for the moment and worn out by its own exertions the storm abated, the wind died, but the great seas rose and fell and the great ship rolled, helpless. At the bottom of each watery gorge it seemed that it must be engulfed by the gray green cliff toppling above it and at the crest of each liquid mountain certain destruction loomed inescapable.

Bohar, still screaming, scrambled to the lower deck. He found men, by some miracle still alive in the open, and others cringing in terror below deck. By dint of curses and blows and the threat of his pistol he gathered them together and though they whimpered in fright he forced them to make a boat ready.

There were twenty of them and their gods or their devils must have been with them, for they lowered a boat and got clear of the floundering hulk in safety and without the loss of a man.

The Cid, seeing what Bohar contemplated, had tried to prevent the seemingly suicidal act by bellowing orders at him from above, but they had no effect and at the last moment The Cid had descended to the lower deck to enforce his commands, but he had arrived too late.

Now he stood staring unbelievingly at the small boat riding the great seas in seeming security while the dismasted ship, pounded by the stumps of its masts, seemed doomed to destruction.

From corners where they had been hiding came the balance of the ship's company and when they saw Bohar's boat and the seemingly relative safety of the crew they clamored for escape by the other boats. With the idea once implanted in their minds there followed a mad panic as the half-brutes fought for places in the remaining boats.

"Come!" cried Stellara. "We must hurry or they will go without us." She started to move toward the companionway, but Tanar restrained her.

"Look at them," he said. "We are safer at the mercy of the sea and the storm."

Stellara shrank back close to him. She saw men knifing one another—those behind knifing those ahead. Men dragging others from the boats and killing them on deck or being killed. She saw The Cid pistol a seaman in the back and leap to his place in the first boat to be lowered. She saw men leaping from the rail in a mad effort to reach this boat and falling into the sea, or being thrown in if they succeeded in boarding the tossing shell.

She saw the other boats being lowered and men crushed between them and the ship's side—she saw the depths to which fear can plunge the braggart and the bully as the last of the ship's company, failing to win places in the last boat, deliberately leaped into the sea and were drowned.

Standing there upon the high poop of the rolling derelict, Tanar and Stellara watched the frantic efforts of the oarsmen in the overcrowded small boats. They saw one boat foul another and both founder. They watched the drowning men battling for survival. They heard their hoarse oaths and their screams above the roaring of the sea and the shriek of the wind as the storm returned as though fearing that some might escape its fury.

"We are alone," said Stellara. "They have all gone."

"Let them go," replied Tanar. "I would not exchange places with them."

"But there can be no hope for us," said the girl.

"There is no more for them," replied the Sarian, "and at least we are not crowded into a small boat filled with cutthroats."

"You are more afraid of the men than you are of the sea," she said.

"For you, yes," he replied.

"Why should you fear for me?" she demanded. "Am I not also your enemy?"

He turned his eyes quickly upon her and they were filled with surprise. "That is so," he said; "but, somehow, I had forgotten it—you do not seem like an enemy, as the others do. You do not seem like one of them, even."

Clinging to the rail and supporting the girl upon the lurching deck, Tanar's lips were close to Stellara's ear as he sought to make himself heard above the storm. He sensed the faint aroma of a delicate sachet that was ever after to be a part of his memory of Stellara.

A sea struck the staggering ship throwing Tanar forward so that his cheek touched the cheek of the girl and as she turned her head his lips brushed hers. Each realized that it was an accident, but the effect was none the less surprising. Tanar, for the first time, felt the girl's body against his and consciousness of contact must have been reflected in his eyes for Stellara shrank back and there was an expression of fear in hers.

Tanar saw the fear in the eyes of an enemy, but it gave him no pleasure. He tried to think only of the treatment that would have been accorded a woman of his tribe had one been at the mercy of the Korsars, but that, too, failed to satisfy him as it only could if he were to admit that he was of the same ignoble clay as the men of Korsar.

But whatever thoughts were troubling the minds of Stellara and Tanar were temporarily submerged by the grim tragedy of the succeeding few moments as another tremendous sea, the most gigantic that had yet assailed the broken ship, hurled its countless tons upon her shivering deck.

To Tanar it seemed, indeed, that this must mark the end since it was inconceivable that the unmanageable hulk could rise again from the smother of water that surged completely over her almost to the very highest deck of the towering poop, where the two clung against the tearing wind and the frightful pitching of the derelict.

But, as the sea rolled on, the ship slowly, sluggishly struggled to the surface like an exhausted swimmer who, drowning, struggles weakly against the inevitability of fate and battles upward for one last gasp of air that will, at best, but prolong the agony of death.

As the main deck slowly emerged from the receding waters, Tanar was horrified by the discovery that the forward hatch had been stove in. That the ship must have taken in considerable water, and that each succeeding wave that broke over it would add to the quantity, affected the Sarian less than knowledge of the fact that it was beneath this hatch that his fellow prisoners were confined.

Through the black menace of his almost hopeless situation had shone a single bright ray of hope that, should the ship weather the storm, there would be aboard her a score of his fellow Pellucidarians and that together they might find the means to rig a makeshift sail and work their way back to the mainland from which they had embarked; but with the gaping hatch and the almost certain conclusion to be drawn from it he realized that it would, indeed, be a miracle if there remained alive aboard the derelict any other than Stellara and himself.

The girl was looking down at the havoc wrought below and now she turned her face toward his.

"They must all be drowned," she said, "and they were your people. I am sorry."

"Perhaps they would have chosen it in preference to what might have awaited them in Korsar," he said.

"And they have been released only a little sooner than we shall be," she continued. "Do you notice how low the ship rides now and how sluggish she is? The hold must be half filled with water—another such sea as the last one will founder her."

For some time they stood in silence, each occupied with his own thoughts. The hulk rolled in the trough and momentarily it seemed that she might not roll back in time to avert the disaster of the next menacing comber, yet each time she staggered drunkenly to oppose a high side to the hungry waters.

"I believe the storm has spent itself," said Tanar.

"The wind has died and there has been no sea like the great one that stove in the forward hatch," said Stellara, hopefully.

The noonday sun broke from behind the black cloud that had shrouded it and the sea burst into a blaze of blue and silver beauty. The storm had passed. The seas diminished. The derelict rolled heavily upon the great swells, low in the water, but temporarily relieved of the menace of immediate disaster.

Tanar descended the companionway to the lower

deck and approached the forward hatch. A single glance below revealed only what he could have anticipated—floating corpses rolling with the roll of the derelict. All below were dead. With a sigh he turned away and returned to the upper deck.

The girl did not even question him for she could read in his demeanor the story of what his eyes had beheld.

"You and I are the only living creatures that remain aboard," he said.

She waved a hand in a broad gesture that took in the sea about them. "Doubtless we alone of the entire ship's company have survived," she said. "I see no other ship nor any of the small boats."

Tanar strained his eyes in all directions. "Nor I," said he; "but perhaps some of them have escaped."

She shook her head. "I doubt it."

"Yours has been a heavy loss," sympathized the Sarian. "Beside so many of your people, you have lost your father and your mother."

Stellara looked up quickly into his eyes. "They were not my people," she said.

"What?" exclaimed Tanar. "They were not your people? But your father, The Cid, was Chief of the Korsars."

"He was not my father," replied the girl.

"And the woman was not your mother?"

"May the gods forbid!" she exclaimed.

"But The Cid! He treated you like a daughter."

"He thought I was his daughter, but I am not."

"I do not understand," said Tanar; "yet I am glad that you are not. I could not understand how you, who are so different from them, could be a Korsar."

"My mother was a native of the island of Amiocap and there The Cid, raiding for women, seized her. She told me about it many times before she died.

"Her mate was absent upon a great tandor hunt and she never saw him again. When I was born The Cid thought that I was his daughter, but my mother knew better for I bore upon my left shoulder a small, red birthmark identical with one upon the left shoulder of the mate from whom she had been stolen—my father.

"My mother never told The Cid the truth, for fear that he would kill me in accordance with the custom the Korsars follow of destroying the children of their captives if a Korsar is not the father."

"And the woman who was with you on board was not your mother?"

"No, she was The Cid's mate, but not my mother, who is dead."

Tanar felt a distinct sense of relief that Stellara was not a Korsar, but why this should be so he did not know, nor, perhaps, did he attempt to analyze his feelings.

"I am glad," he said again.

"But why?" she asked.

"Now we do not have to be enemies," he replied.

"Were we before?"

He hesitated and then he laughed. "I was not your enemy," he said, "but you reminded me that you were mine."

"It has been the habit of a lifetime to think of

myself as a Korsar," exclaimed Stellara, "although I knew that I was not. I felt no enmity toward you."

"Whatever we may have been we must of necessity be friends now," he told her.

"That will depend upon you," she replied.

Chapter Three

AMIOCAP

THE blue waters of the great sea known as Korsar Az wash the shores of a green island far from the mainland—a long, narrow island with verdure clad hills and plateaus, its coast line indented by coves and tiny bays—Amiocap, an island of mystery and romance.

At a distance, and when there is a haze upon the waters, it looks like two islands, rather than one, so low and narrow it is at one point, where coves run in on either side and the sea almost meets.

Thus it appeared to the two survivors from the deck of the Korsar derelict drifting helplessly with the sluggish run of an ocean current and at the whim of vagrant winds.

Time is not even a word to the people of Pellucidar, so Tanar had given no thought to that. They had eaten many times, but as there was still an ample supply of provisions, even for a large ship's company, he felt no concern upon that score, but he had been worried by the depletion of their supply of good water, for the contents of many casks that he had broached had been undrinkable.

They had slept much, which is the way of Pellucidarians when there is naught else to do, storing energy for possible future periods of long drawn exertion.

They had been sleeping thus, for how long who may say in the measureless present of Pellucidar. Stellara was the first to come on deck from the cabin she had occupied next to that of The Cid. She looked about for Tanar, but not seeing him she let her eyes wander out over the upcurving expanse of water that merged in every direction with the blue domed vault of the brilliant sky, in the exact center of which hung the great noonday sun.

But suddenly her gaze was caught and held by something beside the illimitable waters and the ceaseless sun. She voiced a surprised and joyous cry and, turning, ran across the deck toward the cabin in which Tanar slept.

"Tanar! Tanar!" she cried, pounding upon the paneled door. "Land, Tanar, land!"

The door swung open and the Sarian stepped out upon the deck where Stellara stood pointing across the starboard rail of the drifting derelict.

Close by rose the green hills of a long shore line that stretched away in both directions for many miles, but whether it was the mainland or an island they could not tell.

"Land!" breathed Tanar. "How good it looks!"

"The pleasant green of the soft foliage often hides terrible beasts and savage men," Stellara reminded him.

"But they are the dangers that I know—it is the unknown dangers of the sea that I do not like. I am not of the sea."

"You hate the sea?"

"No," he replied, "I do not hate it; I do not understand it—that is all. But there is something that I do understand," and he pointed toward the land.

There was that in Tanar's tone that caused Stellara to look quickly in the direction that he indicated.

"Men!" she exclaimed.

"Warriors," said Tanar.

"There must be twenty of them in that canoe," she said.

"And here comes another canoeful behind them."

From the mouth of a narrow cove the canoes were paddling out into the open sea.

"Look!" cried Stellara. "There are many more coming."

One after another twenty canoes moved in a long column out upon the quiet waters and as they drew steadily toward the ship the survivors saw that each was filled with almost naked warriors. Short, heavy spears, bone-tipped, bristled menacingly; stone knives protruded from every G-string and stone hatchets swung at every hip.

As the flotilla approached, Tanar went to a cabin and returned with two of the heavy pistols left behind by a fleeing Korsar when the ship had been abandoned.

"Do you expect to repulse four hundred warriors with those?" asked the girl.

Tanar shrugged. "If they have never heard the report of a firearm a few shots may suffice to frighten them away, for a time at least," he explained, "and if we do not go on the shore the current will carry us away from them in time."

"But suppose they do not frighten so easily?" she demanded.

"Then I can do no more than my best with the crude weapons and the inferior powder of the Korsars," he said with the conscious superiority of one who had, with his people, so recently emerged from the stone age that he often instinctively grasped a pistol by the muzzle and used it as a war club in sudden emergencies when at close quarters.

"Perhaps they will not be unfriendly," suggested Stellara.

Tanar laughed. "Then they are not of Pellucidar," he said, "but of some wondrous country inhabited by what Perry calls angels."

"Who is Perry?" she demanded. "I never heard of him."

"He is a madman who says that Pellucidar is the inside of a hollow stone that is as round as the strange world that hangs forever above the Land of Awful Shadow, and that upon the outside are seas and mountains and plains and countless people and a great country from which he comes."

"He must be quite mad," said the girl.

"Yet he and David, our Emperor, have brought us many advantages that were before unknown in Pellucidar, so that now we can kill more warriors in a single battle than was possible before during the course of a whole war. Perry calls this civilization and it is indeed a very wonderful thing."

"Perhaps he came from the frozen world from which the ancestors of the Korsars came," suggested the girl. "They say that that country lies outside of Pellucidar."

"Here is the enemy," said Tanar. "Shall I fire at that big fellow standing in the bow of the first canoe?" Tanar raised one of the heavy pistols and took aim, but the girl laid a hand upon his arm.

"Wait," she begged. "They may be friendly. Do not fire unless you must—I hate killing."

"I can well believe that you are no Korsar," he said, lowering the muzzle of his weapon.

There came a hail from the leading canoe. "We are prepared for you, Korsars," shouted the tall warrior standing in the bow. "You are few in numbers. We are many. Your great canoe is a useless wreck; ours are manned by twenty warriors each. You are helpless. We are strong. It is not always thus and this time it is not we who shall be taken prisoners, but you, if you attempt to land.

"But we are not like you, Korsars. We do not want to kill or capture. Go away and we shall not harm you."

"We cannot go away," replied Tanar. "Our ship is helpless. We are only two and our food and water are nearly exhausted. Let us land and remain until we can prepare to return to our own countries."

The warrior turned and conversed with the others in his canoe. Presently he faced Tanar again.

"No," he said; "my people will not permit Korsars to come among us. They do not trust you. Neither do I. If you do not go away we shall take

you as prisoners and your fate will be in the hands
of the Council of the Chiefs."

"But we are not Korsars," explained Tanar.

The warrior laughed. "You speak a lie," he said.
"Do you think that we do not know the ships of
Korsar?"

"This is a Korsar ship," replied Tanar; "but we
are not Korsars. We were prisoners and when they
abandoned their ship in a great storm they left us
aboard."

Again the warriors conferred and those in other
canoes that had drawn alongside the first joined in
the discussion.

"Who are you then?" demanded the spokesman.

"I am Tanar of Pellucidar. My father is King
of Sari."

"We are all of Pellucidar," replied the warrior;
"but we never heard of a country called Sari. And
the woman—she is your mate?"

"No!" cried Stellara, haughtily. "I am not his
mate."

"Who are you? Are you a Sarian, also?"

"I am no Sarian. My father and mother were of
Amiocap."

Again the warriors talked among themselves,
some seeming to favor one idea, some another.

"Do you know the name of this country?" finally
demanded the leading warrior, addressing Stellara.

"No," she replied.

"We were about to ask you that very question,"
said Tanar.

"And the woman is from Amiocap?" demanded
the warrior.

"No other blood flows in my veins," said Stellara, proudly.

"Then it is strange that you do not recognize your own land and your own people," cried the warrior. "This is the island of Amiocap!"

Stellara voiced a low cry of pleased astonishment. "Amiocap!" she breathed softly, as to herself. The tone was a caress, but the warriors in the canoes were too far away to hear her. They thought she was silent and embarrassed because they had discovered her deception.

"Go away!" they cried again.

"You will not send me away from the land of my parents!" cried Stellara, in astonishment.

"You have lied to us," replied the tall warrior. "You are not of Amiocap. You do not know us, nor do we know you."

"Listen!" cried Tanar. "I was a prisoner aboard this ship and, being no Korsar, the girl told me her story long before we sighted this land. She could not have known that we were near your island. I do not know that she even knew its location, but nevertheless I believe that her story is true.

"She has never said that she was from Amiocap, but that her parents were. She has never seen the island before now. Her mother was stolen by the Korsars before she was born."

Again the warriors spoke together in low tones for a moment and then, once more, the spokesman addressed Stellara. "What was your mother's name?" he demanded. "Who was your father?"

"My mother was called Allara," replied the girl. "I never saw my father, but my mother said that

he was a chief and a great tandor hunter, called
Fedol."

At a word from the tall warrior in the bow of the
leading canoe the warriors paddled slowly nearer
the drifting hulk, and as they approached the ship's
waist Tanar and Stellara descended to the main
deck, which was now almost awash, so deep the ship
rode because of the water in her hold, and as the
canoe drifted alongside, the warriors, with the exception of a couple, laid down their paddles and
stood ready with their bone-tipped spears.

Now the two upon the ship's deck and the tall
warrior in the canoe stood almost upon the same
level and face to face. The latter was a smooth-
faced man with finely molded features and clear,
gray eyes that bespoke intelligence and courage.
He was gazing intently at Stellara, as though he
would search her very soul for proof of the veracity
or falsity of her statements. Presently he spoke.

"You might well be her daughter," he said; "the
resemblance is apparent."

"You knew my mother?" exclaimed Stellara.

"I am Vulhan. You have heard her speak of
me?"

"My mother's brother!" exclaimed Stellara, with
deep emotion, but there was no answering emotion
in the manner of the Amiocap warrior. "My
father, where is he? Is he alive?"

"That is the question," said Vulhan, seriously.
"Who is your father! Your mother was stolen by a
Korsar. If the Korsar is your father, you are a
Korsar."

"But he is not my father. Take me to my own

father—although he has never seen me he will know me and I shall know him."

"It will do no harm," said a warrior who stood close to Vulhan. "If the girl is a Korsar we shall know what to do with her."

"If she is the spawn of the Korsar who stole Allara, Vulhan and Fedol will know how to treat her," said Vulhan savagely.

"I am not afraid," said Stellara.

"And this other," said Vulhan, nodding toward Tanar. "What of him?"

"He was a prisoner of war that the Korsars were taking back to Korsar. Let him come with you. His people are not sea people. He could not survive by the sea alone."

"You are sure that he is no Korsar?" demanded Vulhan.

"Look at him!" exclaimed the girl. "The men of Amiocap must know the people of Korsar well by sight. Does this one look like a Korsar?"

Vulhan was forced to admit that he did not. "Very well," he said, "he may come with us, but whatever your fate, he must share it."

"Gladly," agreed Tanar.

The two quit the deck of the derelict as places were made for them in the canoe and as the little craft was paddled rapidly toward shore neither felt any sorrow at parting from the drifting hulk that had been their home for so long. The last they saw of her, just as they were entering the cove, from which they had first seen the canoes emerge, she was drifting slowly with the ocean current parallel with the green shore of Amiocap.

At the upper end of the cove the canoes were beached and dragged beneath the concealing foliage of the luxuriant vegetation. Here they were turned bottom side up and left until occasion should again demand their use.

The warriors of Amiocap conducted their two prisoners into the jungle that grew almost to the water's edge. At first there was no sign of trail and the leading warriors forced their way through the lush vegetation, which fortunately was free from thorns and briers, but presently they came upon a little path which opened into a broad, well beaten trail along which the party moved in silence.

During the march Tanar had an opportunity to study the men of Amiocap more closely and he saw that almost without exception they were symmetrically built, with rounded, flowing muscles that suggested a combination of agility and strength. Their features were regular, and there was not among them one who might be termed ugly. On the whole their expressions were open rather than cunning and kindly rather than ferocious; yet the scars upon the bodies of many of them and their well worn and efficient looking, though crude, weapons suggested that they might be bold hunters and fierce warriors. There was a marked dignity in their carriage and demeanor which appealed to Tanar as did their taciturnity, for the Sarians themselves are not given to useless talk.

Stellara, walking at his side, appeared unusually happy and there was an expression of contentment upon her face that the Sarian had never seen there before. She had been watching him as well as the

Amiocapians, and now she addressed him in a whisper.

"What do you think of my people?" she asked, proudly. "Are they not wonderful?"

"They are a fine race," he replied, "and I hope for your sake that they will believe that you are one of them."

"It is all just as I have dreamed it so many times," said the girl, with a happy sigh. "I have always known that some day I should come to Amiocap and that it would be just as my mother told me that it was—the great trees, the giant ferns, the gorgeous, flowering vines and bushes. There are fewer savage beasts here than in other parts of Pellucidar and the people seldom war among themselves, so that for the most part they live in peace and contentment, broken only by the raids of the Korsars or an occasional raid upon their fields and villages by the great tandors. Do you know what tandors are, Tanar? Do you have them in your country?"

Tanar nodded. "I have heard of them in Amoz," he said, "though they are rare in Sari."

"There are thousands of them upon the island of Amiocap," said the girl, "and my people are the greatest tandor hunters in Pellucidar."

Again they walked on in silence, Tanar wondering what the attitude of the Amiocapians would be towards them, and if friendly whether they would be able to assist him in making his way back to the distant mainland, where Sari lay. To this primitive mountaineer it seemed little short of hopeless even to dream of returning to his native land, for the sea appalled him, nor did he have any conception as to how he might set a course across its savage bosom, or navigate any craft that he might later find at his disposal; yet so powerful is the homing instinct in the Pellucidarians that there was no doubt in his mind that so long as he lived he would always be searching for a way back to Sari.

He was glad that he did not have to worry about Stellara, for if it was true that she was among her own people she could remain upon Amiocap and there would rest upon him no sense of responsibility for her return to Korsar; but if they did not accept her—that was another matter; then Tanar would have to seek for means of escape from an island peopled by enemies and he would have to take Stellara with him.

But this train of thought was interrupted by a sudden exclamation from Stellara. "Look!" she cried. "Here is a village; perhaps it is the very village of my mother."

"What did you say?" inquired a warrior, walking near them.

"I said that perhaps this is the village where my mother lived before she was stolen by the Korsars."

"And you say that your mother was Allara?" inquired the warrior.

"Yes."

"This was indeed the village in which Allara lived," said the warrior; "but do not hope, girl, that you will be received as one of them, for unless your father also was of Amiocap, you are not an Amiocapian. It will be hard to convince any one that you are not the daughter of a Korsar father, and as such you are a Korsar and no Amiocapian."

"But how can you know that my father was a Korsar?" demanded Stellara.

"We do not have to know," replied the warrior; "it is merely a matter of what we believe, but that is a question that will have to be settled by Zural, the chief of the village of Lar."

"Lar," repeated Stellara. "That is the village of my mother! I have heard her speak of it many times. This, then, must be Lar."

"It is," replied the warrior, "and presently you shall see Zural."

The village of Lar consisted of perhaps a hundred thatched huts, each of which was divided into two or more rooms, one of which was invariably an open sitting room without walls, in the center of which was a stone fireplace. The other rooms were ordinarily tightly walled and windowless, affording the necessary darkness for the Amiocapians when they wished to sleep.

The entire clearing was encircled by the most remarkable fence that Tanar had ever seen. The posts, instead of being set in the ground, were suspended from a heavy fiber rope that ran from tree to tree, the lower ends of the posts hanging at least four feet above the ground. Holes had been bored through the posts at intervals of twelve or eighteen inches and into these were inserted hardwood stakes, four or five feet in length and sharpened at either end. These stakes protruded from the posts in all directions, parallel with the ground, and the posts were hung at such a distance from one another that the points of the stakes, protruding from contiguous posts, left intervals of from two to four feet between. As a safeguard against an attacking enemy they seemed futile to Tanar, for in entering the village the party had passed through the open spaces between the posts without being hindered by the barrier.

But conjecture as to the purpose of this strange barrier was crowded from his thoughts by other more interesting occurrences, for no sooner had they entered the village than they were surrounded by a horde of men, women and children.

"Who are these?" demanded some.

"They say that they are friends," replied Vulhan, "but we believe that they are from Korsar."

"Korsars!" cried the villagers.

"I am no Korsar," cried Stellara, angrily. "I am the daughter of Allara, the sister of Vulhan."

"Let her tell that to Zural. It is his business to listen, not ours," cried one. "Zural will know what to do with Korsars. Did they not steal his daughter and kill his son?"

"Yes, take them to Zural," cried another.

"It is to Zural that I am taking them," replied Vulhan.

The villagers made way for the warriors and their prisoners and as the latter passed through the aisles thus formed many were the ugly looks cast upon them and many the expressions of hatred that they overheard, but no violence was offered them and presently they were conducted to a large hut near the center of the village.

Like the other dwellings of the village of Lar,

the floors of the chief's house were raised a foot or eighteen inches above the ground. The thatched roof of the great, open living room, into which they were conducted, was supported by enormous ivory tusks of the giant tandors. The floor, which appeared to be constructed of unglazed tile, was almost entirely covered by the hides of wild animals.. There were a number of low, wooden stools standing about the room, and one higher one that might almost have been said to have attained the dignity of a chair.

Upon this larger stool was seated a stern faced man, who scrutinized them closely and silently as they were halted before him. For several seconds no one spoke, and then the man upon the chair turned to Vulhan.

"Who are these," he demanded, "and what do they in the village of Lar?"

"We took them from a Korsar ship that was drifting helplessly with the ocean current," said Vulhan, "and we have brought them to Zural, chief of the village of Lar, that he may hear their story and judge whether they be the friends they claim to be, or the Korsar enemies that we believe them to be. This one," and Vulhan pointed to Stellara, "says that she is the daughter of Allara."

"I am the daughter of Allara," said Stellara.

"And who was your father?" demanded Zural.

"My father's name is Fedol," replied Stellara.

"How do you know?" asked Zural.

"My mother told me."

"Where were you born?" demanded Zural.

"In the Korsar city of Allaban," replied Stellara.

"Then you are a Korsar," stated Zural with finality. "And this one, what has he to say for himself?" asked Zural, indicating Tanar with a nod.

"He claims that he was a prisoner of the Korsars and that he comes from a distant kingdom called Sari."

"I have never heard of such a kingdom," said Zural. "Is there any warrior here who has ever heard of it?" he demanded. "If there is, let him in justice to the prisoner, speak." But the Amiocapians only shook their heads for there was none who had ever heard of the kingdom of Sari. "It is quite plain," continued Zural, "that they are enemies and that they are seeking by falsehood to gain our confidence. If there is a drop of Amiocapian blood in one of them, we are sorry for that drop. Take them away, Vulhan. Keep them under guard until we decide how they shall be destroyed."

"My mother told me that the Amiocapians were a just and kindly people," said Stellara; "but it is neither just nor kindly to destroy this man who is not an enemy simply because you have never heard of the country from which he comes. I tell you that he is no Korsar. I was on one of the ships of the fleet when the prisoners were brought aboard. I heard The Cid and Bohar the Bloody when they were questioning this man, and I know that he is no Korsar and that he comes from a kingdom known as Sari. They did not doubt his word, so why should you? If you are a just and kindly people how can you destroy me without giving me an opportunity to talk with Fedol, my father. He will believe me; he will know that I am his daughter."

"The gods frown upon us if we harbor enemies in our village," replied Zural. "We should have bad luck, as all Amiocapians know. Wild beasts would kill our hunters and the tandors would trample our fields and destroy our villages. But worst of all the Korsars would come and rescue you from us. As for Fedol, no man knows where he is. He is not of this village and the people of his own village have slept and eaten many times since they saw Fedol. They have slept and eaten many times since Fedol set forth upon his last tandor hunt. Perhaps the tandors have avenged the killing of many of their fellows, or perhaps Fedol fell into the clutches of the Buried People. These things we do not know, but we do know that Fedol went away to hunt tandors and that he never came back and that we do not know where to find him. Take them away, Vulhan, and we shall hold a council of the chiefs and then we shall decide what shall be done with them."

"You are a cruel and wicked man, Zural," cried Stellara, "and no better than the Korsars themselves."

"It is useless, Stellara," said Tanar, laying a hand upon the girl's arm. "Let us go quietly with Vulhan"; and then in a low whisper, "do not anger them, for there is yet hope for us in the council of the chiefs if we do not antagonize them." And so without further word Stellara and Tanar were led from the house of Zural the chief surrounded by a dozen stalwart warriors.

Chapter Four

LETARI

STELLARA and Tanar were conducted to a
small hut in the outskirts of the village. The
building consisted of but two rooms; the open living room with the fireplace and a small dark, sleeping apartment. Into the latter the prisoners were
thrust and a single warrior was left on guard in
the living room to prevent their escape.

In a world where the sun hangs perpetually at
zenith there is no darkness and without darkness
there is little opportunity to escape from the
clutches of a watchful enemy. Yet never for a moment was the thought of escape absent from the
mind of Tanar the Sarian. He studied the sentries
and as each one was relieved he tried to enter into
conversation with his successor, but all to no avail
—the warriors would not talk to him. Sometimes
the guards dozed, but the village and the clearing
about it were always alive with people so that it
appeared unlikely that any opportunity for escape
might present itself.

The sentries were changed, food was brought to
the prisoners and when they felt so inclined they
slept. Thus only might they measure the lapse of
time, if such a thing occurred to them, which doubt-

less it did not. They talked together and sometimes Stellara sang—sang the songs of Amiocap that her mother had taught her, and they were happy and contented, although each knew that the specter of death hovered constantly above them. Presently he would strike, but in the meantime they were happy.

"When I was a youth," said Tanar, "I was taken prisoner by the black people with tails. They build their villages among the high branches of lofty trees and at first they put me in a small hut as dark as this and much dirtier and I was very miserable and very unhappy for I have always been free and I love my freedom, but now I am again a prisoner in a dark hut and in addition I know that I am going to die and I do not want to die, yet I am not unhappy. Why is it, Stellara, do you know?"

"I have wondered about the same thing myself," replied the girl. "It seems to me that I have never been so happy before in my life, but I do not know the reason."

They were sitting close together upon a fiber mat that they had placed near the doorway that they might obtain as much light and air as possible. Stellara's soft eyes looked thoughtfully out upon the little world framed by the doorway of their prison cell. One hand rested listlessly on the mat between them. Tanar's eyes rested upon her profile, and slowly his hand went out and covered hers.

"Perhaps," he said, "I should not be happy if you were not here."

The girl turned half frightened eyes upon him and withdrew her hand. "Don't," she said.

"Why?" he asked.

"I do not know, only that it makes me afraid."

The man was about to speak again when a figure darkened the opening in the doorway. A girl had come bringing food. Heretofore it had been a man —a taciturn man who had replied to none of Tanar's questions. But there was no suggestion of taciturnity upon the beautiful, smiling countenance of the girl.

"Here is food," she said. "Are you hungry?"

"Where there is nothing else to do but eat I am always hungry," said Tanar. "But where is the man who brought our food before?"

"That was my father," replied the girl. "He has gone to hunt and I have brought the food in his stead."

"I hope that he never returns from the hunt," said Tanar.

"Why?" demanded the girl. "He is a good father. Why do you wish him harm?"

"I wish him no harm," replied Tanar, laughing. "I only wish that his daughter would continue to bring our food. She is far more agreeable and much better looking."

The girl flushed, but it was evident that she was pleased.

"I wanted to come before," she said, "but my father would not let me. I saw you when they brought you into the village and I have wanted to see you again. I never before saw a man who looked like you. You are different from the Amiocapians. Are all the men of Sari as good looking as you?"

Tanar laughed. "I am afraid I have never given much thought to that subject," he replied. "In Sari we judge our men by what they do and not by what they look like."

"But you must be a great hunter," said the girl. "You look like a great hunter."

"How do great hunters look?" demanded Stellara with some asperity.

"They look like this man," replied the girl. "Do you know," she continued, "I have dreamed about you many times."

"What is your name?" asked Tanar.

"Letari," replied the girl.

"Letari," repeated Tanar. "That is a pretty name. I hope, Letari, that you will bring our food to us often."

"I shall never bring it again," she said, sadly.

"And why?" demanded Tanar.

"Because no one will bring it again," she said.

"And why is that? Are they going to starve us to death?"

"No, the council of the chiefs has decided that you are both Korsars and that you must be destroyed."

"And when will that be?" asked Stellara.

"As soon as the hunters return with food. We are going to have a great feast and dance, but I shall not enjoy it. I shall be very unhappy for I do not wish to see Tanar die."

"How are they going to destroy us?" asked the man.

"Look," said the girl, pointing through the open doorway. There, in the distance, the two prisoners saw men setting two stakes into the ground. "There were many who wanted to give you to the Buried People," said Letari, "but Zural said that it has been so long since we have had a feast and a dance that he thought that we should celebrate the killing of two Korsars rather than let the Buried People have all the pleasure, and so they are going to tie you to those two stakes and pile dry wood and brush around you and burn you to death."

Stellara shuddered. "And my mother taught me that you were a kindly people," she said.

"Oh, we do not mean to be unkind," said Letari, "but the Korsars have been very cruel to us and Zural believes that the gods will take word to the Korsars that you were burned to death and that perhaps it will frighten them and keep them away from Amiocap."

Tanar arose to his feet and stood very straight and stiff. The horror of the situation almost overwhelmed him. He looked down at Stellara's golden head and shuddered. "You cannot mean," he said, "that the men of Amiocap intend to burn this girl alive?"

"Why, yes," said Letari. "It would do no good to kill her first for then her spirit could not tell the gods that she was burned and they could not tell the Korsars."

"It is hideous," cried Tanar; "and you, a girl yourself, have you no sympathy; have you no heart?"

"I am very sorry that they are going to burn you," said Letari, "but as for her, she is a Korsar and I feel nothing but hatred and loathing for her, but you are different. I know that you are not a Korsar and I wish that I could save you."

"Will you—would you, if you could?" demanded Tanar.

"Yes, but I cannot."

The conversation relative to escape had been carried on in low whispers, so that the guard would not overhear, but evidently it had aroused his suspicion for now he arose and came to the doorway of the hut. "What are you talking about?" he demanded. "Why do you stay in here so long, Letari, talking with these Korsars? I heard what you said and I believe that you are in love with this man."

"What if I am?" demanded the girl. "Do not our gods demand that we love? What else do we live for upon Amiocap but love?"

"The gods do not say that we should love our enemies."

"They do not say that we should not," retorted Letari. "If I choose to love Tanar it is my own affair."

"Clear out!" snapped the warrior. "There are plenty of men in Lar for you to love."

"Ah!" sighed the girl as she passed through the doorway, "but there is none like Tanar."

"The hateful little wanton," cried Stellara after the girl had left.

"She does not hesitate to reveal what is in her heart," said Tanar. "The girls of Sari are not like that. They would die rather than reveal their love before the man had declared his. But perhaps she is only a child and did not realize what she said."

"A child nothing," snapped Stellara. "She knew perfectly well what she was saying and it is quite apparent that you liked it. Very well, when she comes to save you, go with her."

"You do not think that I intended to go with her alone even though an opportunity for escape presented itself through her, do you?" demanded Tanar.

"She told you that she would not help me to escape," Stellara reminded him.

"I know that, but it would be only in the hope of helping you to escape that I would take advantage of her help."

"I would rather be burned alive a dozen times than to escape with her help."

There was a venom in the girl's voice that had never been there before and Tanar looked at her in surprise. "I do not understand you, Stellara," he said.

"I do not understand myself," said the girl, and burying her face in her hands she burst into tears.

Tanar knelt quickly beside her and put an arm about her. "Don't," he begged, "please don't."

She pushed him from her. "Go away," she cried. "Don't touch me. I hate you."

Tanar was about to speak again when he was interrupted by a great commotion at the far end of the village. There were shouts and yells from men, mingled with a thunderous noise that fairly shook the ground, and then the deep booming of drums.

Instantly the men setting the stakes in the ground, where Tanar and Stellara were to be burned, stopped their work, seized their weapons and rushed in the direction from which the noise was coming.

The prisoners saw men, women and children running from their huts and all directed their steps toward the same point. The guard before their door leaped to his feet and stood for a moment looking at the running villagers. Then, without a word or backward glance, he dashed off after them.

Tanar, realizing that for the moment at least they were unguarded, stepped from the dark cell out into the open living apartment and looked in the direction toward which the villagers were running. There he saw the cause of the disturbance and also an explanation of the purpose for which the strange hanging barrier had been erected.

Just beyond the barrier loomed two gigantic mammoths—huge tandors, towering sixteen feet or more in height—their wicked eyes red with hate and rage; their great tusks gleaming in the sunlight; their long, powerful trunks seeking to drag down the barrier from the sharpened stakes of which their flesh recoiled. Facing the mammoths was a shouting horde of warriors, screaming women and children, and above all rose the thundering din of the drums.

Each time the tandors sought to force their way through the barrier, or brush aside its posts, these swung about so that the sharpened stakes threatened their eyes or pricked the tender flesh of their trunks, while bravely facing them the shouting warriors hurled their stone-tipped spears.

But however interesting or inspiring the sight might be, Tanar had no time to spare to follow the course of this strange encounter. Turning to Stellara, he seized her hand. "Come," he cried. "Now is our chance!" And while the villagers were engrossed with the tandors at the far end of the village, Tanar and Stellara ran swiftly across the clearing and entered the lush vegetation of the forest beyond.

There was no trail and it was with difficulty that they forced their way through the underbrush for a short distance before Tanar finally halted.

"We shall never escape them in this way," he said. "Our spoor is as plain as the spoor of a dyryth after a rain."

"How else then may we escape?" asked Stellara.

Tanar was looking upward into the trees examining them closely. "When I was a prisoner among the black people with long tails," he said, "I had to learn to travel through the trees and this knowledge and the ability have stood me in good stead many times since and I believe that they may prove our salvation now."

"You go then," said Stellara, "and save yourself, for certainly I cannot travel through the trees, and there is no reason why we should both be recaptured when one of us can escape."

Tanar smiled. "You know that I would not do that," he said.

"But what else may you do?" demanded Stellara. "They will follow the trail we are making and recapture us before we are out of hearing of the village."

"We shall leave no trail," said Tanar. "Come," and leaping lightly to a lower branch he swung himself into the tree that spread above them. "Give me your hand," he said, reaching down to Stellara, and a moment later he had drawn the girl to his side. Then he stood erect and steadied the girl while she arose to her feet. Before them a maze of branches stretched away to be lost in the foliage.

"We shall leave no spoor here," said Tanar.

"I am afraid," said Stellara. "Hold me tightly."

"You will soon become accustomed to it," said Tanar, "and then you will not be afraid. At first I was afraid, but later I could swing through the trees almost as rapidly as the black men themselves."

"I cannot even take a single step," said Stellara. "I know that I shall fall."

"You do not have to take a step," said Tanar. "Put your arms around my neck and hold on tightly," and then he stooped and lifted her with his left arm while she clung tightly to him, her soft white arms encircling his neck.

"How easily you lifted me!" she said; "how strong you are; but no man living could carry my weight through these trees and not fall."

Tanar did not reply, but instead he moved off among the branches seeking sure footing and secure handholds as he went. The girl's soft body was pressed close to his and in his nostrils was the delicate sachet that he had sensed in his first contact with Stellara aboard the Korsar ship and which now seemed a part of her.

As Tanar swung through the forest, the girl marveled at the strength of the man. She had always considered him a weakling by comparison with the beefy Korsars, but now she realized that in those smoothly rolling muscles was concealed the power of a superman.

She found a fascination in watching him. He moved so easily and he did not seem to tire. Once she let her lips fall until they touched his thick, black hair and then, just a little, almost imperceptibly, she tightened her arms about his neck.

Stellara was very happy and then, of a sudden, she recalled Letari and she straightened up and relaxed her hold. "The vile wanton," she said.

"Who?" demanded Tanar. "What are you talking about?"

"That creature, Letari," said Stellara.

"Why she is not vile," said Tanar. "I thought she was very nice and she is certainly beautiful."

"I believe you are in love with her," snapped Stellara.

"That would not be difficult," said Tanar. "She seemed very lovable."

"Do you love her?" demanded Stellara.

"Why shouldn't I?" asked Tanar.

"Do you?" insisted the girl.

"Would you care if I did?" asked Tanar, softly.

"Most certainly not," said Stellara.

"Then why do you ask?"

"I didn't ask," said Stellara. "I do not care."

"Oh," said Tanar. "I misunderstood," and he moved on in silence, for the men of Sari are not talkative, and Stellara did not know what was in his mind for his face did not reflect the fact that he was laughing inwardly, and, anyway, Stellara could not see his face.

Tanar moved always in one direction and his homing instinct assured him that the direction lay toward Sari. As far as the land went he could move unerringly toward the spot in Pellucidar where he was born. Every Pellucidarian can do that, but put them on the water, out of sight of land, and that instinct leaves them and they have no more conception of direction than would you or I if we were transported suddenly to a land where there are no points of compass since the sun hangs perpetually at zenith and there is no moon and no stars. Tanar's only wish at present was to put them as far as possible from the village of Lar. He would travel until they reached the coast for, knowing that Amiocap was an island, he knew that eventually they must come to the ocean. What they should do then was rather vague in his mind. He had visions of building a boat and embarking upon the sea, although he knew perfectly well that this would be madness on the part of a hill dweller such as he.

Presently he felt hungry and he knew that they must have traveled a considerable distance.

Sometimes Tanar kept track of distance by computing the number of steps that he took, for by much practice he had learned to count them almost mechanically, leaving his mind free for other perceptions and thoughts, but here among the branches of the trees, where his steps were not of uniform length, he had thought it not worth the effort to count them and so he could only tell by the recurrence of hunger that they must have covered considerable distance since they left the village of Lar.

During their flight through the forest they had seen birds and monkeys and other animals and, on several occasions, they had paralleled or crossed game trails, but as the Amiocapians had stripped him of his weapons he had no means of obtaining meat until he could stop long enough to fashion a bow and some arrows and a spear.

How he missed his spear! From childhood it had been his constant companion and for a long time he had felt almost helpless without it. He had never become entirely accustomed or reconciled to carrying firearms, feeling in the bottom of his primitive and savage heart that there was nothing more dependable than a sturdy, stone shod spear.

He had rather liked the bow and arrows that Innes and Perry had taught him to make and use, as the arrows had seemed like little spears. At least one could see them, whereas with the strange and noisy weapons, which belched forth smoke and flame, one could not see the projectile at all. It was most unnatural and uncanny.

But Tanar's mind was not occupied with such thoughts at this time. Food was dominant.

Presently they came to a small, natural clearing beside a crystal brook and Tanar swung lightly to the ground.

"We shall stop here," he said, "until I can make weapons and get meat for us."

With the feel of the ground beneath her feet again Stellara felt more independent. "I am not hungry," she said.

"I am," said Tanar.

"There are berries and fruits and nuts in plenty,"

she insisted. "We should not wait here to be overtaken by the warriors from Lar."

"We shall wait here until I have made weapons," said Tanar, with finality, "and then I shall not only be in a position to make a kill for meat, but I shall be able better to defend you against Zural's warriors."

"I wish to go on," said Stellara. "I do not wish to stay here," and she stamped her little foot.

Tanar looked at her in surprise. "What is the matter with you, Stellara? You were never like this before."

"I do not know what is the matter with me," said the girl. "I only know that I wish I were back in Korsar, in the house of The Cid. There, at least, I should be among friends. Here I am surrounded only by enemies."

"Then you would have Bohar the Bloody One as a mate, if he survived the storm, or if not he another like him," Tanar reminded her.

"At least he loved me," said Stellara.

"And you loved him?" asked Tanar.

"Perhaps," said Stellara.

There was a peculiar look on Tanar's face as his eyes rested upon the girl. He did not understand her, but he seemed to be trying to. She was looking past him, a strange expression upon her face when suddenly she voiced an exclamation of dismay and pointed past him.

"Look!" she cried. "Oh, God, look!"

Chapter Five

THE TANDOR HUNTER

SO FILLED with fear was Stellara's tone that Tanar felt the hair rise upon his scalp as he wheeled about to face the thing that had so filled the girl with horror, but even had he had time to conjure in his imagination a picture worthy of her fright, he could not have imagined a more fearsome or repulsive thing than that which was advancing upon them.

In conformation it was primarily human, but there the similarity ended. It had arms and legs and it walked erect upon two feet; but such feet! They were huge, flat things with nailless toes— short, stubby toes with webs between them. Its arms were short and in lieu of fingers its hands were armed with three heavy claws. It stood somewhere in the neighborhood of five feet in height and there was not a vestige of hair upon its entire naked body, the skin of which was of the sickly pallor of a corpse.

But these attributes lent to it but a fraction of its repulsiveness—it was its head and face that were appalling. It had no external ears, there being only two small orifices on either side of its head where these organs are ordinarily located. Its mouth was large with loose, flabby lips that were drawn back now into a snarl that exposed two rows of heavy fangs. Two small openings above the center of the mouth marked the spot where a nose should have been and, to add further to the hideousness of its appearance, it was eyeless, unless bulging protuberances forcing out the skin where the eyes should have been might be called eyes. Here the skin upon the face moved as though great, round eyes were rolling beneath. The hideousness of that blank face without eyelids, lashes or eyebrows shocked even the calm and steady nerves of Tanar.

The creature carried no weapons, but what need had it for weapons, armed as it was with those formidable claws and fangs? Beneath its pallid skin surged great muscles that attested its giant strength and upon its otherwise blank face the mouth alone was sufficient to suggest its diabolical ferocity.

"Run, Tanar!" cried Stellara. "Take to the trees! It is one of the Buried People." But the thing was too close to him to admit of escape even if Tanar had been minded to desert Stellara, and so he stood there quietly awaiting the encounter and then suddenly, as though to add to the uncanny horror of the situation, the thing spoke. From its flabby, drooling lips issued sounds—mumbled, ghastly sounds that yet took on the semblance of speech until it became intelligible in a distorted way to Tanar and Stellara.

"It is the woman I want," mumbled the creature. "Give me the woman, and the man may go." To Tanar's shocked sensibilities it was as though a mutilated corpse had risen from the grave and spoken, and he fell back a step with a sensation as nearly akin to horror as he had ever experienced.

"You cannot have the woman," said Tanar. "Leave us alone, or I will kill you."

An uncanny scream that was a mixture of laugh and shriek broke from the lips of the thing. "Then die!" it cried, as it launched itself upon the Sarian.

As it closed it struck upward with its heavy claws in an attempt to disembowel its antagonist, but Tanar eluded its first rush by leaping lightly to one side and then, turning quickly, he hurled himself upon the loathsome body and circling its neck with one powerful arm Tanar turned suddenly and, bending his body forward and downward, hurled the creature over his head and heavily to the ground.

But instantly it was up again and at him. Screaming with rage and frothing at the mouth it struck wildly with its heavy claws, but Tanar had learned certain things from David Innes that men of the stone age ordinarily do not know, for David had taught him, as he had taught many another young Pellucidarian, the art of self-defense, including boxing, wrestling and jiu-jitsu, and now again they came into good stead as they had upon other occasions since he had mastered them and once more he gave thanks for the fortunate circumstance that had brought David Innes from the outer crust to Pellucidar to direct the destinies of its human race as first emperor.

Combined with his knowledge, training and agility was Tanar's great strength, without which these other accomplishments would have been of far lesser value, and so as the creature struck, Tanar parried the blows, fending the wicked talons from his flesh and with a strength that surprised his antagonist since it was fully as great as his own.

But what was still more surprising to the monster was the frequency with which Tanar was able to step in and deliver telling blows to the body and head that, in its awkwardness and lack of skill, it was unable to properly protect.

To one side, watching the battle for which she was the stake, stood Stellara. She might have run away and hidden; she might have made good her escape, but no such thoughts entered her courageous little head. It would have been as impossible for her to desert her champion in the hour of his need as it would have been for him to leave her to her fate and so she stood there, helpless, awaiting the outcome.

To and fro across the clearing the battlers moved, trampling down the lush vegetation that sometimes grew so thickly as to hamper their movements, and now it became apparent to both Stellara and Tanar from the labored breathing of the creature that it was being steadily worn down and that it lacked the endurance of the Sarian. However, probably sensing something of this itself, it now redoubled its efforts and the ferocity of its attack, and, at the same time, Tanar discovered a vulnerable spot at which to aim his blows.

Striking for the face he had accidentally touched one of the bulging protuberances that lay beneath the skin where the eyes should have been. At the impact of the blow, light as it was, the creature

screamed and leaped backward, instinctively rais-
ing one of its claws to the injured organ and there-
after Tanar directed all his efforts toward placing
further and heavier blows upon those two bulging
spots.

He struck again and landed cleanly a heavy blow
upon one of them. With a shriek of pain the creature stepped back and clamped both paws to its
hurt.

They were fighting very close to where Stellara
stood. The creature's back was toward her and
she could have reached out and touched him, so
near was he to her. She saw Tanar spring forward
to strike again. The creature dropped back quite
abreast of her and then suddenly lowering its head
it gave vent to a horrid shriek and charged the Sarian with all the hideous ferocity that it could
gather.

It seemed as though it had mustered all its remaining vitality and thrown it into this last, mad
charge. Tanar, his mind and muscles coördinating
perfectly, quick to see openings and take advantage
of them and equally quick to realize the advantages
of retreat, leaped backward to avoid the mad
charge and the flailing claws, but as he did so one of
his heels struck a low bush and he fell heavily to
the ground upon his back.

For the moment he was helpless and in that brief
moment the creature could be upon him with those
horrid fangs and ripping claws.

Tanar knew it. The thing charging him knew it
and Stellara, standing so close to them, knew it,
and so quickly did she act that Tanar had scarcely

struck the ground as she launched herself bodily upon the charging monster from behind.

As a football player hurls himself forward to tackle an opponent so Stellara hurled herself at the creature. Her arms encircled its knees and then slipped down, as he kicked and struggled to free himself, until finally she secured a hold upon one of his skinny ankles just above its huge foot. There she clung and the creature lunged forward just short of Tanar, but instantly, with a howl of rage, it turned to rend the girl. But that brief instant of delay had been sufficient to permit Tanar to regain his feet and ere ever the talons or fangs could sink into the soft flesh of Stellara, Tanar was upon the creature's back. Fingers of steel encircled its throat and though it struggled and struck out with its heavy claws it was at last helpless in the clutches of the Sarian.

Slowly, relentlessly, Tanar choked the life from the monster and then, with an expression of disgust, he cast the corpse aside and stepped quickly to where Stellara was staggering weakly to her feet.

He put his arm about her and for a moment she buried her face in his shoulder and sobbed. "Do not be afraid," he said; "the thing is dead."

She raised her face toward his. "Let us go away from here," she said. "I am afraid. There may be more of the Buried People about. There must be an entrance to their underworld near here, for they do not wander far from such openings."

"Yes," he said, "until I have weapons I wish to see no more of them."

"They are horrible creatures," said Stellara,

"and if there had been two of them we should both have been lost."

"What are they?" asked Tanar. "You seem to know about them. Where had you ever seen one before?"

"I have never seen one until just now," said she, "but my mother told me about them. They are feared and hated by all Amiocapians. They are Coripies and they inhabit dark caverns and tunnels beneath the surface of the ground. That is why we call them the Buried People. They live on flesh and wandering about the jungle they gather up the remains of our kills and devour the bodies of wild beasts that have died in the forest, but being afraid of our spears they do not venture far from the openings that lead down into their dark world. Occasionally they waylay a lone hunter and less often they come to one of our villages and seize a woman or child. No one has ever entered their world and escaped to tell about it, so that what my mother has told me about them is only what our people have imagined as to the underworld where the Buried People dwell for there has never been any Amiocapian warrior brave enough to venture into the dark recesses of one of their tunnels, or if there has been such he has not returned to tell of it."

"And if the kindly Amiocapians had not decided to burn us to death, they might have given us to the Buried People?" asked Tanar.

"Yes, they would have taken us and bound us to trees close to one of the entrances to the underworld, but do not blame my mother's people for that as they would have been doing only that which they considered right and proper."

"Perhaps they are a kindly people," said Tanar, with a grin, "for it was certainly far more kindly to accord us death by burning at the stake than to have left us to the horrid attentions of the Coripies. But come, we will take to the trees again, for this spot does not look as beautiful to me now as it did when we first looked upon it."

Once more they took up their flight among the branches and just as they were commencing to feel the urge to sleep Tanar discovered a small deer in a game trail beneath them, and making his kill the two satisfied their hunger, and then with small branches and great leaves Tanar constructed a platform in a tree—a narrow couch, where Stellara lay down to sleep while he stood guard, and after she had slept he slept, and then once more they resumed their flight.

Strengthened and refreshed by food and sleep they renewed their journey in higher spirits and greater hopefulness. The village of Lar lay far behind and since they had left it they had seen no other village nor any sign of man.

While Stellara had slept Tanar had busied himself in fashioning crude weapons against the time when he might find proper materials for the making of better ones. A slender branch of hard wood, gnawed to a point by his strong, white teeth, must answer him for a spear. His bow was constructed of another branch and strung with tendons taken from the deer he had killed, while his arrows were slender shoots cut from a tough shrub that grew plentifully throughout the forest. He fashioned a second, lighter spear for Stellara, and thus armed each felt a sense of security that had been entirely wanting before.

On and on they went, three times they ate and once again they slept, and still they had not reached the seacoast.

The great sun hung overhead; a gentle, cooling breeze moved through the forest; birds of gorgeous plumage and little monkeys unknown to the outer world flew or scampered, sang or chattered as the man and the woman disturbed them in their passage. It was a peaceful world and to Tanar, accustomed to the savage, carnivorous beasts that overran the great mainland of his birth, it seemed a very safe and colorless world; yet he was content that nothing was interfering with their progress toward escape.

Stellara had said no more about desiring to return to Korsar and the plan that always hovered among his thoughts included taking Stellara back to Sari with him.

The peaceful trend of Tanar's thoughts was suddenly shattered by the sound of shrill trumpeting. So close it sounded that it might almost have been directly beneath him, and an instant later as he parted the foliage ahead of him he saw the cause of the disturbance.

The jungle ended here upon the edge of open meadowland that was dotted with small clumps of trees. In the foreground there were two figures—a warrior fleeing for his life and behind him a huge tandor, which, though going upon three legs, was sure soon to overtake the man.

Tanar took the entire scene in at a glance and was aware that here was a lone tandor hunter who had failed to hamstring his prey in both hind legs.

It is seldom that man hunts the great tandor single-handed and only the bravest or the most rash would essay to do so. Ordinarily there are several hunters, two of whom are armed with heavy, stone axes. While the others make a noise to attract the attention of the tandor and hide the sound of the approach of the axe men, the latter creep cautiously through the underbrush from the rear of the great animal until each is within striking distance of a hind leg. Then simultaneously they hamstring the monster, which, lying helpless, they dispatch with heavy spears and arrows.

He who would alone hamstring a tandor must be endowed not only with great strength and courage, but must be able to strike two unerring blows with his axe in such rapid succession that the beast is crippled almost before it realizes that it has been attacked.

It was evident to Tanar that this hunter had failed to get in his second blow quickly enough and now he was at the mercy of the great beast.

Since they had started upon their flight through the trees Stellara had overcome her fear and was now able to travel alone with only occasional assistance from Tanar. She had been following the Sarian and now she stood at his side, watching the tragedy being enacted below them.

"He will be killed," she cried. "Can we not save him?"

This thought had not occurred to Tanar, for was the man not an Amiocapian and an enemy; but there was something in the girl's tone that spurred the Sarian to action. Perhaps it was the instinct in the male to exhibit his prowess before the female. Perhaps it was because at heart Tanar was brave and magnanimous, or perhaps it was because that among all the other women in the world it was Stellara who had spoken. Who may know? Perhaps Tanar did not know himself what prompted his next act.

Shouting a word that is familiar to all tandor hunters and which is most nearly translatable into English as "Reverse!" he leaped to the ground almost at the side of the charging tandor and simultaneously he carried his spear hand back and drove the heavy shaft deep into the beast's side, just behind its left shoulder. Then he leaped back into the forest expecting that the tandor would do precisely what it did do.

With a squeal of pain it turned upon its new tormentor.

The Amiocapian, who still clung to his heavy axe, had heard, as though it was a miracle from the gods, the familiar signal that had burst so suddenly from Tanar's lips. It had told him what the other would attempt and he was ready, with the result that he turned back toward the beast at the instant that it wheeled to charge after Tanar, and as it crashed into the undergrowth of the jungle in pursuit of the Sarian the Amiocapian overtook it. The great axe moved swiftly as lightning and the huge beast, trumpeting with rage, sank helplessly to the ground and rolled over on its side.

"Down!" shouted the Amiocapian, to advise Tanar that the attack had been successful.

The Sarian returned and together the two warriors dispatched the great beast, while above them Stellara remained among the concealing verdure of the trees, for the women of Pellucidar do not rashly expose themselves to view of enemy warriors. In this instance she knew that it would be safer to wait and discover the attitude of the Amiocapian toward Tanar. Perhaps he would be grateful and friendly, but there was the possibility that he might not.

The beast dispatched, the two men faced one another. "Who are you," demanded the Amiocapian, "who came so bravely to the rescue of a stranger? I do not recognize you. You are not of Amiocap."

"My name is Tanar and I am from the kingdom of Sari, that lies far away on the distant mainland. I was captured by the Korsars, who invaded the empire of which Sari is a part. They were taking me and other prisoners back to Korsar when the fleet was overtaken by a terrific storm and the ship upon which I was confined was so disabled that it was deserted by its crew. Drifting helplessly with the wind and current it finally bore us to the shores of Amiocap, where we were captured by warriors from the village of Lar. They did not believe our story, but thought that we were Korsars and they were about to destroy us when we succeeded in making our escape.

"If you do not believe me," continued the Sarian,

"then one of us must die for under no circumstances will we return to Lar to be burned at the stake."

"Whether I believe you or not," replied the Amiocapian, "I should be beneath the contempt of all men were I to permit any harm to befall one who has just saved my life at the risk of his own."

"Very well," said Tanar. "We shall go our way in the knowledge that you will not reveal our whereabouts to the men of the village of Lar."

"You say 'we,'" said the Amiocapian. "You are not alone then?"

"No, there is another with me," replied Tanar.

"Perhaps I can help you," said the Amiocapian. "It is my duty to do so. In what direction are you going and how do you plan to escape from Amiocap?"

"We are seeking the coast where we hope to be able to build a craft and to cross the ocean to the mainland."

The Amiocapian shook his head. "That will be difficult," he said. "Nay, impossible."

"We may only make the attempt," said Tanar, "for it is evident that we cannot remain here among the people of Amiocap, who will not believe that we are not Korsars."

"You do not look at all like the Korsars," said the warrior. "Where is your companion? Does he look like one?"

"My companion is a woman," replied Tanar.

"If she looks no more like a Korsar than you, then it were easy to believe your story and, I, for one, am willing to believe it and willing to help you.

There are other villages upon Amiocap than Lar and other chiefs than Zural. We are all bitter against the Korsars, but we are not all blinded by our hate as is Zural. Fetch your companion and if she does not appear to be a Korsar, I will take you to my own village and see that you are well treated. If I am in doubt I will permit you to go your way; nor shall I mention the fact to others that I have seen you."

"That is fair enough," said Tanar, and then, turning, he called to the girl. "Come, Stellara! Here is a warrior who would see if you are a Korsar."

The girl dropped lightly to the ground from the branches of the tree above the two men.

As the eyes of the Amiocapian fell upon her he stepped back with an exclamation of shock and surprise.

"Gods of Amiocap!" he cried. "Allara!"

The two looked at him in amazement. "No, not Allara," said Tanar, "but Stellara, her daughter. Who are you that you should so quickly recognize the likeness?"

"I am Fedol," said the man, "and Allara was my mate."

"Then this is your daughter, Fedol," said Tanar.

The warrior shook his head, sadly. "No," he said, "I can believe that she is the daughter of Allara, but her father must have been a Korsar for Allara was stolen from me by the men of Korsar. She is a Korsar and though my heart urges me to accept her as my daughter, the customs of Amio-

cap forbid. Go your way in peace. If I can protect you I shall, but I cannot accept you, or take
you to my village."

Stellara came close to Fedol, her eyes searching
the tan skin upon his left shoulder. "You are
Fedol," she said, pointing to the red birthmark
upon his skin, "and here is the proof that my
mother gave me, transmitted to me through your
blood, that I am the daughter of Fedol," and she
turned her left shoulder to him, and there lay upon
the white skin a small, round, red mark identical
with that upon the left shoulder of the Amiocapian.

For a moment Fedol stood spellbound, his eyes
fixed upon Stellara's shoulder and then he took her
into his arms and held her closely.

"My daughter!" he murmured. "Allara come
back to me in the blood of our blood and the flesh
of our flesh!"

Chapter Six

THE ISLAND OF LOVE

THE noonday sun of Pellucidar shone down upon a happy trio as Fedol guided Stellara and Tanar towards the village of Paraht, where he ruled as chief.

"Will they receive us there as friends," asked Stellara, "or will they wish to destroy us as did the men of Lar?"

"I am chief," said Fedol. "Even if they questioned you, they will do as I command, but there will be no question for the proof is beyond dispute and they will accept you as the daughter of Fedol and Allara, as I have accepted you."

"And Tanar?" asked Stellara, "will you protect him, too?"

"Your word is sufficient that he is not a Korsar," replied Fedol. "He may remain with us as long as he wishes."

"What will Zural think of this?" asked Tanar. "He has condemned us to die. Will he not insist that the sentence be carried out?"

"Seldom do the villagers of Amiocap war one against the other," replied Fedol; "but if Zural wishes war he shall have it ere ever I shall give up you or my daughter to the burning stake of Lar."

Great was the rejoicing when the people of Paraht saw their chief, whom they had thought lost to them forever, returning. They clustered about him with glad cries of welcome, which were suddenly stilled by loud shouts of "The Korsars! The Korsars!" as the eyes of some of the people alighted upon Tanar and Stellara.

"Who cried 'Korsars'?" demanded Fedol. "What know you of these people?"

"I know them," replied a tall warrior. "I am from Lar. There are six others with me and we have been searching for these Korsars, who escaped just before they were to have been burned at the stake. We will take them back with us and Zural will rejoice that you have captured them."

"You will take them nowhere," said Fedol. "They are not Korsars. This one," and he placed a hand upon Stellara's shoulder, "is my daughter, and the man is a warrior from distant Sari. He is the son of the king of that country, which lies far away upon a mainland unknown to us."

"They told that same story to Zural," said the warrior from Lar; "but he did not believe them. None of us believed them. I was with Vulhan and his party when we took them from the Korsar ship that brought them to Amiocap."

"At first I did not believe them," said Fedol, "but Stellara convinced me that she is my daughter, just as I can convince you of the truth of her statement."

"How?" demanded the warrior.

"By the birthmark on my left shoulder," replied

Fedol. "Look at it, and then compare it with the one upon her left shoulder. No one who knew Allara can doubt that Stellara is her daughter, so closely does the girl resemble her mother, and being Allara's daughter how could she inherit the birthmark upon her left shoulder from any other sire than me?"

The warriors from Lar scratched their heads. "It would seem the best of proof," replied the warriors' spokesman.

"It is the best of proof," said Fedol. "It is all that I need. It is all the people of Paraht need. Take the word to Zural and the people of Lar and I believe that they will accept my daughter and Tanar as we are accepting them, and I believe that they will be willing to protect them as we intend to protect them from all enemies, whether from Amiocap or elsewhere."

"I shall take your message to Zural," replied the warrior, and shortly afterward they departed on the trail toward Lar.

Fedol prepared a room in his house for Stellara and assigned Tanar to a large building that was occupied solely by bachelors.

Plans were made for a great feast to celebrate the coming of Stellara and a hundred men were dispatched to fetch the ivory and the meat of the tandor that Fedol and Tanar had slain.

Fedol decked Stellara with ornaments of bone and ivory and gold. She wore the softest furs and the gorgeous plumage of rare birds. The people of Paraht loved her and Stellara was happy.

Tanar was accepted at first by the men of the

tribe with some reservations, not untinged with suspicion. He was their guest by the order of their chief and they treated him as such, but presently, when they came to know him and particularly after he had hunted with them, they liked him for himself and made him one of them.

The Amiocapians were, at first, an enigma to Tanar. Their tribal life and all their customs were based primarily upon love and kindness. Harsh words, bickering and scolding were practically unknown among them. These attributes of the softer side of man appeared at first weak and effeminate to the Sarian, but when he found them combined with great strength and rare courage his admiration for the Amiocapians knew no bounds, and he soon recognized in their attitude toward one another and toward life a philosophy that he hoped he might make clear to his own Sarians.

The Amiocapians considered love the most sacred of the gifts of the gods, and the greatest power for good and they practiced liberty of love without license. So that while they were not held in slavery by senseless man-made laws that denied the laws of God and nature, yet they were pure and virtuous to a degree beyond that which he had known in any other people.

With hunting and dancing and feasting, with tests of skill and strength in which the men of Amiocap contended in friendly rivalry, life for Stellara and Tanar was ideally happy.

Less and less often did the Sarian think of Sari. Sometime he would build a boat and return to his native country, but there was no hurry; he would

wait, and gradually even that thought faded almost
entirely from his mind. He and Stellara were often
together. They found a measure of happiness and
contentment in one another's society that was lacking at other times or with other people. Tanar had
never spoken of love. Perhaps he had not thought
of love for it seemed that he was always engaged
upon some enterprise of the hunt, or contending in
some of the sports and games of the men. His
body and his mind were occupied—a condition
which sometimes excludes thoughts of love, but
wherever he went or whatever he did the face and
figure of Stellara hovered ever in the background
of his thoughts.

Without realizing it, perhaps, his every thought,
his every act was influenced by the sweet loveliness
of the chief's daughter. Her friendship he took
for granted and it gave him great happiness, but
yet he did not speak of love. But Stellara was a
woman, and women live on love.

In the village of Paraht she saw the girls openly
avowing their love to men, but she was still bound
by the customs of Korsar and it would have been
impossible for her to bring herself to tell a man
that she loved him until he had avowed his love.
And so hearing no word of love from Tanar, she
was content with his friendship. Perhaps she, too,
had given no more thought to the matter of love
than he.

But there was another who did harbor thoughts
of love. It was Doval, the Adonis of Paraht. In
all Amiocap there was no handsomer youth than
Doval. Many were the girls who had avowed their

love to him, but his heart had been unmoved until he looked upon Stellara.

Doval came often to the house of Fedol the chief. He brought presents of skin and ivory and bone to Stellara and they were much together. Tanar saw and he was troubled, but why he was troubled he did not know.

The people of Paraht had eaten and slept many times since the coming of Tanar and Stellara and as yet no word had come from Zural, or the village of Lar, in answer to the message that Fedol had sent, but now, at last, there entered the village a party of warriors from Lar, and Fedol, sitting upon the chief's chair, received them in the tiled living room of his home.

"Welcome, men of Lar," said the chief. "Fedol welcomes you to the village of Paraht and awaits with impatience the message that you bring him from his friend, Zural the chief."

"We come from Zural and the people of Lar," said the spokesman, "with a message of friendship for Fedol and Paraht. Zural, our chief, has commanded us to express to you his deep sorrow for the unintentional wrong that he did your daughter and the warrior from Sari. He is convinced that Stellara is your daughter and that the man is no Korsar if you are convinced of these facts, and he has sent presents to them and to you and with these presents an invitation for you to visit the village of Lar and bring Stellara and Tanar with you that Zural and his people may make amends for the wrong that they unwittingly did them."

Fedol and Tanar and Stellara accepted the proffered friendship of Zural and his people, and a feast was prepared in honor of the visitors.

While these preparations were in progress a girl entered the village from the jungle. She was a dark-haired girl of extraordinary beauty. Her soft skin was scratched and soiled as from a long journey. Her hair was disheveled, but her eyes were bright with happiness and her teeth gleamed from between lips that were parted in a smile of triumph and expectation.

She made her way directly through the village to the house of Fedol and when the warriors of Lar descried her they exclaimed with astonishment.

"Letari!" cried one of them. "Where did you come from? What are you doing in the village of Paraht?"

But Letari did not answer. Instead she walked directly to where Tanar stood and halted before him.

"I have come to you," she said. "I have died many a death from loneliness and sorrow since you ran away from the village of Lar, and when the warriors returned and said that you were safe in the village of Paraht I determined to come here. And so when Zural sent these warriors to bear his message to Fedol I followed them. The way has been hard and though I kept close behind them there were many times when wild beasts menaced me and I feared that I should never reach you, but at last I am here."

"But why have you come?" demanded Tanar.

"Because I love you," replied Letari. "Before

the men of Lar and all the people of Paraht I pro-
claim my love."

Tanar flushed. In all his life he had never
been in so embarrassing a position. All eyes were
turned upon him and among them were the eyes of
Stellara.

"Well?" demanded Fedol, looking at Tanar.

"The girl is mad," said the Sarian. "She cannot love me for she scarcely knows me. She never
spoke to me but once before and that was when she
brought food to Stellara and me when we were
prisoners in the village of Lar."

"I am not mad," said Letari. "I love you."

"Will you have her?" asked Fedol.

"I do not love her," said Tanar.

"We will take her back to the village of Lar
with us when we go," said one of the warriors.

"I shall not go," cried Letari. "I love him and
I shall stay here forever."

The girl's declaration of love for Tanar seemed
not to surprise any one but the Sarian. It aroused
little comment and no ridicule. The Amiocapians,
with the possible exception of Stellara, took it as a
matter of course. It was the most natural thing in
the world for the people of this island of love to
declare themselves publicly in matters pertaining to
their hearts or to their passions.

That the general effect of such a policy was not
nor never had been detrimental to the people as a
race was evident by their high intelligence, the per-
fection of their physique, their great beauty and
their unquestioned courage. Perhaps the opposite
custom, which has prevailed among most of the peo-

ple of the outer crust for so many ages, is responsible for the unnumbered millions of unhappy human
beings who are warped or twisted mentally, morally
or physically.

But with such matters the mind of Letari was not
concerned. It was not troubled by any consideration of posterity. All she thought of was that she
loved the handsome stranger from Sari and that
she wanted to be near him. She came close to him
and looked up into his face.

"Why do you not love me?" she asked. "Am I
not beautiful?"

"Yes, you are very beautiful," he said; "but no
one can explain love, least of all I. Perhaps there
are qualities of mind and character—things that
we can neither see nor feel nor hear—that draw
one heart forever to another."

"But I am drawn to you," said the girl. "Why
are not you attracted to me?"

Tanar shook his head for he did not know. He
wished that the girl would go away and leave him
alone for she made him feel uneasy and restless and
entirely uncomfortable, but Letari had no idea of
leaving him alone. She was near him and there she
intended to stay until they dragged her away and
took her back to Lar, if they were successful in so
doing, but she had determined in her little head
that she should run away from them at the first
opportunity and hide in the jungle until she could
return to Paraht and Tanar.

"Will you talk to me?" she asked. "Perhaps
if you talk to me you will love me."

"I will talk to you," said Tanar, "but I shall not love you."

"Let us walk a little way from these people where we may talk," she said.

"Very well," said Tanar. He was only too anxious himself to get away where he might hide his embarrassment.

Letari led the way down the village street, her soft arm brushing his. "I should be a good mate," she said, "for I should love only you, and if, after a while, you did not like me you could send me away for that is one of the customs of Amiocap— that when one of two people ceases to love they shall no longer be mates."

"But they do not become mates unless they both love," insisted Tanar.

"That is true," admitted Letari, "but presently you shall love me. I know that, for all men love me. I could have for my mate any man in Lar that I choose."

"You do not feel unkindly towards yourself," said Tanar, with a grin.

"Why should I?" asked Letari. "Am I not beautiful and young?"

Stellara watched Tanar and Letari walking down the village street. She saw how close together they walked and it seemed that Tanar was very much interested in what Letari had to say to him. Doval was standing at her side. She turned to him.

"It is noisy here," she said. "There are too many people. Walk with me to the end of the village."

It was the first time that Stellara had ever indicated a desire to be alone with him and Doval felt a strange thrill of elation. "I will walk with you to the end of the village, Stellara, or to the end of Pellucidar, forever, because I love you," he said.

The girl sighed and shook her head. "Do not talk about love," she begged. "I merely wish to walk and there is no one else here to walk with me."

"Why will you not love me?" asked Doval, as they left the house of the chief and entered the main street of the village. "Is it because you love another?"

"No," cried Stellara, vehemently. "I love no one. I hate all men."

Doval shook his head in perplexity. "I cannot understand you," he said. "Many girls have told me that they loved me. I think that I could have almost any girl in Amiocap as my mate if I asked her; but you, the only one that I love, will not have me."

For a few moments Stellara was silent in thought. Then she turned to the handsome youth at her side. "You are very sure of yourself, Doval," she said, "but I do not believe that you are right. I would be willing to bet that I could name a girl who would not have you; who, no matter how hard you tried to make her, would not love you."

"If you mean yourself, then there is one," he said, "but there is no other."

"Oh, yes, there is," insisted Stellara.

"Who is she?" demanded Doval.

"Letari, the girl from Lar," said Stellara.

Doval laughed. "She throws her love at the first stranger that ·comes to Amiocap," he said. "She would be too easy."

"Nevertheless you cannot make her love you," insisted Stellara.

"I do not intend to try," said Doval. "I do not love her. I love only you, and if I made her love me of what good would that be toward making you love me? No, I shall spend my time trying to win you."

"You are afraid," said Stellara. "You know that you would fail."

"It would do me no good if I succeeded," insisted Doval.

"It would make me like you very much better than I do now," said Stellara.

"You mean that?" asked Doval.

"I most certainly do," said Stellara.

"Then I shall make the girl love me," said Doval. "And if I do you promise to be mine?"

"I said nothing of the kind," said Stellara. "I only said that I should like you very much better than I do now."

"Well, that is something," said Doval. "If you will like me very much better than you do now that is at least a step in the right direction."

"However, there is no danger of that," said Stellara, "for you cannot make her love you."

"Wait, and see," said Doval.

As Tanar and Letari turned to come back along the village street they passed Doval and Stellara, and Tanar saw that they were walking very close together and whispering in low tones. The Sarian scowled; and suddenly he discovered that he did not like Doval and he wondered why because always he had thought Doval a very fine fellow. Presently it occurred to him that the reason was that Doval was not good enough for Stellara, but then if Stellara loved him that was all there was to it and with the thought that perhaps Stellara loved him Tanar became angry with Stellara. What could she see in this Doval, he wondered, and what business had Doval to walk alone with her in the village streets? Had not he, Tanar, always had Stellara to himself? Never before had any one interfered, although all the men liked Stellara. Well, if Stellara liked Doval better than she did him, he would show her that he did not care. He, Tanar the Sarian, son of Ghak, king of Sari, would not let any woman make a fool of him and so he ostentatiously put his arm around the slim shoulders of Letari and walked thus slowly the length of the village street; nor did Stellara fail to see.

At the feast that was given in honor of the messengers sent by Zural, Stellara sat by Doval and Tanar had Letari at his side, and Doval and Letari were happy.

After the feast was over most of the villagers returned to their houses and slept, but Tanar was restless and unhappy and could not sleep so he took his weapons, his heavy spear shod with bone, his bow and his arrows, and his stone knife with the ivory handle, that Fedol the chief had given him, and went alone into the forest to hunt.

If the villagers slept an hour or a day is a matter of no moment, since there was no way of measuring the time. When they awoke—some sooner, some later—they went about the various duties of their life. Letari sought for Tanar, but she could not find him; instead she came upon Doval.

"You are very beautiful," said the man.

"I know it," replied Letari.

"You are the most beautiful girl that I have ever seen," insisted Doval.

Letari looked at him steadily for a few moments. "I never noticed you before," she said. "You are very handsome. You are quite the handsomest man that I ever saw."

"That is what every one says," replied Doval. "Many girls have told me that they loved me, but still I have no mate."

"A woman wants something beside a handsome face in her mate," said Letari.

"I am very brave," said Doval, "and I am a great hunter. I like you. Come, let us walk together," and Doval put his arm about the girl's shoulders and together they walked along the village street, while, from the doorway of her sleeping apartment in the home of her father, the chief, Stellara watched, and as she watched, a smile touched her lips.

Over the village of Paraht rested the peace of Amiocap and the calm of eternal noon. The children played at games beneath the shade of the trees that had been left dotting the village here and there when the clearing had been made. The women worked upon skins, strung beads or prepared food. The men looked to their weapons against the next hunt, or lolled idly on furs in their open living rooms—those who were not still sleeping off the effects of the heavy feast. Fedol, the chief, was bidding farewell to Zural's messengers and entrusting to them a gift for the ruler of Lar, when suddenly the peace and quiet was shattered by hoarse cries and a shattering burst of musketry.

Instantly all was pandemonium. Then women and warriors rushed from their homes; shouts, curses and screams filled the air.

"Korsars! Korsars!" rang through the village, as the bearded ruffians, taking advantage of the surprise and confusion of the villagers, rushed rapidly forward to profit by the advantage they had gained.

Chapter Seven

"KORSARS!"

TANAR the Sarian hunted through the primeval forest of Amiocap. Already his repute as a hunter stood high among the men of Paraht, but it was not to add further luster to his fame that he hunted now. It was to quiet a restlessness that would not permit him to sleep—restlessness and a strange depression that was almost unhappiness, but his thoughts were not always upon the hunt. Visions of Stellara often walked in front of him, the golden sunlight on her golden hair, and then beside her he saw the handsome Doval with an arm about her shoulder. He closed his eyes and shook his head to dispel the vision, but it persisted and he tried thinking of Letari, the beautiful maiden from Lar. Yes, Letari was beautiful. What eyes she had; and she loved him. Perhaps, after all, it would be as well to mate with her and remain forever upon Amiocap, but presently he found himself comparing Letari with Stellara and he found himself wishing that Letari possessed more of the characteristics of Stellara. She had not the character nor the intelligence of the daughter of Fedol. She offered him none of the restful companionship that had made his association with Stellara so infinitely happy.

124

He wondered if Stellara loved Doval, and if Doval loved Stellara, and with the thoughts he halted in his tracks and his eyes went wide as a sudden realization burst for the first time upon his consciousness.

"God!" he exclaimed aloud. "What a fool I have been. I have loved her always and did not know it," and wheeling about he set off at a brisk trot in the direction of Paraht, all thoughts of his hunt erased from his mind.

Tanar had hunted far, much farther than he had thought, but at last he came to the village of Fedol the chief. As he passed through the hanging barrier of Paraht, the first people that he saw were Letari and Doval. They were walking side by side and very close and the man's arm was about the slim shoulders of the girl.

Letari looked at Tanar in astonishment as she recognized him. "We all thought the Korsars had taken you with them," she cried.

"Korsars!" exclaimed Tanar. "What Korsars?"

"They were here," said Doval. "They raided the village, but we drove them off with just a small loss. There were not many of them. Where were you?"

"After the feast I went into the forest to hunt," said Tanar. "I did not know that there was a Korsar upon the island of Amiocap."

"It is just as well that you were not here," said Letari, "for while you were away I have learned that I love Doval."

"Where is Stellara?" demanded Tanar.

"She was taken by the Korsars," said Doval.

"Thank God that it was not you, Letari," and, stooping, he kissed the girl upon the lips.

With a cry of grief and rage Tanar ran swiftly to the house of Fedol the chief. "Where is Stellara?" he demanded, springing unceremoniously into the center of the living room.

An old woman looked up from where she sat with her face buried in her hands. She was the sole occupant of the room. "The Korsars took her," she said.

"Where is Fedol then?" demanded Tanar.

"He has gone with warriors to try to rescue her," said the old woman, "but it is useless. They, who are taken by the Korsars, never come back."

"Which way did they go?" asked Tanar.

Sobbing with grief, the old woman pointed in the direction taken by the Korsars, and again she buried her face in her hands, grieving for the misfortune that had overtaken the house of Fedol the chief.

Almost immediately Tanar picked up the trail of the Korsars, which he could identify by the imprints of their heeled boots, and he saw that Fedol and his warriors had not followed the same trail, evidencing the fact that they must have gone in the wrong direction to succor Stellara successfully.

Sick with anguish, maddened by hate, the Sarian plunged on through the forest. Plain to his eyes lay the spoor of his quarry. In his heart was a rage that gave him the strength of many men.

In a little glade, partially surrounded by limestone cliffs, a small company of ragged, bewhiskered men had halted to rest. Where they had halted a tiny spring broke from the base of the cliff and trickled along its winding channel for a short distance to empty into a natural, circular opening in the surface of the ground. From deep in the bottom of this natural well the water falling from the rim could be heard splashing upon the surface of the water far below. It was dark down there— dark and mysterious, but the bearded ruffians gave no heed either to the beauty or the mystery of the spot.

One huge, fierce-visaged fellow, his countenance disfigured by an ugly scar, confronted a slim girl, who sat upon the turf, her back against a tree, her face buried in her arms.

"You thought me dead, eh?" he exclaimed. "You thought Bohar the Bloody dead? Well he is not dead. Our boat weathered the storm and passing close to Amiocap we saw the wreck of The Cid's ship lying upon the sand. Knowing that you and the prisoners had been left aboard when we quit the ship, I guessed that perhaps you might be somewhere upon Amiocap; nor was I wrong, Stellara. Bohar the Bloody is seldom wrong.

"We hid close to a village which they call Lar and at the first opportunity we captured one of the villagers—a woman—and from her we learned that you had indeed come ashore, but that you were then in the village of your father and we made the woman guide us there. The rest you know and now be cheerful for at last you are to mate with Bohar the Bloody and return to Korsar."

"Rather than that I shall die," cried the girl.

"But how?" laughed Bohar. "You have no

weapons. Perhaps, however, you will choke yourself to death," and he laughed uproariously at his
own joke.

"There is a way," cried the girl, and before he
could guess what she intended, or stay her, she
dodged quickly around him and ran toward the
natural well that lay a few hundred feet away.

"Quick!" shouted Bohar. "Stop her!" And
instantly the entire twenty sprang in pursuit. But
Stellara was swift and there was likelihood that
they would not overtake her in the short distance
that lay before her and the edge of the abyss.

Fortune, however, was with Bohar the Bloody
that day and almost at her goal Stellara's foot
caught in a tangle of grasses and she stumbled forward upon her face. Before she could recover her
feet the nearest Korsar had seized her, and then
Bohar the Bloody ran to her side and, taking her
from the grasp of the other Korsar, shook her
violently.

"You she tarag!" he cried. "For this I shall fix
you so that never again will you run away. When
we reach the sea I shall cut off one of your feet
and then I shall know that you will not run away
from me again," and he continued to shake her
violently.

Breaking suddenly and unexpectedly from the
dense jungle into the opening of the glade a warrior came upon the scene being enacted at the edge
of the well. At the moment he thought that Stellara was being killed and he went mad with rage;
nor was his rage any the less when he recognized
Bohar the Bloody as the author of the assault.

With an angry shout he leaped forward, his heavy spear ready in his hand. What mattered it that twenty men with firearms opposed him? He saw only Stellara in the cruel grip of the bestial Bohar.

At the sound of his voice the Korsar looked up and instantly Bohar recognized the Sarian.

"Look, Stellara," he said, with a sneer. "Your lover has come. It is well, for with no lover and only one foot you will have no reason at all for running away."

A dozen harquebuses had already been raised in readiness and the men stood looking toward Bohar.

Tanar had reached the opposite edge of the well, only a few yards distant, when Bohar nodded and there was a roar of musketry and a flash of flame accompanied by so dense a pall of black smoke that for an instant the figure of the Sarian was entirely obliterated from view.

Stellara, wide-eyed and trembling with pain and horror, tried to penetrate the smoke cloud with her frightened eyes. Quickly it lifted, revealing no sign of Tanar.

"Well done," cried Bohar to his men. "Either you blew him all to pieces, or his body fell into the hole," and going to the edge of the opening he looked down, but it was very dark there and he saw nothing. "Wherever he is, at least he is dead," said Bohar. "I should like to have crushed his life out with my own hands, but at least he is dead by my command and the blow that he struck me is wiped out, as Bohar wipes out the blows of all his enemies."

As the Korsars resumed the march toward the ocean, Stellara walked among them with bent head and moist, unseeing eyes. Often she stumbled and each time she was jerked roughly to her feet and shaken, at the same time being admonished in hoarse tones to watch her footing.

By the time they reached the seashore Stellara was sick with a high fever and she lay in the camp of the Korsars for what may have been a day or a month, too sick to move, while Bohar and his men felled timbers, hewed planks and constructed a boat to carry them to the distant shores of Korsar.

Rushing forward to rescue Stellara from the clutches of Bohar, Tanar's mind and eyes had been fixed on nothing but the figure of the girl. He had not seen the opening in the ground and at the instant that the Korsars fired their harquebuses he had stepped unwittingly into the opening and plunged to the water far below.

The fall had not hurt him. It had not even stunned him and when he came to the surface he saw before him a quiet stream moving gently through an opening in the limestone wall about him. Beyond the opening was a luminous cavern and into this Tanar swam, clambering to its rocky floor the moment that he had found a low place in the bank of the stream. Looking about him he found himself in a large cavern, the walls of which shone luminously, so considerable was their content of phosphorus.

There was a great deal of rubbish on the floor of the cave—the bones of animals and men, broken weapons, bits of hide. It might have been the dumping ground of some grewsome charnal house.

The Sarian walked back to the opening through which the little stream had borne him into the grotto, but a careful investigation revealed no avenue of escape in this direction, although he reëntered the stream and swam into the bottom of the well where he found the walls worn so smooth by the long continued action of falling water that they gave no slightest indication of handhold or foothold.

Then slowly he made a circuit of the outer walls of the grotto, but only where the stream passed out at its far end was there any opening—a rough archway that rose some six feet above the surface of the underground stream.

Along one side was a narrow ledge and looking through the opening he saw a dim corridor leading away into the distance and obscurity.

There being no other way in which to search for freedom Tanar passed along the narrow ledge beneath the archway to find himself in a tunnel that followed the windings of the stream.

Only here and there small patches of the rock that formed the walls and ceiling of the corridor threw out a luminosity that barely relieved the inky darkness of the place, yet relieve it it did so that at least one might be sure of his footing, though at points where the corridor widened its walls were often lost in darkness.

For what distance he followed the tunnel Tanar did not know, but presently he came to a low and narrow opening through which he could pass only upon his hands and knees. Beyond there seemed to be a much lighter chamber and as Tanar came into this, still upon all fours, a heavy body dropped upon his back from above and then another at each side of him and he felt cold, clammy claws seizing his arms and legs, and arms encircled his neck— arms that felt against his flesh like the arms of a corpse.

He struggled but there were too many for him and in a moment he was disarmed and his ankles and wrists securely bound with tough thongs of raw- hide. Then he was rolled over on his side and lay looking up into the horrid faces of Coripies, the Buried People of Amiocap.

The blank faces, the corpse-like skin, the bulg- ing protuberances where the eyes would have been, the hairless bodies, the claw-like hands combined to produce such a hideous aspect in the monsters as to make the stoutest of hearts quail.

And when they spoke! The mumbled mouthing revealing yellow fangs withered the heart in the breast of the Sarian. Here, indeed, was a hideous end, for he knew that it was the end, since never in all the many tales the Amiocapians had told him of the Buried People was there any record of a human being escaping from their clutches.

Now they were addressing him and presently, in their hollow mewing, he discerned words. "How did you get into the land of the Coripies?" de- manded one.

"I fell into a hole in the ground," replied Tanar. "I did not seek to come here. Take me out and I will reward you."

"What have you to give the Coripies more than your flesh?" demanded another.

"Do not think to get out for you never shall," said a third.

Now two of them lifted him lightly and placed him upon the back of one of their companions. So easily the creature carried him that Tanar wondered that he had ever overcome the Coripi that he had met upon the surface of the ground.

Through long corridors, some very dark and others partially lighted by outcroppings of phosphorescent rock, the creature bore him. At times they passed through large grottoes, beautifully wrought in intricate designs by nature, or climbed long stairways carved in the limestone, probably by the Coripies themselves, only presently to descend other stairways and follow winding tunnels that seemed interminable.

But at last the journey ended in a huge cavern, the ceiling of which rose at least two hundred feet above them. This stupendous grotto was more brilliantly lighted than any other section of the subterranean world that Tanar had passed through. Into its limestone walls were cut pathways that zigzagged back and forth upward toward the ceiling, and the entire surface of the surrounding walls was pierced by holes several feet in diameter that appeared to be the mouths of caves.

Squatting about on the floor of the cavern were hundreds of Coripies of all ages and both sexes.

At one end of the grotto, in a large opening, a few feet above the floor, squatted a single, large Coripi. His skin was mottled with a purplish hue that suggested a corpse in which mortification had progressed to a considerable degree. The protuberances that suggested huge eyeballs beneath the skin protruded much further and were much larger than those in any other of the Coripies that Tanar had examined. The creature was, by far, the most repulsive of all the repulsive horde.

On the floor of the grotto, directly before this creature, were gathered a number of male Coripies and toward this congregation Tanar's captors bore him.

Scarcely had they entered the grotto when it became apparent to Tanar that these creatures could see, a thing that he had commenced to suspect shortly after his capture, for now, at sight of him, they commenced to scream and make strange, whistling sounds, and from the openings of many of the high flung caves within the walls heads protruded and the hideous, eyeless faces seemed to be bending eyes upon him.

One cry seemed to rise above all others as he was borne across the grotto towards the creature sitting in the niche. It was "Flesh! Flesh!" and it sounded grewsome and horrible in its suggestiveness.

Flesh! Yes, he knew that they ate human flesh and it seemed now that they were but awaiting a signal to leap upon him and devour him alive, tearing pieces from him with their heavy claws. But when one did rush upon him there came a scream from the creature in the niche and the fellow desisted, even as one of his captors had turned to defend him.

The cavern crossed at last, Tanar was deposited upon his feet in front of the creature squatting in the niche. Tanar could see the great eyeballs revolving beneath the pulsing skin of the protuberances and though he could see no eyes, he knew that he was being examined coldly and calculatingly.

"Where did you get it?" finally demanded the creature, addressing Tanar's captors.

"He tumbled into the Well of Sounding Water," replied one.

"How do you know?"

"He told us so."

"Do you believe him?"

"There was no other way in which he could enter the land of the Coripies," replied one of the captors.

"Perhaps he was leading a party in to slay us," said the creature in the niche. "Go, many of you, and search the corridors and the tunnels about the Well of Sounding Water." Then the creature turned to Tanar's captors. "Take this and put it with the others; we have not yet enough."

Tanar was now again placed upon the back of a Coripi, who carried him across the grotto and up one of the pathways cut into the face of the limestone wall. Ascending this pathway a short distance the creature turned into one of the cave openings, and Tanar found himself again in a narrow, dark, winding tunnel.

The tunnels and corridors through which he had already been conducted had impressed upon Tanar the great antiquity of this underground labyrinthian world, since there was every evidence that the majority of these tunnels had been hewn from the limestone rock or natural passageways enlarged to accommodate the Coripies, and as these creatures appeared to have no implements other than their heavy, three-toed claws the construction of the tunnels must have represented the labor of countless thousands of individuals over a period of many ages.

Tanar, of course, had only a hazy conception of what we describe as the measurable aspect of duration. His consideration of the subject concerned itself with the countless millions of times that these creatures must have slept and eaten during the course of their stupendous labors.

But the mind of the captive was also occupied with other matters as the Coripi bore him through the long tunnel. He thought of the statement of the creature in the niche, as he had ordered Tanar taken into confinement, to the effect that there were not yet enough. What did he mean? Enough of what? Enough prisoners? And when there were enough to what purpose would they be devoted?

But perhaps, to a far greater extent, his mind was occupied with thoughts of Stellara; with fears for her safety and with vain regret that he had been unable to accomplish her rescue.

From the moment that he had been so unexpectedly precipitated into the underground world of the Buried People, his dominant thought, of course, had been that of escape; but the further into the bowels of the earth he was carried the more hopeless appeared the outcome of any venture in this direction, yet he never for once abandoned it though he realized that he must wait until they had reached the place of his final confinement before he could intelligently consider any plan at all.

How far the tireless Coripi bore Tanar the Sarian could not guess, but presently they emerged into a dimly lighted grotto, before the narrow entrance to which squatted a dozen Coripies. Within the chamber were a score more and one human being—a man with sandy hair, close-set eyes and a certain mean, crafty expression of countenance that repelled the Sarian immediately.

"Here is another," said the Coripi who had carried Tanar to the cavern, and with that he dumped the Sarian unceremoniously upon the stone floor at the feet of the dozen Coripies who stood guard at the entrance.

With teeth and claws they severed the bonds that secured his wrists and ankles.

"They come slowly," grumbled one of the guards. "How much longer must we wait?"

"Old Xax wishes to have the greatest number that has ever been collected," remarked another of the Coripies.

"But we grow impatient," said the first speaker. "If he makes us wait much longer he may be one of the number here himself."

"Be careful," cautioned one of his fellows. "If Xax heard that you had said such a thing as that the number of our prisoners would be increased by one."

As Tanar arose to his feet, after his bonds were severed, he was pushed roughly toward the other inmates of the room, who he soon was to discover were prisoners, like himself, and quite naturally the first to approach him was the other human captive.

"Another," said the stranger. "Our numbers increase but slowly, yet each one brings us closer to our inevitable doom and so I do not know whether I am sorry to see you here or glad because of the human company that I shall now have. I have eaten and slept many times since I was thrown into this accursed place and always nothing but these hideous, mumbling things for company. God, how I hate and loathe them, yet they are in the same predicament as we for they, too, are doomed to the same fate."

"And what may that be?" asked Tanar.

"You do not know?"

"I may only guess," replied the Sarian.

"These creatures seldom get flesh with warm blood in it. They subsist mostly upon the fish in their underground rivers and upon the toads and lizards that inhabit their caves. Their expeditions to the surface ordinarily yield nothing more than the carcasses of dead beasts, yet they crave flesh and warm blood. Heretofore they had killed their condemned prisoners one by one as they were available, but this plan gave only a mouthful of flesh to a very few Coripies. Recently Xax hit upon the plan of preserving his own condemned and the prisoners from the outer world until he had accumulated a sufficient number to feast the entire population of the cavern of which he is chief. I do not know how many that will be, but steadily the numbers grow and perhaps it will not be long now before there are enough of us to fill the bellies of Xax's tribe."

"Xax!" repeated Tanar.   "Was he the creature sitting in the niche in the great cavern to which I was first taken?"

"That was Xax.   He is ruler of that cavern.   In the underground world of the Buried People there are many tribes, each of which occupies a large cavern similar to that in which you saw Xax.   These tribes are not always friendly and the most of the prisoners that you see in this cavern are members of other tribes, though there are a few from the tribe of Xax who have been condemned to death for one reason or another."

"And there is no escape?" asked Tanar.

"None," replied the other.   "Absolutely none; but tell me who are you and from what country? I cannot believe that you are a native of Amiocap, for what Amiocapian is there who would need ask questions about the Buried People?"

"I am not of Amiocap," replied Tanar.   "I am from Sari, upon the far distant mainland."

"Sari!   I never heard of such a country," said the other.   "What is your name?"

"Tanar, and yours?"

"I am Jude of Hime," replied the man.   "Hime is an island not far from Amiocap.   Perhaps you have heard of it."

"No," said Tanar.

"I was fishing in my canoe, off the coast of Hime," continued Jude, "when a great storm arose which blew me across the waters and hurled me upon the coast of Amiocap.   I had gone into the forest to hunt for food when three of these creatures fell upon me and dragged me into their underworld."

"And you think that there is no escape?" demanded Tanar.

"None—absolutely none," replied Jude.

Chapter Eight

Mow

IMPRISONMENT in the dark, illy lighted, poorly ventilated cavern weighed heavily upon Tanar of Pellucidar, and he knew that it was long for he had eaten and slept many times and though other Coripi prisoners were brought from time to time there seemed not to be enough to satisfy Xax's bloody craving for flesh.

Tanar had been glad of the companionship of Jude, though he never thoroughly understood the man, whose sour and unhappy disposition was so unlike his own. Jude apparently hated and mistrusted everyone, for even in speaking of the people of his own island he mentioned no one except in terms of bitterness and hatred, but this attitude Tanar generously attributed to the effect upon the mind of the Himean of his long and terrible incarceration among the creatures of the underworld, an experience which he was fully convinced might easily affect and unbalance a weak mind.

Even in the breasts of some of the Coripi prisoners Tanar managed to arouse sentiments somewhat analogous to friendship.

Among the latter was a young Coripi named Mow from the grotto of Ictl, who hated all the Coripies from the grotto of Xax and seemed suspicious of those from other grottoes.

Though the creatures seemed endowed with few human attributes or characteristics, yet it was apparent to Tanar that they set a certain value upon companionship, and being denied this among the creatures of his own kind Mow gradually turned to Tanar, whose courageous and happy spirit had not been entirely dampened by his lot.

Jude would have nothing to do with Mow or any other of the Coripies and he reproached Tanar for treating them in a friendly manner.

"We are all prisoners together," Tanar reminded him, "and they will suffer the same fate as we. It will neither lessen our danger nor add to our peace of mind to quarrel with our fellow prisoners, and I, for my part, find it interesting to talk with them about this strange world which they inhabit."

And, indeed, Tanar had learned many interesting things about the Coripies. Through his association with Mow he had discovered that the creatures were color blind, seeing everything in blacks and whites and grays through the skin that covered their great eyeballs. He learned also that owing to the restricted amount of food at their command it had been necessary to restrict their number, and to this end it had become customary to destroy women who gave birth to too many children, the third child being equivalent to a death sentence for the mother.

He learned also that among these unhappy Coripies there were no diversions and no aim in life other than eating. So meager and unvaried was their diet of fish and toads and lizards that the promise of warm flesh was the only great event in the tiresome monotony of their deadly existence.

Although Mow had no words for love and no conception of its significance, Tanar was able to gather from his remarks that this sentiment did not exist among the Buried People. A mother looked upon each child as a threat to her existence and a prophecy of death, with the result that she loathed children from birth; nor is this strange when the fact is considered that the men chose as the mothers of their children the women whom they particularly loathed and hated, since the custom of destroying a woman who had borne three children deterred them from mating with any female for whom they might have entertained any degree of liking.

When not hunting or fishing the creatures squatted around upon their haunches staring stupidly and sullenly at the floor of their cavern.

"I should think," said Tanar to Mow, "that, confronted by such a life, you would welcome death in any form."

The Coripi shook his head. "I do not want to die," he said.

"Why?" demanded Tanar.

"I do not know," replied Mow. "I simply wish to live."

"Then I take it that you would like to escape from this cavern, if you could," suggested Tanar.

"Of course I should like to escape," said Mow, "but if I try to escape and they catch me they will kill me."

"They are going to kill you anyway," Tanar reminded him.

"Yes, I never thought of that," said Mow. "That is quite true; they are going to kill me anyhow."

"Could you escape?" asked Tanar.

"I could if I had someone to help me," said Mow.

"This cavern is filled with men who will help you," said Tanar.

"The Coripies from the grotto of Xax will not help me," said Mow, "because if they escape there is no place where they may go in safety. If Xax recaptures them they will be killed, and the same is true if the ruler of any other grotto captures them."

"But there are men from other grottoes here," insisted Tanar, "and there are Jude and I."

Mow shook his head. "I would not save any of the Coripies. I hate them. They are all enemies from other grottoes."

"But you do not hate me," said Tanar, "and I will help you, and so will Jude."

"I need but one," said Mow, "but he must be very strong, stronger than you, stronger than Jude."

"How strong?" asked Tanar.

"He must be able to lift my weight," replied the Coripi.

"Look then," said Tanar, and seizing Mow he held him high above his head.

When he had set him down upon the floor again the Coripi gazed at Tanar for some time. "You are, indeed, strong," he said.

"Then let us make our plans for escape," said Tanar.

"Just you and I," said the Coripi.

"We must take Jude with us," insisted Tanar.

Mow shrugged his shoulders. "It is all the same to me," he said. "He is not a Coripi, and if we become hungry and cannot find other food we can eat him."

Tanar made no reply as he felt that it would be unwise to voice his disgust at this proposal and he was sure that he and Jude together could prevent the Coripi from succumbing to his lust for flesh.

"You have noticed at the far end of the cavern, where the shadows are so dense, that one may scarcely see a figure moving there?" asked Mow.

"Yes," said Tanar.

"There the dim shadows hide the rough, rocky walls and the ceiling there is lost in total darkness, but in the ceiling is an opening that leads through a narrow shaft into a dark tunnel."

"How do you know this?" asked Tanar.

"I discovered it once when I was hunting. I came upon a strange tunnel leading from that along which I was making my way to the upper world. I followed it to see where it led and I came at last to the opening in the ceiling of this cavern, from whence one may see all that takes place below without being himself seen. When I was brought here as a prisoner I recognized the spot immediately. That is how I know that one may escape if he has proper help."

"Explain," said Tanar.

"The wall beneath the opening is, as I have discovered, inclined backward from the floor to a considerable height and so rough that it can easily be scaled to a little ledge beneath the opening in the ceiling, but just so far beneath that one may not reach it unaided. If, however, I could lift you into the opening you could, in turn, reach down and help me up."

"But how may we hope to climb the wall without being seen by the guards?" demanded Tanar.

"That is the only chance of capture that we shall have to take," replied Mow. "It is very dark there and if we wait until another prisoner is brought and their attention is diverted we may be able to succeed in reaching the opening in the ceiling before we are discovered, and once there they cannot capture us."

Tanar discussed the plan with Jude, who was so elated at the prospect of escape that he almost revealed a suggestion of happiness.

And now commenced an interminable wait for the moment when a new prisoner might be brought into the cavern. The three conspirators made it a practice to spend most of their time in the shadows at the far end of the cavern so that the guards might become accustomed to seeing them there, and as no one other than themselves was aware of the opening in the ceiling at this point no suspicions were aroused, as the spot where they elected to be was at the opposite end of the cavern from the entrance, which was, in so far as the guards knew, the only opening into the cavern.

Tanar, Jude and Mow ate and slept several times until it began to appear that no more prisoners ever would be brought to the cavern; but if no prisoners came, news trickled in and one item filled them with such alarm that they determined to risk all upon the hazard of a bold dash for freedom.

Some Coripies coming to relieve a part of the guard reported that it had been with difficulty that Xax had been able to suppress an uprising among his infuriated tribesmen, many of whom had conceived the conviction that Xax was saving all of the prisoners for himself.

The result had been that a demand had been made upon Xax for an immediate feast of flesh. Perhaps already other Coripies were on their way to conduct the unfortunate prisoners to the great cavern of Xax, where they would be torn limb from limb by the fierce, hunger-mad throng.

And, true enough, there had been time for but one hunger before the party arrived to conduct them back to the main grotto of the tribe.

"Now is the time," whispered Tanar to Mow and Jude, seeing that the guard was engaged in conversation with the newcomers, and in accordance with their previously made plan the three started without an instant's hesitation to scale the far wall of the cavern.

Upon a little ledge, twenty-five feet from the floor, Tanar halted, and an instant later Mow and Jude stood upon either side of him. Without a word the Coripi lifted Tanar to his shoulders and in the darkness above Tanar groped for a handhold.

He soon found the opening into the shaft leading into the tunnel above, and, too, he found splendid handholds there so that an instant later he had drawn himself up into the opening and was sitting upon a small ledge that entirely encircled it.

Bracing himself, he reached down and seized the hand of Jude, who was standing upon Mow's shoulders, and drew the Himean to the ledge beside him.

At that instant a great shouting arose below them, and glancing down Tanar saw that one of the guards had discovered them and that now a general rush of both guard and prisoners was being made in their direction.

Even as Tanar reached down to aid Mow to the safety of the shaft's mouth, some of the Coripies were already scaling the wall below them. Mow hesitated and turned to look at the enemies clambering rapidly toward him.

The ledge upon which Mow stood was narrow and the footing precarious. The surprise and shock of their discovery may have unnerved him, or, in turning to look downward he may have lost his balance, but whatever it was Tanar saw him reel, topple and then lunge downward upon the ascending Coripies, scraping three of them from the wall in his descent as he crashed to the stone floor below, where he lay motionless.

Tanar turned to Jude. "We cannot help him," he said. "Come, we had better get out of this as quickly as possible."

Feeling for each new handhold and foothold the two climbed slowly up the short shaft and presently found themselves in the tunnel, which Mow had described. Darkness was absolute.

"Do you know the way to the surface?" asked Jude.

"No," said Tanar. "I was depending upon Mow to lead us."

"Then we might as well be back in the cavern," said Jude.

"Not I," said Tanar, "for at least I am satisfied now that the Coripies will not eat me alive, if they eat me at all."

Groping his way through the darkness and followed closely by Jude, Tanar crept slowly through the Stygian darkness. The tunnel seemed interminable. They became very hungry and there was no food, though they would have relished even the filthy fragments of decayed fish that the Coripies had hurled them while they were prisoners.

"Almost," said Tanar, "could I eat a toad."

They became exhausted and slept, and then again they crawled and stumbled onward. There seemed no end to the interminable, inky corridor.

For long distances the floor of the tunnel was quite level, but then again it would pitch downward, sometimes so steeply that they had difficulty in clinging to the sloping floor. It turned and twisted as though its original excavators had been seldom of the same mind as to the direction in which they wished to proceed.

On and on the two went; again they slept, but whether that meant that they had covered a great distance, or that they were becoming weak from hunger, neither knew.

When they awoke they went on again for a long time in silence, but the sleep did not seem to have refreshed them much, and Jude especially was soon exhausted again.

"I cannot go much further," he said. "Why did you lure me into this crazy escapade?"

"You need not have come," Tanar reminded him, "and if you had not you would by now be out of your misery since doubtless all the prisoners have long since been torn to pieces and devoured by the Coripies of the grotto of Xax."

Jude shuddered. "I should not mind being dead," he said, "but I should hate to be torn to pieces by those horrible creatures."

"This is a much nicer death," said Tanar, "for when we are sufficiently exhausted we shall simply sleep and awake no more."

"I do not wish to die," wailed Jude.

"You have never seemed very happy," said Tanar. "I should think one as unhappy as you would be glad to die."

"I enjoy being unhappy," said Jude. "I know that I should be most miserable were I happy and anyway I should much rather be alive and unhappy than dead and unable to know that I was unhappy."

"Take heart," said Tanar. "It cannot be much further to the end of this long corridor. Mow came through it and he did not say that it was so great a length that he became either exhausted or hungry and he not only traversed it from end to end in one direction, but he had to turn around and retrace his steps after he reached the opening into the cavern which we left."

"The Coripies do not eat much; they are accustomed to starving," said Jude, "and they sleep less than we."

"Perhaps you are right," said Tanar, "but I am sure that we are nearing the end."

"I am," said Jude, "but not the end that I had wished."

Even as they discussed the matter they were moving slowly along, when far ahead Tanar discerned a slight luminosity.

"Look," he said, "there is light. We are nearing the end."

The discovery instilled new strength into both the men and with quickened steps they hastened along the tunnel in the direction of the promised escape. As they advanced, the light became more apparent until finally they came to the point where the tunnel they had been traversing opened into a large corridor, which was filled with a subdued light from occasional patches of phosphorescent rock in walls and ceiling, but neither to the right nor the left could they see any sign of daylight.

"Which way now?" demanded Jude.

Tanar shook his head. "I do not know," he said.

"At least I shall not die in that awful blackness," wailed Jude, and perhaps that factor of their seemingly inevitable doom had weighed most heavily upon the two Pellucidarians, for, living as these people do beneath the brilliant rays of a perpetual noonday sun, darkness is a hideous and abhorrent thing to them, so unaccustomed are they to it.

"In this light, however slight it may be," said Tanar, "I can no longer be depressed. I am sure that we shall escape."

"But in which direction?" again demanded Jude.

"I shall turn to the right," said Tanar.

Jude shook his head. "That probably is the wrong direction," he said.

"If you know that the right direction lies to the left," said Tanar, "let us go to the left."

"I do not know," said Jude; "doubtless either direction is wrong."

"All right," said Tanar, with a laugh. "We shall go to the right," and, turning, he set off at a brisk walk along the larger corridor.

"Do you notice anything, Jude?" asked Tanar.

"No. Why do you ask?" demanded the Himean.

"I smell fresh air from the upper world," said Tanar, "and if I am right we must be near the mouth of the tunnel."

Tanar was almost running now; exhaustion was forgotten in the unexpected hope of immediate deliverance. To be out in the fresh air and the light of day! To be free from the hideous darkness and the constant menace of recapture by the hideous monsters of the underworld! And across that bright hope, like a sinister shadow, came the numbing fear of disappointment.

What, if, after all, the breath of air which was now clear and fresh in their nostrils should prove to be entering the corridor through some unscalable shaft, such as the Well of Sounding Water into which he had fallen upon his entrance into the country of the Buried People, or what, if, at the moment of escape, they should meet a party of the Coripies?

So heavily did these thoughts weigh upon Tanar's mind that he slackened his speed until once again he moved in a slow walk.

"What is the matter?" demanded Jude. "A moment ago you were running and now you are barely crawling along. Do not tell me that you were mistaken and that, after all, we are not approaching the mouth of the corridor."

"I do not know," said Tanar. "We may be about to meet a terrible disappointment and if that is true I wish to delay it as long as possible. It would be a terrible thing to have hope crushed within our breasts now."

"I suppose it would," said Jude, "but that is precisely what I have been expecting."

"You, I presume, would derive some satisfaction from disappointment," said Tanar.

"Yes," said Jude, "I suppose I would. It is my nature."

"Then prepare to be unhappy," cried Tanar, suddenly, "for here indeed is the mouth of the tunnel."

He had spoken just as he had rounded a turn in the corridor, and when Jude came to his side the latter saw daylight creeping into the corridor through an opening just in front of them—an opening beyond which he saw the foliage of growing things and the blue sky of Pellucidar.

Emerging again to the light of the sun after their long incarceration in the bowels of the earth, the two men were compelled to cover their eyes with their hands, while they slowly accustomed themselves again to the brilliant light of the noon-day sun of Pellucidar.

When he was able to uncover his eyes and look about him, Tanar saw that the mouth of the tunnel was high upon the precipitous side of a lofty mountain. Below them wooded ravines ran down to a mighty forest, just beyond which lay the sparkling waters of a great ocean that, curving upward, merged in the haze of the distance.

Faintly discernible in the mid-distance an island raised its bulk out of the waters of the ocean.

"That," said Jude, pointing, "is the island of Hime."

"Ah, if I, too, could but see my home from here," sighed Tanar, "my happiness would be almost complete. I envy you, Jude."

"It gives me no happiness to see Hime," said Jude. "I hate the place."

"Then you are not going to try to go back to it?" demanded Tanar.

"Certainly, I shall," said Jude.

"But, why?" asked Tanar.

"There is no other place where I may go," grumbled Jude. "At least in Hime they will not kill me for no reason at all as strangers would do if I went elsewhere."

Jude's attention was suddenly attracted by something below them in a little glade that lay at the upper end of the ravine, which started a little distance below the mouth of the tunnel.

"Look," he cried, "there are people."

Tanar looked in the direction in which Jude was pointing, and when his eyes found the figures far below they first went wide with incredulity and then narrowed with rage.

"God!" he exclaimed, and as he voiced that single exclamation he leaped swiftly downward in the direction of the figures in the glade.

Chapter Nine

LOVE AND TREACHERY

STELLARA, lying upon a pallet of grasses beneath the shade of a large tree, above the beach where the Korsars were completing the boat in which they hoped to embark for Korsar, knew that the fever had left her and that her strength was rapidly returning, but having discovered that illness, whether real or feigned, protected her from the attentions of Bohar, she continued to permit the Korsars to believe that she was quite ill. In her mind there constantly revolved various plans for escape, but she wished to delay the attempt as long as possible, not only that she might have time to store up a greater amount of reserve strength, but also because she realized that if she waited until the Korsar boat was completed it would be unlikely that the majority of the men would brook delay in departure for the purpose of gratifying any desire that Bohar might express to pursue and recapture her.

Again, it was necessary to choose a time when none of the Korsars was in camp and as one of the two, who were detailed to prepare food and stand guard, was invariably on duty it appeared possible that she might never have the opportunity she hoped for, though she had determined that this fact would not prevent her from making an attempt at escape.

All of her hopes in this direction were centered upon one contingency, which her knowledge of nautical matters made to appear almost a certainty of the near future, and this was the fact that the launching of the boat would require the united efforts and strength of the entire party.

She knew from the discussions and conversations that she had overheard that it was Bohar's intention to launch the boat the moment that the hull was completed and to finish the balance of the work upon it while it floated in the little cove upon the beach of which it was being constructed.

This work would require no great amount of time or effort, since the mast, spars, rigging and sail were ready and at hand; bladders and gourds already prepared to receive fresh water, and food provisions for the trip, accumulated by the hunters detailed for this purpose, were neatly sewn up in hides and stored away in a cool, earth-covered dugout.

And so from her couch of grasses beneath the great tree Stellara watched the work progressing upon the hull of the boat that was to carry Bohar and his men to Korsar, and, as she watched, she planned her method of escape.

Above the camp rose the forested slopes of the hills which she must cross in her return to Paraht. For some distance the trees were scattered and then commenced the dense forest. If she could reach this unobserved she felt that she might entertain high hope of successful escape, for once in the denser growth she could take advantage of the skill and experience she had acquired under Tanar's tutorage and prosecute her flight along the leafy pathways of the branches, leaving no spoor that Bohar might follow and at the same time safeguarding herself from the attacks of the larger and more dangerous beasts of the forest, for, though few, there were still dangerous beasts upon Amiocap. Perhaps the most fearsome was the tarag, the giant, saber-toothed tiger that once roamed the hills of the outer crust. For the tandor she felt less concern since they seldom attack an individual unless molested; but in the hills which she must cross the greatest danger lay in the presence of the tarag and the ryth, the gigantic cave bear or Ursus Stelaeus, long since extinct upon the outer crust. Of the men of Amiocap whom she might possibly encounter she entertained little fear, even though they might be members of tribes other than hers, though she shuddered at the thought that she might fall into the hands of the Coripies, as these grotesque monsters engendered within her far greater fear than any of the other dangers that might possibly beset her way.

The exhilaration of contemplated flight and the high hopes produced within her at prospects of successfully returning to her father and her friends were dampened by the realization that Tanar would not be there to greet her. The supposed death of the Sarian had cast a blight upon her happiness that naught ever could remove and her sorrow was the deeper, perhaps, because no words of love had passed between them, and, therefore, she had not the consolation of happy memories to relieve the gnawing anguish of her grief.

The work upon the hull of the boat was at last completed and the men, coming to camp to eat, spoke hopefully of early departure for Korsar. Bohar approached Stellara's couch and stood glaring down upon her, his repulsive face darkened by a malignant scowl.

"How much longer do you intend to lie here entirely useless to me?" he demanded. "You eat and sleep and the flush of fever has left your skin. I believe that you are feigning illness in order to escape fulfilling your duties as my mate and if that is true, you shall suffer for it. Get up!"

"I am too weak," said Stellara. "I cannot rise."

"That can be remedied," growled Bohar, and seizing her roughly by the hair, he dragged her from her couch and lifted her to her feet.

As Bohar released his hold upon her, Stellara staggered, her legs trembled, her knees gave beneath her and she fell back upon her couch, and so realistic was the manner in which she carried out the deception that even Bohar was fooled.

"She is sick and dying," growled one of the Korsars. "Why should we take her along in an overcrowded boat to eat the food and drink the water that some of us may be dying for before we reach Korsar?"

"Right," cried another. "Leave her behind."

"Stick a knife into her," said a third. "She is good for nothing."

"Shut up!" cried Bohar. "She is going to be my mate and she is going with us." He drew his two huge pistols. "Whoever objects will stay here with a bullet in his guts. Eat now, you filthy hounds, and be quick about it for I shall need all hands and all your strength to launch the hull when you have eaten."

So they were going to launch the hull! Stellara trembled with excitement as the moment for her break for liberty drew near. With impatience she watched the Korsars as they bolted their food like a pack of hungry wolf-dogs. She saw some of them throw themselves down to sleep after they had eaten, but Bohar the Bloody kicked them into wakefulness, and, at the point of his pistol, herded them to the beach, taking every available man and leaving Stellara alone and unguarded for the first time since he had seized her in the village of Fedol the chief.

She watched them as they descended to the hull and she waited until they seemed to be wholly engrossed in their efforts to shove the heavy boat into the sea; then she rose from her pallet and scurried like a frightened rabbit toward the forest on the slopes above the camp.

The hazards of fate, while beyond our control, are the factors in life which oftentimes make for the success or failure of our most important ventures. Upon them hang the fruition of our most cherished hope. They are, in truth, in the lap of the gods, where lies our future, and it was only by the merest hazard that Bohar the Bloody chanced to glance back toward the camp at the very moment that Stellara rose from her couch to make her bid for freedom.

With an oath he abandoned the work of launching the hull, and, calling his men to follow him, ran hurriedly up the steep slope in pursuit.

His fellows took in the situation at a glance and hesitated. "Let him chase his own woman," growled one. "What have we to do with it? Our business is to launch the boat and get her ready to sail to Korsar."

"Right," said another, "and if he is not back by the time that we are ready we shall sail without him."

"Good," cried a third. "Let us make haste then in the hope that we may be prepared to sail before he returns."

And so Bohar the Bloody, unaccompanied by his men, pursued Stellara alone. Perhaps it was as well for the girl that this was true for there were many fleeter among the Korsars than the beefy Bohar.

The girl was instantly aware that her attempt to escape had been discovered, for Bohar was shouting in stentorian tones demanding that she halt, but his words only made her run the faster until presently she had darted into the forest and was lost to his view.

Here she took to the trees, hoping thereby to elude him even though she knew that her speed would be reduced. She heard the sound of his advance as he crashed through the underbrush and she knew that he was gaining rapidly upon her, but this did not unnerve her since she was confident that he could have no suspicion that she was in the branches of the trees and just so long as she kept among thick foliage he might pass directly beneath her without being aware of her close presence, and that is precisely what he did, cursing and puffing as he made his bull-like way up the steep slope of the hillside.

Stellara heard him pass and go crashing on in pursuit, and then she resumed her flight, turning to the right away from the direction of Bohar's advance until presently the noise of his passing was lost in the distance; then she turned upward again toward the height she must cross on her journey to Paraht.

Bohar sweated upward until finally almost utter exhaustion forced him to rest. He found himself in a little glade and here he lay down beneath a shrub that not only protected him from the rays of the sun, but hid him from sight as well, for in savage Pellucidar it is always well to seek rest in concealment.

Bohar's mind was filled with angry thoughts. He cursed himself for leaving the girl alone in camp and he cursed the girl for escaping, and he cursed the fate that had forced him to clamber up this steep hillside upon his futile mission, and most of all he cursed his absent followers whom he now realized had failed to accompany him. He knew that he had lost the girl and that it would be like looking for a particular minnow in the ocean to continue his search for her, and so, having rested, he was determined to hasten back to his camp when

his attention was suddenly attracted by a noise at
the lower end of the glade. Instinctively he
reached for one of his pistols and to his dismay
he found that both were gone, evidently having
slipped from his sash or been scraped from it as
he wallowed upward through the underbrush.

Bohar, despite his bluster and braggadocio, was
far from courageous. Without his weapons he was
an arrant coward and so now he cringed in his
concealment as he strained his eyes to discover the
author of the noise he had heard, and as he watched
a cunning leer of triumph curled his hideous mouth,
for before him, at the far end of the glade, he saw
Stellara drop from the lower branches of a tree and
come upward across the glade toward him.

As the girl came abreast of his hiding place,
Bohar the Bloody leaped to his feet and confronted
her. With a stifled exclamation of dismay Stellara
turned and sought to escape, but the Korsar was
too close and too quick and reaching forth he seized
her roughly by the hair.

"Will you never learn that you cannot escape
Bohar the Bloody?" he demanded. "You are mine
and for this I shall cut off both your feet at the
ankles when I get you into the boat, so that there
will be no chance whatever that you may again
run away from me. But come, mate willingly with
me and it will go less hard with you," and he drew
her slim figure into his embrace.

"Never," cried Stellara, and she struck him in
the face with her two clenched fists.

With an oath Bohar seized the girl by the throat
and shook her. "You she-ryth," he cried, "if I did

not want you so badly I should kill you, and by the god of Korsar if ever you strike me again I shall kill you."

"Then kill me," cried Stellara, "for I should rather die than mate with you," and again she struck him with all her strength full in the face.

Bohar frothed with rage as he closed his fingers more tightly upon the girl's soft neck. "Die, then, you——"

The words died upon his lips and he wheeled about as there fell upon his ears a man's loud voice raised in anger.

As he stood there hesitating and looking in the direction of the sound, the underbrush at the upper end of the glade parted and a warrior, leaping into the clearing, ran swiftly toward him.

Bohar blanched as though he had seen a ghost, and then, hurling the girl roughly to the ground, he faced the lone warrior.

Bohar would have fled had he not realized the futility of flight, for what chance had he in a race with this lithe man, who leaped toward him with the grace and speed of a deer.

"Go away," shouted Bohar. "Go away and leave us alone. This is my mate."

"You lie," growled Tanar of Pellucidar as he leaped upon the Korsar.

Down went the two men, the Sarian on top, and as they fell each sought a hold upon the other's throat, and, failing to secure it, they struck blindly at one another's face.

Tanar was mad with rage. He fought like a wild beast, forgetting all that David Innes had taught him. His one thought was to kill; it mattered not how just so long as he killed, and Bohar, on the defensive fighting for his life, battled like a cornered rat. To his advantage were his great weight and his longer reach, but in strength and agility as well as courage Tanar was his superior.

Stellara slowly opened her eyes as she recovered from the swoon into which she had passed beneath the choking fingers of Bohar the Bloody. At first she did not recognize Tanar, seeing only two warriors battling to the death on the sward of the glade and guessing that she would be the prey of him who was victorious. But presently, in the course of the duel, the face of the Sarian was turned toward her.

"Tanar!" she cried. "God is merciful. I thought you were dead and He has given you back to me."

At her words the Sarian redoubled his efforts to overcome his antagonist, but Bohar succeeded in getting his fingers upon Tanar's throat.

Horrified, Stellara looked about her for a rock or a stick with which to come to the succor of her champion, but before she had found one she realized that he needed no outside assistance. With a single Herculean movement he tore himself loose from Bohar and leaped to his feet.

Instantly the Korsar sprang to an upright position and lowering his head he charged the Sarian —charged like a mad bull.

Now Tanar was fighting with cool calculation. The blood-madness of the first moment following the sight of Stellara in the choking murderous fingers of the Korsar had passed. He awaited Bohar's rush, and as they came together he clamped an arm around the Korsar's head, and, turning swiftly, hurled the man over his shoulder and heavily to the ground. Then he waited.

Once more Bohar, shaking his head, staggered to his feet. Once more he rushed the Sarian, and once more that deadly arm was locked about his head, and once more he was hurled heavily to the ground.

This time he did not arise so quickly nor so easily. He came up staggering and feeling of his head and neck.

"Prepare to die," growled Tanar. "For the suffering you have inflicted upon Stellara you are about to die."

With a shriek of mingled rage and fright Bohar, gone mad, charged the Sarian again, and for the third time his great body flew through the air, to alight heavily upon the hard ground, but this time it did not arise; it did not stir, for Bohar the Bloody lay dead with a broken neck.

For a moment Tanar of Pellucidar stood ready over the body of his fallen foe, but when he realized that Bohar was dead he turned away with a sneer of disgust.

Before him stood Stellara, her beautiful eyes filled with incredulity and with happiness.

"Tanar!" It was only a whisper, but it carried to him a world of meaning that sent thrill after thrill through his body.

"Stellara!" he cried, as he took the girl in his arms. "Stellara, I love you."

Her soft arms stole around his neck and drew

his face to hers. His mouth covered her mouth in a long kiss, and, as he raised his face to look down into hers, from her parted lips burst a single exclamation, "Oh, God!" and from the depth of her half-closed eyes burned a love beyond all understanding.

"My mate," he cried, as he pressed her form to him.

"My mate," breathed Stellara, "while life remains in my body and after life, throughout death, forever!"

Suddenly she looked up and drew away.

"Who is that, Tanar?" she asked.

As Tanar turned to look in the direction indicated by the girl he saw Jude emerging from the forest at the upper end of the glade. "It is Jude," he said to Stellara, "who escaped with me from the country of the Buried People."

Jude approached them, his sullen countenance clouded by its habitual scowl.

"He frightens me," said Stellara, pressing closer to Tanar.

"You need not fear him," said the Sarian. "He is always scowling and unhappy; but he is my friend and even if he were not he is harmless."

"I do not like him," whispered Stellara.

Jude approached and stopped before them. His eyes wandered for a moment to the body of Bohar and then came back and fastened themselves in a steady gaze upon Stellara, appraising her from head to foot. There was a crafty boldness in his gaze that disturbed Stellara even more than his sullen scowl.

"Who is the woman?" he demanded, without taking his eyes from her face.

"My mate," replied Tanar.

"Then she is going with us?" asked Jude.

"Of course," replied the Sarian.

"And where are we going?" demanded Jude.

"Stellara and I will return to Paraht, where her father, Fedol, is chief," replied Tanar. "You may come with us if you wish. We will see that you are received as a friend and treated well until you can find the means to return to Hime."

"Is he from Hime?" asked Stellara, and Tanar felt her shudder.

"I am from Hime," said Jude, "but I do not care if I never return there if your people will let me live with them."

"That," said Tanar, "is something that must be decided by Fedol and his people, but I can promise you that they will let you remain with them, if not permanently, at least until you can find the means of returning to Hime. And now, before we set out for Paraht, let us renew our strength with food and sleep."

Without weapons it was not easy to obtain game and they had traveled up the mountain slopes for some distance before the two men were able to bring down a brace of large birds, which they knocked over with well aimed stones. The birds closely resembled wild turkeys, whose prototypes were doubtless the progenitors of the wild turkeys of the outer crust. The hunt had brought them to a wide plateau, just below the summit of the hills. It was a rolling table-land, waist deep in lush grasses, with here and there a giant tree or a group of trees offering shade from the vertical rays of the noonday sun.

Beside a small stream, which rippled gayly downward toward the sea, they halted to eat and sleep.

Jude gathered firewood while Tanar made fire by the primitive method of rapidly revolving a sharpened stick in a tinder-filled hole in a larger piece of dry wood. As these preparations were going forward Stellara prepared the birds and it was not long before the turkeys were roasting over a hot fire.

Their hunger appeased, the urge to sleep took possession of them, and now Jude insisted that he stand the first watch, arguing that he had not been subjected to the fatigue of battle as had Tanar, and so Stellara and the Sarian lay down beneath the shade of the tree while the scowling Himean stood watch.

Even in the comparative safety of Amiocap danger might always be expected to lurk in the form of carnivorous beast or hunting man, but the watcher cast no solicitous glances beyond the camp. Instead, he squatted upon his haunches, devouring Stellara with his eyes. Not once did he remove them from the beautiful figure of the girl except occasionally to glance quickly at Tanar, where the regular rising and falling of his breast denoted undisturbed slumber.

Whatever thoughts the beauty of the sleeping girl engendered in the breast of the Himean, they were reflected only in the unremitting scowl that never lifted itself from the man's dark brows.

Presently he arose noiselessly and gathered a handful of soft grasses, which he rolled into a small ball. Then he crept stealthily to where Stellara lay and kneeled beside her.

Suddenly he leaned over her and grasped her by the throat, at the same time clamping his other hand, in the palm of which lay the ball of grass, over her mouth.

Thus rudely awakened from deep slumber, her first glance revealing the scowling features of the Himean, Stellara opened her mouth to scream for help, and, as she did so, Jude forced the ball of grass between her teeth and far into her mouth, dragged her to her feet, and, throwing her across his shoulder, bore her swiftly downward across the table-land.

Stellara struggled and fought to free herself, but Jude was a powerful man and her efforts were of no avail against his strength. He held her in such a way that both her arms were confined. The ball of grass expanded in her mouth and she could not force it out with her tongue alone. A single scream she knew would awaken Tanar and bring him to her rescue, but she could not scream.

Down across the rolling table-land the Himean carried Stellara to the edge of a steep cliff that overhung the sea at the upper end of a deep cove which cut far into the island at this point. Here Jude lowered Stellara to her feet, but he still clung tightly to one of her wrists.

"Listen, woman," he growled, "you are coming to Hime to be the mate of Jude. If you come peaceably, no harm will befall you and if you will promise to make no outcry I shall remove the gag from your mouth. Do you promise?"

Stellara shook her head determinedly in an unquestionable negative and at the same time struggled to free herself from Jude's grasp.

With an ugly growl the man struck her and as she fell unconscious he gathered long grasses and twisted them into a rope and bound her wrists and ankles; then he lifted her again to his shoulder and started down over the edge of the cliff, where a narrow trail now became discernible.

It was evident that Jude had had knowledge of this path since he had come to it so unerringly, and the ease and assurance with which he descended it strengthened this conviction.

The descent was not over a hundred feet to a little ledge almost at the water's edge.

It was here that Stellara gained consciousness, and, as she opened her eyes, she saw before her a water-worn cave that ran far back beneath the cliff.

Into this, along the narrow ledge, Jude carried her to the far end of the cavern, where, upon a narrow, pebbly beach, were drawn up a half dozen dugouts—the light, well-made canoes of the Himeans.

In one of these Jude placed the girl, and, pushing it off into the deep water of the cove, leaped into it himself, seized the paddle and directed its course out toward the open sea.

Chapter Ten

PURSUIT

AWAKENING from a deep and refreshing slumber, Tanar opened his eyes and lay gazing up into the foliage of the tree above him. Happy thoughts filled his mind, a smile touched his lip and then, following the trend of his thoughts, his eyes turned to feast upon the dear figure of his mate.

She was not there, where he had last seen her huddled snugly in her bed of grasses, but still he felt no concern, thinking merely that she had awakened before him and arisen.

Idly his gaze made a circuit of the little camp, and then with a startled exclamation he leaped to his feet for he realized that both Stellara and Jude had disappeared. Again he looked about him, this time extending the field of his enquiring gaze, but nowhere was there any sign of either the man or the woman that he sought.

He called their names aloud, but there was no response, and then he fell to examining the ground about the camp. He saw where Stellara had been sleeping and to his keen eyes were revealed the tracks of the Himean as he had approached her couch. He saw other tracks leading away, the tracks of Jude alone, but in the crushed grasses where the man had gone he read the true story, for they told him that more than the weight of a single man had bent and bruised them thus; they told him that Jude had carried Stellara off, and Tanar knew that it had been done by force.

Swiftly he followed the well marked spoor through the long grass, oblivious of all else save the prosecution of his search for Stellara and the punishment of Jude. And so he was unaware of the sinister figure that crept along the trail behind him.

Down across the table-land they went—the man and the great beast following silently in his tracks. Down to a cliff overhanging the sea the trail led, and here as Tanar paused an instant to look out across the ocean he saw hazily in the distance a canoe and in the canoe were two figures, but who they were he could only guess since they were too far away for him to recognize.

As he stood there thus, stunned for a moment, a slight noise behind him claimed his attention, recalled him momentarily from the obsession of his sorrow and his rage so that he turned a quick, scowling glance in the direction from which the interruption had come, and there, not ten paces from him, loomed the snarling face of a great tarag.

The fangs of the saber-tooth gleamed in the sunlight; the furry snout was wrinkled in a snarl of anger; the lashing tail came suddenly to rest, except for a slight convulsive twitching of its tip; the beast crouched and Tanar knew that it was about to charge.

Unarmed and single-handed as he was, the man seemed easy prey for the carnivore; nor to right nor to left was there any avenue of escape.

All these things passed swiftly through the mind of the Sarian, yet never did they totally obliterate the memory of the two figures in the canoe far out at sea behind him; nor of the cliff overhanging the waters of the cove beneath. And then the tarag charged.

A hideous scream broke from the savage throat as the great beast hurled itself forward with lightning-like rapidity. Two great bounds it took, and in mid-spring of the second Tanar turned and dove head foremost over the edge of the cliff, for the only alternative that remained to him was death beneath the rending fangs and talons of the saber-tooth.

For all he knew jagged rocks might lie just beneath the surface of the water, but there was one chance that the water was deep, while no chance for life remained to him upon the cliff top.

The momentum of the great cat's spring, unchecked by the body of his expected prey, carried him over the edge of the cliff also so that man and beast hurtled downward almost side by side to the water far below.

Tanar cut the water cleanly with extended hands and turning quickly upwards came to the surface scarcely a yard from where the great cat had alighted.

The two faced one another and at sight of the man the tarag burst again into hideous screams and struck out swiftly toward him.

Tanar knew that he might outdistance the tarag in the water, but at the moment that they reached the beach he would be at the mercy of the great carnivore. The snarling face was close to his; the great talons were reaching for him as Tanar of Pellucidar dove beneath the beast.

A few, swift strokes brought him up directly behind the cat and an instant later he had reached out and seized the furry hide. The tarag turned swiftly to strike at him, but already the man was upon his shoulders and his weight was carrying the snarling face below the surface.

Choking, struggling, the maddened animal sought to reach the soft flesh of the man with his raking talons, but in the liquid element that filled the sea its usual methods of offense and defense were worthless. Quickly realizing that death stared it in the face, unless it could immediately overcome this handicap, the tarag now strained its every muscle to reach the solid footing of the land, while Tanar on his part sought to prevent it. Now his fingers had crept from their hold upon the furry shoulders down to the white furred throat and like claws of steel they sank into the straining muscles.

No longer did the beast attempt to scream and the man, for his part, fought in silence.

It was a grim duel; a terrible duel; a savage encounter that might be enacted only in a world that was very young and between primitive creatures who never give up the stern battle for life until the scythe of the Grim Reaper has cut them down.

Deep into the gloomy cavern beneath the cliff the tarag battled for the tiny strip of beach at the far end and grimly the man fought to hold it back and force its head beneath the water. He felt the efforts of the beast weakening and yet they were very close to the beach. At any instant the great claws might strike bottom and Tanar knew that there was still left within that giant carcass enough vitality to rend him to shreds if ever the tarag got four feet on solid ground and his head above the water.

With a last supreme effort he tightened his fingers upon the throat of the tarag and sliding from its back sought to drag it from its course, and the animal upon its part made one, last supreme effort for life. It reared up in the water and wheeling about struck at the man. The raking talons grazed his flesh, and then he was back upon the giant shoulders forcing the head once more beneath the surface of the sea. He felt a spasm pass through the great frame of the beast beneath him; the muscles relaxed and the tarag floated limp.

A moment later Tanar dragged himself to the pebbly beach, where he lay panting from exhaustion.

Recovered, nor did it take him long to recover, so urgent were the demands of the pursuit upon which he was engaged, Tanar rose and looked about him. Before him were canoes, such as he had never seen before, drawn up upon the narrow beach. Paddles lay in each of the canoes as though they but awaited the early return of their owners. Whence they had come and what they were doing here in this lonely cavern, Tanar could not guess. They were unlike the canoes of the Amiocapians, which fact convinced him that they belonged to a people from some other island, or possibly from the mainland itself. But these were questions which did not concern him greatly at the time. Here were canoes. Here was the means of pursuing the two that he had seen far out at sea and whom he was convinced were none other than Jude and Stellara.

Seizing one of the small craft he dragged it to the water's edge and launched it. Then, leaping into it, he paddled swiftly down the cove out towards the sea, and as he paddled he had an opportunity to examine the craft more closely.

It was evidently fashioned from a single log of very light wood and was all of one piece, except a bulkhead at each end of the cockpit, which was large enough to accommodate three men.

Rapping with his paddle upon the surface of the deck and upon the bulkheads convinced him that the log had been entirely hollowed out beneath the deck and as the bulkheads themselves gave every appearance of having been so neatly fitted as to be watertight, Tanar guessed that the canoe was unsinkable.

His attention was next attracted by a well-tanned and well-worn hide lying in the bottom of the cockpit. A rawhide lacing ran around the entire periphery of the hide and as he tried to determine the purpose to which the whole had been put his eyes fell upon a series of cleats extending entirely around the edge of the cockpit, and he guessed that the hide was intended as a covering for it. Examining it more closely he discovered an opening in it about the size of a man's body and immediately its purpose became apparent to him. With the covering in place and laced tightly around the cockpit and also laced around the man's body the canoe could ship no water and might prove a seaworthy craft, even in severe storms.

As the Sarian fully realized his limitations as a seafaring man, he lost no time in availing himself of this added protection against the elements, and when he had adjusted it and laced it tightly about the outside of the cockpit and secured the lacing which ran around the opening in the center of the hide about his own body, he experienced a feeling of security that he had never before felt when he had been forced to surrender himself to the unknown dangers of the sea.

Now he paddled rapidly in the direction in which he had last seen the canoe with its two occupants, and when he had passed out of the cove into the open sea he espied them again, but this time so far out that the craft and its passengers appeared only as a single dot upon the broad waters. But beyond them hazily loomed the bulk of the island that Jude had pointed out as Hime and this tended to crystallize Tanar's assurance that the canoe ahead of him was being guided by Jude toward the island of his own people.

The open seas of Pellucidar present obstacles to the navigation of a small canoe that would seem insurmountable to men of the outer crust, for their waters are ofttimes alive with saurian monsters of a long past geologic epoch and it was encounters with these that the Sarian mountaineer apprehended with more acute concern than consideration of adverse wind or tempest aroused within him.

He had noticed that one end of the long paddle
he wielded was tipped with a piece of sharpened
ivory from the end of a tandor's tusk, but the thing
seemed an utterly futile weapon with which to combat a tandoraz or an azdyryth, two of the might-
iest and most fearsome inhabitants of the deep, but
as far as he could see ahead the long, oily swells
of a calm ocean were unruffled by marine life of
any description.

Well aware of his small experience and great
deficiency as a paddler, Tanar held no expectation
of being able to overhaul the canoe manned by the
experienced Jude. The best that he could hope was
that he might keep it in view until he could mark
the spot upon Hime where it landed. And once
upon solid ground again, even though it was an
island peopled by enemies, the Sarian felt that he
would be able to cope with any emergency that
might arise.

Gradually the outlines of Hime took definite
shape before him, while those of Amiocap became
correspondingly vague behind.

And between him and the island of Hime the
little dot upon the surface of the sea told him that
his quarry had not as yet made land. The pursuit
seemed interminable. Hime seemed to be receding
almost as rapidly as he approached it. He became
hungry and thirsty, but there was neither food nor
water. There was naught but to bend his paddle
ceaselessly through the monotonous grind of pursuit, but at length the details of the shore-line grew
more distinct. He saw coves and inlets and wooded

hills and then he saw the canoe that he was following disappear far ahead of him beyond the entrance of a cove. Tanar marked the spot well in his mind and redoubled his efforts to reach the shore. And then fate arose in her inexorable perversity and confounded all his hopes and plans.

A sudden flurry on the surface of the water far to his right gave him his first warning. And then, like the hand of a giant, the wind caught his frail craft and turned it at right angles to the course he wished to pursue. The waves rolled; the wind shrieked; the storm was upon him in great fury and there was naught to do but turn and flee before it.

Down the coast of Hime he raced, parallel to the shore, further and further from the spot where Jude had landed with Stellara, but all the time Tanar was striving to drive his craft closer and closer to the wooded slopes of Hime.

Ahead of him, and upon his right, he could see what appeared to be the end of the island. Should he be carried past this he realized that all would be lost, for doubtless the storm would carry him on out of sight of land and if it did he knew that he could never reach Hime nor return to Amiocap, since he had no means whatsoever of ascertaining direction once land slipped from view in the haze of the upcurving horizon.

Straining every muscle, continuously risking being capsized, Tanar strove to drive inward toward the shore, and though he saw that he was gaining he knew that it was too late, for already he was almost abreast of the island's extremity, and still he was a hundred yards off shore. But even so he did not despair, or if he did despair he did not cease to struggle for salvation.

He saw the island slip past him, but there was yet a chance for in its lee he saw calm water and if he could reach that he would be saved.

Straining every muscle the Sarian bent to his crude paddle. Suddenly the breeze stopped and he shot out into the smooth water in the lee of the island, but he did not cease his strenuous efforts until the bow of the canoe had touched the sand of Hime.

Tanar leaped out and dragged the craft ashore. That he should ever need it again he doubted, yet he hid it beneath the foliage of nearby bushes, and alone and unarmed set forth to face the dangers of an unknown country in what appeared even to Tanar as an almost hopeless quest for Stellara.

To the Sarian it seemed wisest to follow the coast-line back until he found the spot at which Jude had landed and then trace his trail inland, and this was the plan that he proceeded to follow.

Being in a strange land and, therefore, in a land of enemies, and being unarmed, Tanar was forced to move with great caution; yet constantly he sacrificed caution to speed. Natural obstacles impeded his progress. A great cliff running far out into the sea barred his way and it was with extreme difficulty that he found a path up the face of the frowning escarpment and then only after traveling inland for a considerable distance.

Beyond the summit rolled a broad table-land dotted with trees. A herd of thags grazed quietly in the sunlight or dozed beneath the shadowy foliage of the trees.

At sight of the man passing among them these great horned cattle became restless. An old bull bellowed and pawed the ground, and Tanar measured the distance to the nearest tree. But on he went, avoiding the beasts as best he could and hoping against hope that he could pass them successfully without further arousing their short tempers. But the challenge of the old bull was being taken up by others of his sex until a score of heavy shouldered mountains of beef were converging slowly upon the lone man, stopping occasionally to paw or gore the ground, while they bellowed forth their displeasure.

There was still a chance that he might pass them in safety. There was an opening among them just ahead of him, and Tanar accelerated his speed, but just at that instant one of the bulls took it into his head to charge and then the whole twenty bore down upon the Sarian like a band of iron locomotives suddenly endowed with the venom of hornets.

There was naught to do but seek the safety of the nearest tree and towards this Tanar ran at full speed, while from all sides the angry bulls raced to head him off.

With scarcely more than inches to spare Tanar swung himself into the branches of the tree just as the leading bull passed beneath him. A moment later the bellowing herd congregated beneath his sanctuary and while some contented themselves with pawing and bellowing, others placed their heavy heads against the bole of the tree and sought to push it down, but fortunately for Tanar it was a young oak and it withstood their sturdiest efforts.

But now, having treed him, the thags showed no disposition to leave him. For a while they milled around beneath him and then several deliberately lay down beneath the tree as though to prevent his escape.

To one accustomed to the daily recurrence of the darkness of night, following the setting of the sun, escape from such a dilemma as that in which Tanar found himself would have seemed merely a matter of waiting for the coming of night, but where the sun does not set and there is no night, and time is immeasurable and unmeasured, and where one may not know whether a lifetime or a second has been encompassed by the duration of such an event, the enforced idleness and delay are maddening.

But in spite of these conditions, or perhaps because of them, the Sarian possessed a certain philosophic outlook upon life that permitted him to accept his fate with marked stoicism and to take advantage of the enforced delay by fashioning a bow, arrows and a spear from the material afforded by the tree in which he was confined.

The tree gave him everything that he needed except the cord for his bow, and this he cut from the rawhide belt that supported his loin cloth—a long, slender strip of rawhide which he inserted in his mouth and chewed thoroughly until it was entirely impregnated with saliva. Then he bent his bow and stretched the wet rawhide from tip to tip.

While it dried, he pointed his arrows with his teeth.

In drying the rawhide shrunk, bending the bow still further and tightening the string until it hummed to the slightest touch.

The weapons were finished and yet the great bulls still stood on guard, and while Tanar remained helpless in the tree Jude was taking Stellara toward the interior of the island.

But all things must end. Impatient of delay, Tanar sought some plan whereby he might rid himself of the short tempered beasts beneath him. He hit upon the plan of yelling and throwing dead branches at them and this did have the effect of bringing them all to their feet. A few wandered away to graze with the balance of the herd, but enough remained to keep Tanar securely imprisoned.

A great bull stood directly beneath him. Tanar jumped up and down upon a small branch, making its leafy end whip through the air, and at the same time he hurled bits of wood at the great thags. And then, suddenly, to the surprise and consternation of both man and beast, the branch broke and precipitated Tanar full upon the broad shoulders of the bull. Instantly his fingers clutched its long hair as, with a bellow of surprise and terror, the beast leaped forward.

Instinct took the frightened animal toward the balance of the herd and when they saw him with a man sitting upon his back they, too, became terrified, with the result that a general stampede ensued, the herd attempting to escape their fellow, while the bull raced to be among them.

Stragglers, that had been grazing at a considerable distance from the balance of the herd, were stringing out to the rear and it was the presence of these that made it impossible for Tanar to slip to the ground and make his escape. Knowing that he would be trampled by those behind if he left the back of the bull, there was no alternative but to remain where he was as long as he could.

The thag, now thoroughly frightened because of his inability to dislodge the man-thing from his shoulders, was racing blindly forward, and presently Tanar found himself carried into the very midst of the lunging herd as it thundered across the table-land toward a distant forest.

The Sarian knew that once they reached the forest he would doubtless be scraped from the back of the thag almost immediately by some low hanging limb, and if he were not killed or injured by the blow he would be trampled to death by the thags behind. But as escape seemed hopeless he could only await the final outcome of this strange adventure.

When the leaders of the herd approached the forest hope was rekindled in Tanar's breast, for he saw that the growth was so thick and the trees so close together that it was impossible for the beasts to enter the woods at a rapid gait.

Immediately the leaders reached the edge of the forest their pace was slowed down and those behind them, pushing forward, were stopped by those in front. Some of them attempted to climb up, or were forced up, upon the backs of those ahead. But, for the most part, the herd slowed down and contented itself with pushing steadily onward toward the woods with the result that when the beast that Tanar was astride arrived at the edge of the dark shadows his gait had been reduced to a walk, and as he passed beneath the first tree Tanar swung lightly into its branches.

He had lost his spear, but his bow and arrows that he had strapped to his back remained with him, and as the herd passed beneath him and he saw the last of them disappear in the dark aisles of the forest, he breathed a deep sigh of relief and turned once more toward the far end of the island.

The thags had carried him inland a considerable distance, so now he cut back diagonally toward the coast to gain as much ground as possible.

Tanar had not yet emerged from the forest when he heard the excited growling of some wild beast directly ahead of him.

He thought that he recognized the voice of a codon, and fitting an arrow to his bow he crept warily forward. What wind was blowing came from the beast toward him and presently brought to his nostrils proof of the correctness of his guess, together with another familiar scent—that of man.

Knowing that the beast could not catch his scent from upwind, Tanar had only to be careful to advance silently, but there are few animals on earth that can move more silently than primitive man when he elects to do so, and so Tanar came in sight of the beast without being discovered by it.

It was, as he had thought, a huge wolf, a prehistoric but gigantic counterpart of our own timber wolf.

No need had the codon to run in packs, for in size, strength, ferocity and courage it was a match for any creature that it sought to bring down, with the possible exception of the mammoth, and this great beast alone it hunted in packs.

The codon stood snarling beneath a great tree, occasionally leaping high against the bole as though he sought to reach something hidden by the foliage above.

Tanar crept closer and presently he saw the figure of a youth crouching among the lower branches above the codon. It was evident that the boy was terror-stricken, but the thing that puzzled Tanar was that he cast affrighted glances upward into the tree more often than he did downward toward the codon, and presently this fact convinced the Sarian that the youth was menaced by something above him.

Tanar viewed the predicament of the boy and then considered the pitiful inadequacy of his own makeshift bow and arrow, which might only infuriate the beast and turn it upon himself. He doubted that the arrows were heavy enough, or strong enough, to pierce through the savage heart and thus only might he hope to bring down the codon.

Once more he crept to a new position, without attracting the attention either of the codon or the youth, and from this new vantage point he could look further up into the tree in which the boy crouched and then it was that he realized the hopelessness of the boy's position, for only a few feet above him and moving steadily closer appeared the head of a great snake, whose wide, distended jaws revealed formidable fangs.

Tanar's consideration of the boy's plight was influenced by a desire to save him from either of the two creatures that menaced him and also by the hope that if successful he might win sufficient gratitude to enlist the services of the youth as a guide, and especially as a go-between in the event that he should come in contact with natives of the island.

Tanar had now crept to within seven paces of the codon, from the sight of which he was concealed by a low shrub behind which he lay. Had the youth not been so occupied between the wolf and the snake he might have seen the Sarian, but so far he had not seen him.

Fitting an arrow to his crude bow and inserting four others between the fingers of his left hand, Tanar arose quietly and drove a shaft into the back of the codon, between its shoulders.

With a howl of pain and rage the beast wheeled about, only to receive another arrow full in the chest. Then his glaring eyes alighted upon the Sarian and, with a hideous growl, he charged.

With such rapidity do events of this nature transpire that they are over in much less time than it takes to record them, for a wounded wolf, charging its antagonist, can cover seven paces in an incredibly short space of time; yet even in that brief interval three more arrows sank deeply into the white breast of the codon, and the momentum of its last stride sent it rolling against the Sarian's feet— dead.

The youth, freed from the menace of the codon, leaped to the ground and would have fled without a word of thanks had not Tanar covered him with another arrow and commanded him to halt.

The snake, seeing another man and realizing, perhaps, that the odds were now against him, hesitated a moment and then withdrew into the foliage of the tree, as Tanar advanced toward the trembling youth.

"Who are you?" demanded the Sarian.

"My name is Balal," replied the youth. "I am the son of Scurv, the chief."

"Where is your village?" asked Tanar.

"It is not far," replied Balal.

"Will you take me there?" asked Tanar.

"Yes," replied Balal.

"Will your father receive me well?" continued the Sarian.

"You saved my life," said Balal. "For that he will treat you well, though for the most part we kill strangers who come to Garb."

"Lead on," said the Sarian.

Chapter Eleven

GURA

BALAL led Tanar through the forest until they came at last to the edge of a steep cliff, which the Sarian judged was the opposite side of the promontory that had barred his way along the beach.

Not far from the cliff's edge stood the stump of a great tree that seemed to have been blasted and burned by lightning. It reared its head some ten feet above the ground and from its charred surface protruded the stub end of several broken limbs.

"Follow me," said Balal, and leaping to the protruding stub, he climbed to the top of the stump and lowered himself into the interior.

Tanar followed and found an opening some three feet in diameter leading down into the bole of the dead tree. Set into the sides of this natural shaft were a series of heavy pegs, which answered the purpose of ladder rungs to the descending Balal.

The noonday sun lighted the interior of the tree for a short distance, but their own shadows, intervening, blotted out everything that lay at a depth greater than six or eight feet.

None too sure that he was not being led into a trap and, therefore, unwilling to permit his guide to get beyond his reach, Tanar hastily entered the hollow stump and followed Balal downward.

The Sarian was aware that the interior of the tree led into a shaft dug in the solid ground and a moment later he felt his feet touch the floor of a dark tunnel.

Along this tunnel Balal led him and presently they emerged into a cave that was dimly lighted through a small opening opposite them and near the floor.

Through this aperture, which was about two feet in diameter and beyond which Tanar could see daylight, Balal crawled, followed closely by the Sarian, who found himself upon a narrow ledge, high up on the face of an almost vertical cliff.

"This," said Balal, "is the village of Garb."

"I see no village nor any people," said Tanar.

"They are here though," said Balal. "Follow me," and he led the way a short distance along the ledge, which inclined downward and was in places so narrow and so shelving that the two men were compelled to flatten themselves against the side of the cliff and edge their way slowly, inch by inch, sideways.

Presently the ledge ended and here it was much wider so that Balal could lie down upon it, and, lowering his body over the edge, he clung a moment by his hands and then dropped.

Tanar looked over the edge and saw that Balal had alighted upon another narrow ledge about ten feet below. Even to a mountaineer, such as the Sarian was, the feat seemed difficult and fraught with danger, but there was no alternative and so, lying down, he lowered himself slowly over the edge of the ledge, clung an instant with his fingers, and then dropped.

As he alighted beside the youth he was about to remark upon the perilous approach to the village of Garb, but it was so apparent that Balal took it as a matter of course and thought nothing of it that Tanar desisted, realizing, in the instant, that among cliff dwellers, such as these, the little feat that they had just accomplished was as ordinary and every-day an occurrence as walking on level ground was to him.

As Tanar had an opportunity to look about him on this new level, he saw, and not without relief, that the ledge was much wider and that the mouths of several caves opened upon it. In places, and more especially in front of the cave entrances, the ledge widened to as much as six or eight feet, and here Tanar obtained his first view of any consider-able number of Himeans.

"Is it not a wonderful village?" asked Balal, and without waiting for an answer, "Look!" and he pointed downward over the edge of the ledge.

Following the direction indicated by the youth, Tanar saw ledge after ledge scoring the face of a lofty cliff from summit to base, and upon every ledge there were men, women and children.

"Come," said Balal, "I will take you to my father," and forthwith he led the way along the ledge.

As the first people they encountered saw Tanar they leaped to their feet, the men seizing their weapons. "I am taking him to my father, the chief," said Balal. "Do not harm him," and with sullen looks the warriors let them pass.

A log into which wooden pegs were driven served as an easy means of descent from one ledge to the next, and after descending for a considerable distance to about midway between the summit and the ground Balal halted at the entrance to a cave, before which sat a man, a woman and two children, a girl about Balal's age and a boy much younger.

As had all the other villagers they had passed, these, too, leaped to their feet and seized weapons when they saw Tanar.

"Do not harm him," repeated Balal. "I have brought him to you, Scurv, my father, because he saved my life when it was threatened simultaneously by a snake and a wolf and I promised him that you would receive him and treat him well."

Scurv eyed Tanar suspiciously and there was no softening of the lines upon his sullen countenance even when he heard that the stranger had saved the life of his son. "Who are you and what are you doing in our country?" he demanded.

"I am looking for one named Jude," replied Tanar.

"What do you know of Jude?" asked Scurv. "Is he your friend?"

There was something in the man's tone that made it questionable as to the advisability of claiming Jude as a friend. "I know him," he said. "We were prisoners together among the Coripies on the island of Amiocap."

"You are an Amiocapian?" demanded Scurv.

"No," replied Tanar, "I am a Sarian from a country on a far distant mainland."

"Then what were you doing on Amiocap?" asked Scurv.

"I was captured by the Korsars and the ship in which they were taking me to their country was wrecked on Amiocap. All that I ask of you is that you give me food and show me where I can find Jude."

"I do not know where you can find Jude," said Scurv. "His people and my people are always at war."

"Do you not know where their country or village is?" demanded Tanar.

"Yes, of course I know where it is, but I do not know that Jude is there."

"Are you going to give him food," asked Balal, "and treat him well as I promised you would?"

"Yes," said Scurv, but his tone was sullen and his shifty eyes looked neither at Balal nor Tanar as he replied.

In the center of the ledge, opposite the mouth of the cave, a small fire was burning beneath an earthen bowl, which was supported by three or four small pieces of stone. Squatting close to this was a female, who, in youth, might have been a fine looking girl, but now her face was lined by bitterness and hate as she glared sullenly into the caldron, the contents of which she was stirring with the rib of some large animal.

"Tanar is hungry, Sloo," said Balal, addressing the woman. "When will the food be cooked?"

"Have I not enough to do preparing hides and cooking food for all of you without having to cook for every enemy that you see fit to bring to the cave of your father?"

"This is the first time I ever brought any one, mother," said Balal.

"Let it be the last, then," snapped the woman.

"Shut up, woman," snapped Scurv, "and hasten with the food."

The woman leaped to her feet, brandishing the rib above her head. "Don't tell me what to do, Scurv," she shrilled. "I have had about enough of you anyway."

"Hit him, mother!" screamed a lad of about eleven, jumping to his feet and dancing about in evident joy and excitement.

Balal leaped across the cook fire and struck the lad heavily with his open palm across the face, sending him spinning up against the cliff wall. "Shut up, Dhung," he cried, "or I'll pitch you over the edge."

The remaining member of the family party, a girl, just ripening into womanhood, remained silent where she was seated, leaning against the face of the cliff, her large, dark eyes taking in the scene being enacted before her. Suddenly the woman turned upon her. "Why don't you do something, Gura?" she demanded. "You sit there and let them attack me and never raise a hand in my defense."

"But no one has attacked you, mother," said the girl, with a sigh.

"But I will," yelled Scurv, seizing a short club that lay beside him. "I'll knock her head off if she doesn't keep a still tongue in it and hurry with that food." At this instant a loud scream attracted the attention of all toward another family group before a cave, a little further along the ledge. Here, a man, grasping a woman by her hair, was beating her with a stick, while several children were throwing pieces of rock, first at their parents and then at one another.

"Hit her again!" yelled Scurv.

"Scratch out his eyes!" screamed Sloo, and for the moment the family of the chief forgot their own differences in the enjoyable spectacle of another family row.

Tanar looked on in consternation and surprise. Never had he witnessed such tumult and turmoil in the villages of the Sarians, and coming, as he just had, from Amiocap, the island of love, the contrast was even more appalling.

"Don't mind them," said Balal, who was watching the Sarian and had noticed the expression of surprise and disgust upon his face. "If you stay with us long you will get used to it, for it is always like this. Come on, let's eat, the food is ready," and drawing his stone knife he fished into the pot and speared a piece of meat.

Tanar, having no knife, had recourse to one of his arrows, which answered the purpose quite as well, and then, one by one, the family gathered around as though nothing unusual had happened, and fell, too, upon the steaming stew with avidity.

During the meal they did not speak other than to call one another vile names, if two chanced to

reach into the caldron simultaneously and one interfered with another.

The caldron emptied, Scurv and Sloo crawled
into the dark interior of their cave to sleep, where
they were presently followed by Balal.

Gura, the daughter, took the caldron and started
down the cliff toward the brook to wash out the
receptacle and return with it filled with water.

As she made her precarious way down rickety
ladders and narrow ledges, little Dhung, her
brother, amused himself by hurling stones at her.

"Stop that," commanded Tanar. "You might
hit her."

"That is what I am trying to do," said the little
imp. "Why else should I be throwing stones at
her? To miss her?" He hurled another missile
and with that Tanar grabbed him by the scruff of
the neck.

Instantly Dhung let out a scream that might have
been heard in Amiocap—a scream that brought
Sloo rushing from the cave.

"He is killing me," shrieked Dhung, and at that
the cave woman turned upon Tanar with flashing
eyes and a face distorted with rage.

"Wait," said Tanar, in a calm voice. "I was not
hurting the child. He was hurling rocks at his
sister and I stopped him."

"What business have you to stop him?" demanded Sloo. "She is his sister, he has a right to
hurl rocks at her if he chooses."

"But he might have struck her, and if he had she
would have fallen to her death below."

"What if she did? That is none of your business," snapped Sloo, and grabbing Dhung by his long hair she cuffed his ears and dragged him into the interior of the cave, where for a long time Tanar could hear blows and screams, mingled with the sharp tongue of Sloo and the curses of Scurv.

But finally these died down to silence, permitting the sounds of other domestic brawls from various parts of the cliff village to reach the ears of the disgusted Sarian.

Far below him Tanar saw the girl, Gura, washing the earthenware vessel in a little stream, after which she filled it with fresh water and lifted the heavy burden to her head. He wondered at the ease with which she carried the great weight and was at a loss to know how she intended to scale the precipitous cliff and the rickety, makeshift ladders with her heavy load. Watching her progress with considerable interest he saw her ascend the lowest ladder, apparently with as great ease and agility as though she was unburdened. Up she came, balancing the receptacle with no evident effort.

As he watched her he saw a man ascending also, but several ledges higher than the girl. The fellow came swiftly and noiselessly to the very ledge where Tanar stood. Paying no attention to the Sarian, he slunk cautiously along the ledge to the mouth of the cave next to that of Scurv. Drawing his stone knife from his loin cloth he crept within, and a moment later Tanar heard the sounds of screams and curses and then two men rolled from the mouth of the cave, locked in a deadly embrace. One of them was the fellow whom Tanar had just seen enter the cave. The other was a younger man and smaller and less powerful than his antagonist. They were slashing desperately at one another with their stone knives, but the duel seemed to be resulting in more noise than damage.

At this juncture, a woman came running from the cave. She was armed with the leg bone of a thag and with this she sought to belabor the older man, striking vicious blows at his head and body.

This attack seemed to infuriate the fellow to the point of madness, and, rather than incapacitating him, urged him on to redoubled efforts.

Presently he succeeded in grasping the knife hand of his opponent and an instant later he had driven his own blade into the heart of his opponent.

With a scream of anguish the woman struck again at the older man's head, but she missed her target and her weapon was splintered on the stone of the ledge. The victor leaped to his feet and seizing the body of his opponent hurled it over the cliff, and then grabbing the woman by the hair he dragged her about, shrieking and cursing, as he sought for some missile wherewith to belabor her.

As Tanar stood watching the disgusting spectacle he became aware that someone was standing beside him and, turning, he saw that Gura had returned. She stood there straight as an arrow, balancing the water vessel upon her head.

"It is terrible," said Tanar, nodding toward the battling couple.

Gura shrugged indifferently. "It is nothing," she said. "Her mate returned unexpectedly. That is all."

"You mean," asked Tanar, "that this fellow is her mate and that the other was not?"

"Certainly," said Gura, "but they all do it. What can you expect where there is nothing but hate," and walking to the entrance to her father's cave she set the water vessel down within the shadows just inside the entrance. Then she sat down and leaned her back against the cliff, paying no more attention to the matrimonial difficulties of her neighbor.

Tanar, for the first time, noticed the girl particularly. He saw that she had neither the cunning expression that characterized Jude and all of the other Himeans he had seen; nor were there the lines of habitual irritation and malice upon her face; instead it reflected an innate sadness and he guessed that she looked much like her mother might have when she was Gura's age.

Tanar crossed the ledge and sat down beside her. "Do your people always quarrel thus?" he asked.

"Always," replied Gura.

"Why?" he asked.

"I do not know," she replied. "They take their mates for life and are permitted but one and though both men and women have a choice in the selection of their mates they never seem to be satisfied with one another and are always quarreling, usually because neither one nor the other is faithful. Do the men and women quarrel thus in the land from which you come?"

"No," replied Tanar. "They do not. If they did they would be thrown out of the tribe."

"But suppose that they find that they do not like one another?" insisted the girl.

"Then they do not live together," replied Tanar. "They separate and if they care to they find other mates."

"That is wicked," said Gura. "We would kill any of our people who did such a thing."

Tanar shrugged and laughed.

"At least we are all a very happy people," he said, "which is more than you can say for yourselves, and, after all, happiness, it seems to me, is everything."

The girl thought for some time, seemingly studying an idea that was new to her.

"Perhaps you are right," she said, presently. "Nothing could be worse than the life that we live. My mother tells me that it was not thus in her country, but now she is as bad as the rest."

"Your mother is not a Himean?" asked Tanar.

"No, she is from Amiocap. My father captured her there when she was young."

"That accounts for the difference," mused Tanar.

"What difference?" she asked. "What do you mean?"

"I mean that you are not like the others, Gura," he replied. "You neither look like them nor act like them—neither you nor your brother, Balal."

"Our mother is an Amiocapian," she replied. "Perhaps we inherited something from her and then again, and most important, we are young and, as yet, have no mates. When that time comes we shall grow to be like the others, just as our mother has grown to be like them."

"Do many of your men take their mates from Amiocap?" asked Tanar.

"Many try to, but few succeed for as a rule they are driven away or killed by the Amiocapian warriors. They have a landing place upon the coast of Amiocap in a dark cave beneath a high cliff and of ten Himean warriors who land there scarce one returns, and he not always with an Amiocapian mate. There is a tribe living along our coast that has grown rich by crossing to Amiocap and bringing back the canoes of the warriors, who have crossed for mates and have died at the hands of the Amiocapian warriors."

For a few moments she was silent, absorbed in thought. "I should like to go to Amiocap," she mused, presently.

"Why?" asked Tanar.

"Perhaps I should find there a mate with whom I might be happy," she said.

Tanar shook his head sadly. "That is impossible, Gura," he said.

"Why?" she demanded. "Am I not beautiful enough for the Amiocapian warriors?"

"Yes," he replied, "you are very beautiful, but if you went to Amiocap they would kill you."

"Why?" she demanded again.

"Because, although your mother is an Amiocapian, your father is not," explained Tanar.

"That is their law?" asked Gura, sadly.

"Yes," replied Tanar.

"Well," she said with a sigh, "then I suppose I must remain here and seek a mate whom I shall learn to hate and bring children into the world who will hate us both."

"It is not a pleasant outlook," said Tanar.

"No," she said, and then after a pause, "unless——"

"Unless, what?" asked the Sarian.

"Nothing," said Gura.

For a time they sat in silence, each occupied with his own thoughts, Tanar's being filled to the exclusion of all else by the face and figure of Stellara.

Presently the girl looked up at him. "What are you going to do after you find Jude?" she asked.

"I am going to kill him," replied Tanar.

"And then?" she queried.

"I do not know," said the Sarian. "If I find the one whom I believe to be with Jude we shall try to return to Amiocap."

"Why do you not remain here?" asked Gura. "I wish that you would."

Tanar shuddered. "I would rather die," he said.

"I do not blame you much," said the girl, "but I believe there is a way in which you might be happy even in Hime."

"How?" asked Tanar.

Gura did not answer and he saw the tears come to her eyes. Then she arose hurriedly and entered the cave.

Tanar thought that Scurv would never be done with his sleep. He wanted to talk to him and arrange for a guide to the village of Jude, but it was Sloo who first emerged from the cave.

She eyed him sullenly. "You still here?" she demanded.

"I am waiting for Scurv to send a guide to direct me to the village of Jude," replied the Sarian. "I shall not remain here an instant longer than is necessary."

"That will be too long," growled Sloo, and turning on her heels she reëntered the cave.

Presently Balal emerged, rubbing his eyes. "When will Scurv send me on my way?" demanded Tanar.

"I do not know," replied the youth. "He has just awakened. When he comes out you should speak to him about it. He has just sent me to fetch the skin of the codon you killed. He was very angry to think that I left it lying in the forest."

After Balal departed, Tanar sat with his own thoughts for a long while.

Presently Gura came from the cave. She appeared frightened and excited. She came close to Tanar and, kneeling, placed her lips close to his ear. "You must escape at once," she said, in a low whisper. "Scurv is going to kill you. That is why he sent Balal away."

"But why does he want to kill me?" demanded Tanar. "I saved the life of his son and I have only asked that he direct me to the village of Jude."

"He thinks Sloo is in love with you," explained Gura, "for when he awakened she was not in the cave. She was out here upon the ledge with you."

Tanar laughed. "Sloo made it very plain to me that she did not like me," he said, "and wanted me to be gone."

"I believe you," said Gura, "but Scurv, filled
with suspicion and hatred and a guilty conscience,
is anxious to believe anything bad that he can of
Sloo, and as he does not wish to be convinced that
he is wrong it stands to reason that nothing can
convince him, so that your only hope is in flight."

"Thank you, Gura," said Tanar. "I shall go at
once."

"No, that will not do," said the girl. "Scurv
is coming out here immediately. He would miss
you, possibly before you could get out of sight, and
in a moment he could muster a hundred warriors to
pursue you, and furthermore you have no proper
weapons with which to start out in search of Jude."

"Perhaps you have a better plan, then," said
Tanar.

"I have," said the girl. "Listen! Do you see
where the stream enters the jungle," and she pointed
across the clearing at the foot of the cliff toward
the edge of a dark forest.

"Yes," said Tanar, "I see."

"I shall descend now and hide there in a large
tree beside the stream. When Scurv comes out,
tell him that you saw a deer there and ask him to
loan you weapons, so that you may go and kill it.
Meat is always welcome and he will postpone his
attack upon you until you have returned with the
carcass of your kill, but you will not return. When
you enter the forest I shall be there to direct you
to the village of Jude."

"Why are you doing this, Gura?" demanded
Tanar.

"Never mind about that," said the girl. "Only

do as I say. There is no time to lose as Scurv may come out from the cave at any moment," and without further words she commenced the descent of the cliff face.

Tanar watched her as, with the agility and grace of a chamois, the girl, oftentimes disdaining ladders, leaped lightly from ledge to ledge. Almost before he could realize it she was at the bottom of the cliff and moving swiftly toward the forest beyond, the foliage of which had scarcely closed about her when Scurv emerged from the cave. Directly behind him were Sloo and Dhung, and Tanar saw that each carried a club.

"I am glad you came out now," said Tanar, losing no time, for he sensed that the three were bent upon immediate attack.

"Why?" growled Scurv.

"I just saw a deer at the edge of the forest. If you will let me take weapons, perhaps I can repay your hospitality by bringing you the carcass."

Scurv hesitated, his stupid mind requiring time to readjust itself and change from one line of thought to another, but Sloo was quick to see the advantage of utilizing the unwelcome guest and she was willing to delay his murder until he had brought back his kill. "Get weapons," she said to Dhung, "and let the stranger fetch the deer."

Scurv scratched his head, still in a quandary, and before he had made up his mind one way or the other, Dhung reappeared with a lance and a stone knife, which, instead of handing to Tanar, he threw at him, but the Sarian caught the weapons, and, without awaiting further permission, clambered down the ladder to the next ledge and from thence downward to the ground. Several of the villagers, recognizing him as a stranger, sought to interfere with him, but Scurv, standing upon the ledge high above watching his descent, bellowed commands that he be left alone, and presently the Sarian was crossing the open towards the jungle.

Just inside the concealing verdure of the forest he was accosted by Gura, who was perched upon the limb of a tree above him.

"Your warning came just in time, Gura," said the man, "for Scurv and Sloo and Dhung came out almost immediately, armed and ready to kill me."

"I knew that they would," she said, "and I am glad that they will be disappointed, especially Dhung—the little beast! He begged to be allowed to torture you."

"It does not seem possible that he can be your brother," said Tanar.

"He is just like Scurv's mother," said the girl. "I knew her before she was killed. She was a most terrible old woman, and Dhung has inherited all of her venom and none of the kindly blood of the Amiocapians, which flows in the veins of my mother, despite the change that her horrid life has brought over her."

"And now," said Tanar, "point the way to Jude's village and I shall be gone. Never, Gura, can I repay you for your kindness to me—a kindness which I can only explain on the strength of the Amiocapian blood which is in you. I shall never see you again, Gura, but I shall carry the recollection of your image and your kindness always in my heart."

"I am going with you," said Gura.

"You cannot do that," said Tanar.

"How else may I guide you to the village of Jude then?" she demanded.

"You do not have to guide me; only tell me the direction in which it lies and I shall find it," replied Tanar.

"I am going with you," said the girl, determinedly. "There is only hate and misery in the cave of my father. I would rather be with you."

"But that cannot be, Gura," said Tanar.

"If I went back now to the cave of Scurv he would suspect me of having aided your escape and they would all beat me. Come, we cannot waste time here for if you do not return quickly, Scurv will become suspicious and set out upon your trail." She had dropped to the ground beside him and now she started off into the forest.

"Have it as you wish, then, Gura," said Tanar, "but I am afraid that you are going to regret your act—I am afraid that we are both going to regret it."

"At least I shall have a little happiness in life," said the girl, "and if I have that I shall be willing to die."

"Wait," said Tanar, "in which direction does the village of Jude lie?" The girl pointed. "Very well," said Tanar, "instead of going on the ground and leaving our spoor plainly marked for Scurv to follow, we shall take to the trees, for after having watched you descend the cliff I know that you must be able to travel as rapidly among the branches as you do upon the ground."

"I have never done it," said the girl, "but wherever you go I shall follow."

Although Tanar had been loath to permit the girl to accompany him, nevertheless he found that her companionship made what would have been otherwise a lonely adventure far from unpleasant.

Chapter Twelve

"I HATE YOU!"

THE companions of Bohar the Bloody had not waited long for him after he had set out in pursuit of Stellara and had not returned. They hastened the work upon their boat to early completion, and, storing provisions and water, sailed out of the cove on the shores of which they had constructed their craft and bore away for Korsar with no regret for Bohar, whom they all cordially hated.

The very storm that had come near to driving Tanar past the island of Hime bore the Korsars down upon the opposite end, carried away their rude sail and finally dashed their craft, a total wreck, upon the rocks at the upper end of Hime.

The loss of their boat, their provisions and one of their number, who was smashed against a rock and drowned, left the remaining Korsars in even a more savage mood than was customary among them, and the fact that the part of the island upon which they were wrecked afforded no timber suitable for the construction of a boat made it necessary for them to cross over land to the opposite shore.

They were faced now with the necessity of entering a land filled with enemies in search of food and material for a new craft, and, to cap the climax of their misfortune, they found themselves with wet powder and forced to defend themselves, if necessity arose, with daggers and cutlasses alone.

The majority of them being old sailors they were well aware of where they were and even knew a great deal concerning the geography of Hime and the manners and customs of its people, for most of them had accompanied raiding parties into the interior on many occasions when the Korsar ships had fallen upon the island to steal furs and hides, in the perfect curing and tanning of which the Himean women were adept with the result that Himean furs and skins brought high prices in Korsar.

A council of the older sailors decided then to set off across country toward a harbor on the far side of the island, where the timber of an adjoining forest would afford them the material for building another craft with the added possibility of the arrival of a Korsar raider.

As these disgruntled men plodded wearily across the island of Hime, Jude led the reluctant Stellara toward his village, and Gura guided Tanar in the same direction.

Jude had been compelled to make wide detours to avoid unfriendly villagers; nor had Stellara's unwilling feet greatly accelerated his pace, for she constantly hung back, and, though he no longer had to carry her, he had found it necessary to make a leather thong fast about her neck and lead her along in this fashion to prevent the numerous, sudden breaks for liberty that she had made before he had devised this scheme.

Often she pulled back, refusing to go further, saying that she was tired and insisting upon lying down to rest, for in her heart she knew that wherever Jude or another took her, Tanar would seek her out.

Already in her mind's eyes she could see him upon the trail behind them and she hoped to delay Jude's march sufficiently so that the Sarian would overtake them before they reached his village and the protection of his tribe.

Gura was happy. Never before in all her life had she been so happy, and she saw in the end of their journey a possible end to this happiness and so she did not lead Tanar in a direct line to Carn, the village of Jude, but led him hither and thither upon various excuses so that she might have him to herself for as long a time as possible. She found in his companionship a gentleness and an understanding that she had never known in all her life before.

It was not love that Gura felt for Tanar, but something that might have easily been translated into love had the Sarian's own passion been aroused toward the girl, but his love for Stellara precluded such a possibility and while he found pleasure in the company of Gura he was yet madly impatient to continue directly upon the trail of Jude that he might rescue Stellara and have her for himself once more.

The village of Carn is not a cliff village, as is

Garb, the village of Scurv. It consists of houses
built of stone and clay and, entirely surrounded by
a high wall, it stands upon the top of a lofty mesa
protected upon all sides by steep cliffs, and over-
looking upon one hand the forests and hills of Hime,
and upon the other the broad expanse of the Korsar Az, or Sea of Korsar.

Up the steep cliffs toward Carn climbed Jude,
dragging Stellara behind him. It was a long and
arduous climb and when they reached the summit
Jude was glad to stop and rest. He also had some
planning to do, since in the village upon the mesa
Jude had left a mate, and now he was thinking of
some plan whereby he might rid himself of her,
but the only plan that Jude could devise was to
sneak into the city and murder her. But what was
he to do with Stellara in the meantime? And then
a happy thought occurred to him.

He knew a cave that lay just below the summit
of the cliff and not far distant and toward this he
took Stellara, and when they had arrived at it he
bound her ankles and her wrists.

"I shall not leave you here long," he said.
"Presently I shall return and take you into the village of Carn as my mate. Do not be afraid. There
are few wild beasts upon the mesa, and I shall return long before any one can find you."

"Do not hurry," said Stellara. "I shall welcome
the wild beast that reaches me before you return."

"You will think differently after you have been
the mate of Jude for a while," said the man, and
then he left her and hurried toward the walled
village of Carn.

Struggling to a sitting posture Stellara could look out across the country that lay at the foot of the cliff and presently, below her, she saw a man and a woman emerge from the forest.

For a moment her heart stood still, for the instant that her eyes alighted upon him she recognized the man as Tanar. A cry of welcome was upon her lips when a new thought stilled her tongue.

Who was the girl with Tanar? Stellara saw how close she walked to him and she saw her look up into his face and though she was too far away to see the girl's eyes or her expression, there was something in the attitude of the slim body that denoted worship, and Stellara turned her face and buried it against the cold wall of the cave and burst into tears.

Gura pointed upward toward the high mesa. "There," she said, "just beyond the summit of that cliff lies Carn, the village where Jude lives, but if we enter it you will be killed and perhaps I, too, if the women get me first."

Tanar, who was examining the ground at his feet, seemed not to hear the girl's words. "Someone has passed just ahead of us," he said; "a man and a woman. I can see the imprints of their feet. The grasses that were crushed beneath their sandals are still rising slowly—a man and a woman—and one of them was Stellara and the other Jude."

"Who is Stellara?" asked the girl.

"My mate," replied Tanar.

The habitual expression of sadness that had marked Gura's face since childhood, but which had been supplanted by a radiant happiness since she had left the village of Garb with Tanar, returned as with tear-filled eyes she choked back a sob, which went unnoticed by the Sarian as he eagerly searched the ground ahead of them. And in the cave above them warm tears bathed the unhappy cheeks of Stellara, but the urge of love soon drew her eyes back to Tanar just at the moment that he turned and called Gura's attention to the well marked spoor he was following.

The eyes of the Sarian noted the despair in the face of his companion and the tears in her eyes.

"Gura!" he cried. "What is the matter? Why do you cry?" and impulsively he stepped close to her and put a friendly arm about her shoulders, and Gura, unnerved by kindness, buried her face upon his breast and wept. And this was what Stellara saw—this scene was what love and jealousy put their own interpretation upon—and the eyes of the Amiocapian maiden flashed with hurt pride and anger.

"Why do you cry, Gura?" demanded Tanar.

"Do not ask me," begged the girl. "It is nothing. Perhaps I am tired; perhaps I am afraid. But now we may not think of either fatigue or fear, for if Jude is taking your mate toward the village of Carn we must hasten to rescue her before it is too late."

"You are right," exclaimed Tanar. "We must not delay," and, followed by Gura, he ran swiftly toward the base of the cliff, tracing the spoor of Jude and Stellara where it led to the precarious ascent of the cliffside. And as they hastened on, brutal eyes watched them from the edge of the jungle from which they had themselves so recently emerged.

Where the steep ascent topped the summit of the cliff bare rock gave back no clew to the direction that Jude had taken, but twenty yards further on where the soft ground commenced again Tanar picked up the tracks of the man to which he called Gura's attention.

"Jude's footprints are here alone," he said.

"Perhaps the woman refused to go further and he was forced to carry her," suggested Gura.

"That is doubtless the fact," said Tanar, and he hastened onward along the plain trail left by the Himean.

The way led now along a well marked trail, which ran through a considerable area of bushes that grew considerably higher than a man's head so that nothing was visible upon either side and only for short distances ahead of them and behind them along the winding trail. But Tanar did not slacken his speed, his sole aim being to overhaul the Himean before he reached his village.

As Tanar and Gura had capped the summit of the cliff and disappeared from view, eighteen hairy men came into view from the forest and followed their trail toward the foot of the cliff.

They were bushy whiskered fellows with gay sashes around their waists and equally brilliant cloths about their heads. Huge pistols and knives bristled from their waist cloths, and cutlasses dangled from their hips—fate had brought these survivors of The Cid's ship to the foot of the cliffs below the village of Carn at almost the same moment that Tanar had arrived. With sensations of surprise, not unmingled with awe, they had recognized the Sarian who had been a prisoner upon the ship and whom they thought they had seen killed by their musket fire at the edge of the natural well upon the island of Amiocap.

The Korsars, prompted by the pernicious stubbornness of ignorance, were moved by a common impulse to recapture Tanar. And with this end in view they waited until Gura and the Sarian had disappeared beyond the summit of the cliff, when they started in pursuit.

The walls of Carn lie no great distance from the edge of the table-land upon which it stands. In timeless Pellucidar events, which are in reality far separated, seem to follow closely, one upon the heels of another, and for this reason one may not say how long Jude was in the village of Carn, or whether he had had time to carry out the horrid purpose which had taken him thither, but the fact remained that as Tanar and Gura reached the edge of the bushes and looked across the clearing toward the walls of Carn they saw Jude sneaking from the city. Could they have seen his face they might have noticed a malicious leer of triumph and could they have known the purpose that had taken him thus stealthily to his native village they might have reconstructed the scenes of the bloody episode which had just been enacted within the house of the Himean. But Tanar only saw that Jude, whom he sought, was coming toward him, and that Stellara was not with him.

The Sarian drew Gura back into the concealment

of the bushes that lined the trail which Jude was approaching.

On came the Himean and while Tanar awaited his coming, the Korsars were making their clumsy ascent of the cliff, while Stellara, sick from jealousy and unhappiness, leaned disconsolately against the cold stone of her prison cave.

Jude, unconscious of danger, hastened back toward the spot where he had left Stellara and as he came opposite Tanar, the Sarian leaped upon him.

The Himean reached for his knife, but he was helpless in the grasp of Tanar, whose steel fingers closed about his wrists with such strength that Jude dropped his weapon with a cry of pain as he felt both of his arms crushed beneath the pressure of the Sarian's grip.

"What do you want?" he cried. "Why do you attack me?"

"Where is Stellara?" demanded Tanar.

"I do not know," replied Jude. "I have not seen her."

"You lie," said Tanar. "I have followed her tracks and yours to the summit of the cliff. Where is she?" He drew his knife. "Tell me, or die."

"I left her at the edge of the cliff while I went to Carn to arrange to have her received in a friendly manner. I did it all for her protection, Tanar. She wanted to go back to Korsar and I was but helping her."

"Again you lie," said the Sarian; "but lead me to her and we shall hear her version of the story."

The Himean held back until the point of Tanar's knife pressed against his ribs; then he gave in. "If

I lead you to her will you promise not to kill me?" asked Jude. "Will you let me return in peace to my village?"

"I shall make no promises until I learn from her own lips how you have treated her," replied the Sarian.

"She has not been harmed," said Jude. "I swear it."

"Then lead me to her," insisted Tanar.

Sullenly the Himean guided them back along the path toward the cave where he had left Stellara, while at the other edge of the bushes eighteen Korsars, warned by the noise of their approach, halted, listening, and presently melted silently from view in the surrounding shrubbery.

They saw Jude and Gura and Tanar emerge from the bushes, but they did not attack them; they waited to see for what purpose they had returned. They saw them disappear over the edge of the cliff at a short distance from the summit of the trail that led down into the valley. And then they emerged from their hiding places and followed cautiously after them.

Jude led Tanar and Gura to the cave where Stellara lay and when Tanar saw her, her dear wrists and ankles bound with thongs and her cheeks still wet with tears, he sprang forward and gathered her into his arms.

"Stellara!" he cried. "My darling!" But the girl turned her face away from him.

"Do not touch me," she cried. "I hate you."

"Stellara!" he exclaimed in amazement. "What has happened?" But before she could reply they were startled by a hoarse command from behind them, and, turning, found themselves looking into the muzzles of the pistols of eighteen Korsars.

"Surrender, Sarian!" cried the leader of the Korsars.

Gazing into the muzzles of about thirty-six huge pistols, which equally menaced the lives of Stellara and Gura, Tanar saw no immediate alternative but to surrender.

"What do you intend to do with us if we do surrender?" he demanded.

"That we shall decide later," growled the spokesman for the Korsars.

"Do you expect ever to return to Korsar?" asked Tanar.

"What is that to you, Sarian?" demanded the Korsar.

"It has a considerable bearing upon whether or not we surrender," replied Tanar. "You have tried to kill me before and you have found that I am hard to kill. I know something about your weapons and your powder and I know that even at such close quarters I may be able to kill some of you before you can kill me. But if you answer my question fairly and honestly and if your answer is satisfactory I shall surrender."

At Tanar's mention of his knowledge of their powder the Korsars immediately assumed that he knew that it was wet, whereas he was only alluding to its uniformly poor quality and so the spokesman decided that it would be better to temporize for the time being at least. "As soon as we can build a boat we shall return to Korsar," he said, "unless in the meantime a Korsar ship anchors in the bay of Carn."

"Good," commented the Sarian. "If you will promise to return the daughter of The Cid safe and unharmed to her people in Korsar I will surrender. And you must also promise that no harm shall befall this other girl and that she shall be permitted to go with you in safety to Korsar or to remain here among her own people as she desires."

"How about the other man?" demanded the Korsar.

"You may kill him when you kill me," replied Tanar.

Stellara's eyes widened in fearful apprehension as she heard the words of the Sarian and she found that jealousy was no match for true love.

"Very well," said the Korsar. "We accept the condition. The women shall return to Korsar with us, and you two men shall die."

"Oh, no," begged Jude. "I do not wish to die. I am a Himean. Carn is my home. You Korsars come there often to trade. Spare me and I shall see that you are furnished with more hides than you can pack in your boat, after you have built it."

The leader of the band laughed in his face. "Eighteen of us can take what we choose from the village of Carn," he said. "We are not such fools as to spare you that you may go and warn your people."

"Then take me along as a prisoner," wailed Jude.

"And have to feed you and watch you all the

time? No, you are worth more to us dead than alive."

As Jude spoke he had edged over into the mouth of the cave, where he stood half behind Stellara as though taking shelter at the expense of the girl.

With a gesture of disgust, Tanar turned toward the Korsars. "Come," he said, impatiently. "If the bargain is satisfactory there is no use in discussing it further. Kill us, and take the women in safety to Korsar. You have given your word."

At the instant that Tanar concluded his appeal to the Korsars, Jude turned before any one could prevent him and disappeared into the cave behind him. Instantly Korsars leaped in pursuit, while the others awaited impatiently their return with Jude. But when they emerged they were empty handed.

"He escaped us," said one of those who had gone after the Himean. "This cave is the mouth of a dark, long tunnel with many branches. We could see nothing and fearful that we should become lost, we returned to the opening. It would be useless to try to find the man within unless one was familiar with the tunnel which honeycombs the cliff beyond this cave. We had better kill this one immediately before he has an opportunity to escape too," and the fellow raised his pistol and aimed it at Tanar, possibly hoping that his powder had dried since they had set out from the beach upon the opposite side of the island.

"Stop!" cried Stellara, jumping in front of the man. "As you all know I am the daughter of The Cid. If you return me to him in safety you will be well rewarded. I will see to that. You all knew that The Cid was taking this man to Korsar, but possibly you did not know why."

"No," said one of the Korsars, who, being only common sailors, had had no knowledge of the plans of their commander.

"He knows how to make firearms and powder far superior to ours and The Cid was taking him back to Korsar that he might teach the Korsars the secrets of powder making and the manufacture of weapons, that we do not know. If you kill him The Cid will be furious with you, and you all know what it means to anger The Cid. But if you return him, also, to Korsar your reward will be much larger."

"How do we know that The Cid is alive?" demanded one of the Korsars; "and if he is not, who is there who will pay reward for your return, or for the return of this man?"

"The Cid is a better sailor than Bohar the Bloody—that you all know. And if Bohar the Bloody brought his boat safely through to Amiocap there is little doubt but that The Cid took his safely to Korsar. But even if he did not, even if The Cid perished, still will you receive your reward if you return me to Korsar."

"Who will pay it?" demanded one of the sailors.

"Bulf," replied Stellara.

"Why should Bulf pay a reward for your return?" asked the Korsar.

"Because I am to be his mate. It was The Cid's wish and his."

By no change of expression did the Sarian reveal the pain that these words inflicted like a knife thrust through his heart. He merely stood with his arms folded, looking straight ahead. Gura's eyes were wide in surprise as she looked, first at Stellara and then at Tanar, for she recalled that the latter had told her that Stellara was his mate, and she had known, with woman's intuition, how much the man loved this woman. Gura was mystified and, too, she was saddened because she guessed the pain that Stellara's words had inflicted upon Tanar, and so her kind heart prompted her to move close to Tanar's side and to lay her hand gently upon his arm in mute expression of sympathy.

For a time the Korsars discussed Stellara's proposition in low whispers and then the spokesman addressed her. "But if The Cid is dead there will be no one to reward us for returning the Sarian; therefore, we might as well kill him for there will be enough mouths to feed during the long journey to Korsar."

"You do not know that The Cid is dead," insisted Stellara; "but if he is, who is there better fitted to be chief of the Korsars than Bulf? And if he is chief he will reward you for returning this man when I explain to him the purpose for which he was brought back to Korsar."

"Well," said the Korsar, scratching his head, "perhaps you are right. He may be more valuable to us alive than dead. If he will promise to help us work the boat and not try to escape we shall take him with us. But how about the girl here?"

"Keep her until we are ready to sail," growled one of the other Korsars, "and then turn her loose."

"If you wish to receive any reward for my return you will do nothing of the sort," said Stellara with finality, and then to Gura, "What do you wish to do?" Her voice was cold and haughty.

"Where Tanar goes there I wish to go," replied Gura.

Stellara's eyes narrowed and for an instant they flashed fire, but immediately they resumed their natural, kindly expression, though tinged with sadness. "Very well, then," she said, turning sadly away, "the girl must return with us to Korsar."

The sailors discussed this question at some length and most of them were opposed to it, but when Stellara insisted and assured them of a still greater reward they finally consented, though with much grumbling.

The Korsars marched boldly across the mesa, past the walls of Carn, their harquebuses ready in their hands, knowing full well the fear of them that past raids had implanted in the breasts of the Himeans. But they did not seek to plunder or demand tribute for they still feared that their powder was useless.

As they reached the opposite side of the mesa, where they could look out across the bay of Carn, a hoarse shout of pleasure arose from the throats of the Korsars, for there, at anchor in the bay, lay a Korsar ship. Not knowing how soon the vessel might weigh anchor and depart, the Korsars fairly tumbled down the precipitous trail to the beach, while in their rear the puzzled villagers watched them over the top of the wall of Carn until the last man had disappeared beyond the summit of the cliff.

Rushing to the edge of the water the Korsars tried to discharge their harquebuses to attract attention from the vessel. A few of the charges had dried and the resulting explosion awakened signs of life upon the anchored ship. The sailors on the shore tore off sashes and handkerchiefs, which they waved frantically as signals of distress, and presently they were rewarded by the sight of the lowering of a boat from the vessel.

Within speaking distance of the shore the boat came to a stop and an officer hailed the men on shore.

"Who are you," he demanded, "and what do you want?"

"We are part of the crew of the ship of The Cid," replied the sailors' spokesman. "Our ship was wrecked in mid-ocean and we made our way to Amiocap and then to Hime, but here we lost the boat that we built upon Amiocap."

Assured that the men were Korsars the officer commanded that the boat move in closer to the shore and finally it was beached close to where the party stood awaiting its coming.

The brief greetings and explanations over, the officer took them all aboard and shortly afterward Tanar of Pellucidar found himself again upon a Korsar ship of war.

The commander of the ship knew Stellara, and after questioning them carefully he approved her plan and agreed to take Tanar and Gura back to Korsar with them.

Following their interview with the officer, Tanar found himself momentarily alone with Stellara.

"Stellara!" he said. "What change has come over you?"

She turned and looked at him coldly. "In Amiocap you were well enough," she said, "but in Korsar you would be only a naked barbarian," and, turning, she walked away from him without another word.

Chapter Thirteen

PRISONERS

THE voyage to Korsar was uneventful and during its entire extent Tanar saw nothing of either Stellara or Gura for, although he was not confined in the dark hold, he was not permitted above the first deck, and although he often looked up at the higher deck at the stern of the ship he never caught a glimpse of either of the girls, from which he concluded that Gura was confined in one of the cabins and that Stellara deliberately avoided him or any sight of him.

As they approached the coast of Korsar Tanar saw a level country curving upward into the mist of the distance. He thought that far away he discerned the outlines of hills, but of that he could not be certain. He saw cultivated fields and patches of forest land and a river running down to the sea —a broad, winding river upon the shore of which a city lay, inland a little from the ocean. There was no harbor at this point upon the coast, but the ship made directly for the mouth of the river, up which it sailed toward the city, which, as he approached it, he saw far surpassed in size and the pretentiousness of its buildings any habitation of man that he had ever seen upon the surface of Pellucidar, not even excepting the new capital of the confederated kingdoms of Pellucidar that the Emperor David was building.

Most of the buildings were white with red-tiled roofs, and there were some with lofty minarets and domes of various colors—blue and red and gold, the last shining in the sunlight like the jewels in the diadem of Dian the Empress.

Where the river widened the town had been built and here there rode at anchor a great fleet of ships of war and many lesser craft—fishing boats and river boats and barges. The street along the river-front was lined with shops and alive with people.

As their ship approached cannon boomed from the deck of the anchored warships, and the salute was returned by their own craft, which finally came to anchor in mid-stream, opposite the city.

Small boats put out from the shore and were paddled rapidly toward the warship, which also lowered some of her own boats, into one of which Tanar was ordered under charge of an officer and a couple of sailors. As he was taken to shore and marched along the street he excited considerable attention among the crowds through which they passed, for he was immediately recognized as a barbarian captive from some uncivilized quarter of Pellucidar.

During the debarkation Tanar had seen nothing of either Stellara or Gura and now he wondered if he was ever to see them again. His mind was filled with the same sad thoughts that had been his companions during the entire course of the long journey from Hime to Korsar and which had finally con-

vinced him that he had never known the true
Stellara until she had avowed herself upon the deck
of the ship in the harbor of Carn. Yes, he was all
right upon Amiocap, but in Korsar he was only a
naked savage, and this fact was borne in upon him
now by the convincing evidence of the haughty contempt with which the natives of Korsar stared at
him or exchanged rude jokes at his expense.

It hurt the Sarian's pride to think that he had
been so deceived by the woman to whom he had
given all his love. He would have staked his life
upon his belief that hers was the sweetest and purest
and most loyal of characters, and to learn at last
that she was shallow and insincere cut him to the
quick and his suffering was lightened by but a single
thought—his unquestioned belief in the sweet and
enduring friendship of Gura.

It was with such thoughts that his mind was occupied as he was led into a building along the water-
front, which seemed to be in the nature of a
guardhouse.

Here he was turned over to an officer in charge,
and, after a few brief questions, two soldiers conducted him into another room, raised a heavy trap
door in the floor and bade him descend a rude
ladder that led downward into darkness below.

No sooner had his head descended below the floor
joists than the door was slammed down above him.
He heard the grating of a heavy bolt as the soldiers
shut it and then the thud of their footsteps as they
left the room above.

Descending slowly for about ten feet Tanar came
at last to the surface of a stone floor. His eyes

becoming accustomed to the change, he realized that the apartment into which he had descended was not in total darkness, but that daylight filtered into it from a small, barred window near the ceiling. Looking about him he saw that he was the only occupant of the room.

In the wall, opposite the window, he discerned a doorway and crossing to it he saw that it opened into a narrow corridor, running parallel with the length of the room. Looking up and down the corridor he discerned faint patches of light, as though other open doorways lined one side of the hallway.

He was about to enter upon a tour of investigation when the noise of something scurrying along the floor of the corridor attracted his attention, and looking back to his left he saw a dark form creeping toward him. It stood about a foot in height and was, perhaps, three feet long, but in the shadows of the corridor it loomed too indistinctly for him to recognize its details. But presently he saw that it had two shining eyes that seemed to be directed upon him.

As it came boldly forward Tanar stepped back into the room he was about to quit, preferring to meet the thing in the lesser darkness of the apartment rather than in the gloomy corridor, if it was the creature's intent to attack him.

On the thing came and turning into the doorway it stopped and surveyed the Sarian. In his native country Tanar had been familiar with a species of wood rat, which the Sarian considered large, but never in all his life had he dreamed that a rat could grow to the enormous proportions of the hideous thing that confronted him with its bold, gleaming, beady eyes.

Tanar had been disarmed when he had been taken aboard the Korsar ship, but even so he had no fear of a rodent, even if the thing should elect to attack him, which he doubted. But the ferocious appearance of the rat gave him pause as he thought what the result might be if a number of them should attack a man simultaneously.

Presently the rat, still standing facing him, squealed. For a time there was silence and then the thing squealed again and, as from a great distance, Tanar heard an answering squeal, and then another and another, and presently they grew louder and greater in volume, and he knew that the rat of the Korsar dungeon was calling its fellows to the attack and the feast.

He looked about him for some weapon of defense, but there was nothing but the bare stone of the floor and the walls. He heard the rat pack coming, and still the scout that had discovered him stood in the doorway, waiting.

But why should he, the man, wait? If he must die, he would die fighting and if he could take the rats as they came, one by one, he might make them pay for their meal and pay dearly. And so, with the agility of a tiger, the man leaped for the rodent, and so sudden and unexpected was his spring that one hand fell upon the loathsome creature before it could escape. With loud squeals it sought to fasten its fangs in his flesh, but the Sarian was too quick and too powerful. His fingers closed once upon the creature's neck. He swung its body around a few times until the neck broke and then he hurled the corpse toward the advancing pack that he could already see in the distance through the dim light in the corridor, in the center of which Tanar now stood awaiting his inevitable doom, but he was prepared to fight until he was dragged down by the creatures.

As he waited he heard a noise behind him and he thought that another pack was taking him in the rear, but as he glanced over his shoulder he saw the figure of a man, standing in front of a doorway further down the corridor.

"Come," shouted the stranger. "You will find safety here." Nor did Tanar lose any time in racing down the corridor to where the man stood, the rats close at his heels.

"Quick, in here," cried his savior, and seizing Tanar by the arm he dragged him through the doorway into a large room in which there were a dozen or more men.

At the doorway the rat pack stopped, glaring in, but not one of them crossed the threshold.

The room in which he found himself was lighted by two larger windows than that in the room which he had just quitted and in the better light he had an opportunity to examine the man who had rescued him. The fellow was a copper-colored giant with fine features.

As the man turned his face a little more toward the light of the windows, Tanar gave an exclamation of surprise and delight. "Ja!" he cried, and before

Ja could reply to the salutation, another man sprang forward from the far end of the room.

"Tanar!" exclaimed the second man. "Tanar, the son of Ghak!" As the Sarian wheeled he found himself standing face to face with David Innes, Emperor of Pellucidar.

"Ja of Anoroc and the Emperor!" cried Tanar. "What has happened? What brought you here?"

"It is well that we were here," said Ja, "and that I heard the rat pack squealing just when I did. These other fellows," and he nodded toward the remaining prisoners, "haven't brains enough to try to save the newcomers that are incarcerated here. David and I have been trying to pound it into their stupid heads that the more of us there are the safer we shall be from the attacks of the rats, but all they think of is that they are safe now, and so they do not care what becomes of the other poor devils that are shoved down here; nor have they brains enough to look into the future and realize that when some of us are taken out or die there may not be enough left to repel the attacks of the hungry beasts. But tell us, Tanar, where you have been and how you came here at last."

"It is a long story," replied the Sarian, "and first I would hear the story of my Emperor."

"There is little of interest in the adventures that befell us," said David, "but there may be points of great value to us in what I have managed to learn from the Korsars concerning a number of problems that have been puzzling me.

"When we saw the Korsars' fleet sail away with

you and others of our people, prisoners aboard them, we were filled with dismay and as we stood upon the shore of the great sea above The Land of Awful Shadow, we were depressed by the hopelessness of ever effecting your rescue. It was then that I determined to risk the venture which is responsible for our being here in the dungeon of the capital of Korsar.

"From all those who volunteered to accompany me I selected Ja, and we took with us to be our pilot a Korsar prisoner named Fitt. Our boat was one of those abandoned by the Korsars in their flight and in it we pursued our course toward Korsar without incident until we were overwhelmed by the most terrific storm that I have ever witnessed."

"Doubtless the same storm that wrecked the Korsars' fleet that was bearing us away," said Tanar.

"Unquestionably," said David, "as you will know in a moment. The storm carried away all our rigging, snapping the mast short off at the deck, and left us helpless except for two pairs of oars.

"As you may know, these great sweeps are so heavy that, as a rule, two or three men handle a single oar, and as there were only three of us we could do little more than paddle slowly along with one man paddling on either side while the third relieved first one and then the other at intervals, and even this could be accomplished only after we had cut the great sweeps down to a size that one man might handle without undue fatigue.

"Fitt had laid a course which my compass showed me to be almost due north and this we followed with little or no deviation after the storm had subsided.

"We slept and ate many times before Fitt announced that we were not far from the island of Amiocap, which he says is half way between the point at which we had embarked and the land of Korsar. We still had ample water and provisions to last us the balance of our journey if we had been equipped with a sail, but the slow progress of paddling threatened to find us facing starvation, or death by thirst, long before we could hope to reach Korsar. With this fate staring us in the face we decided to land on Amiocap and refit our craft, but before we could do so we were overtaken by a Korsar ship and being unable either to escape or defend ourselves, we were taken prisoners.

"The vessel was one of those that had formed the armada of The Cid, and was, as far as they knew, the only one that had survived the storm. Shortly before they had found us they had picked up a boat-load of the survivors of The Cid's ship, including The Cid himself, and from The Cid we learned that you and the other prisoners had doubtless been lost with his vessel, which he said was in a sinking condition at the time that he abandoned it. To my surprise I learned that The Cid had also abandoned his own daughter to her fate and I believe that this cowardly act weighed heavily upon his mind, for he was always taciturn and moody, avoiding the companionship of even his own officers."

"She did not die," said Tanar. "We escaped together, the sole survivors, as far as we knew, of The Cid's ship, though later we were captured by the members of another boat crew that had also made the island of Amiocap and with them we were brought to Korsar."

"In my conversation with The Cid and also with the officers and men of the Korsar ship I sought to sound them on their knowledge of the extent of this sea, which is known as the Korsar Az. Among other things I learned that they possess compasses and are conversant with their use and they told me that to the west they had never sailed to the extreme limits of the Korsar Az, which they state reaches on, a vast body of water, for countless leagues beyond the knowledge of man. But to the east they have followed the shore-line from Korsar southward almost to the shore upon which they landed to attack the empire of Pellucidar.

"Now this suggests, in fact almost proves, that Korsar lies upon the same great continent as the empire of Pellucidar and if we can escape from prison, we may be able to make our way by land back to our own country."

"But there is that 'if,' " said Ja. "We have eaten and slept many times since they threw us into this dark hole, yet we are no nearer escape now than we were at the moment that they put us here; nor do we even know what fate lies in store for us."

"These other prisoners tell us," resumed David, "that the fact that we were not immediately killed, which is the customary fate of prisoners of war among the Korsars, indicates that they are saving us for some purpose; but what that purpose is I cannot conceive."

"I can," said Tanar. "In fact I am quite sure that I know."

"And what is it?" demanded Ja.

"They wish us to teach them how to make fire-arms and powder such as ours," replied the Sarian. "But where do you suppose they ever got firearms and powder in the first place?"

"Or the great ships they sail," added Ja; "ships that are even larger than those which we build? These things were unknown in Pellucidar before David and Perry came to us, yet the Korsars appear to have known of them and used them always."

"I have an idea," said David; "yet it is such a mad idea that I have almost hesitated to entertain it, much less to express it."

"What is it?" asked Tanar.

"It was suggested to me in my conversations with the Korsars themselves," replied the Emperor. "Without exception they have all assured me that their ancestors came from another world—a world above which the sun did not stand perpetually at zenith, but crossed the heavens regularly, leaving the world in darkness half the time. They say that a part of this world is very cold and that their ancestors, who were seafaring men, became caught with their ships in the frozen waters; that their compasses turned in all directions and became use-less to them and that when finally they broke through the ice and sailed away in the direction that they thought was south, they came into Pelluci-dar, which they found inhabited only by naked sav-ages and wild beasts. And here they set up their city and built new ships, their numbers being augmented from time to time by other seafaring men from this world from which they say they originally came.

"They intermarried with the natives, which in this part of Pellucidar seemed to have been of a very low order." David paused.

"Well," asked Tanar, "what does it all mean?"

"It means," said David, "that if their legend is true, or based upon fact, that their ancestors came from the same outer world from which Perry and I came, but by what avenue?—that is the astounding enigma."

Many times during their incarceration the three men discussed this subject, but never were they able to arrive at any definite solution of the mystery. Food was brought them many times and several times they slept before Korsar soldiers came and took them from the dungeon.

They were led to the palace of The Cid, the architecture of which but tended to increase the mystery of the origin of this strange race in the mind of David Innes, for the building seemed to show indisputable proof of Moorish influence.

Within the palace they were conducted to a large room, comfortably filled with bewhiskered Korsars decked out in their gaudiest raiment, which far surpassed in brilliancy of coloring and ornamentation the comparatively mean clothes they had worn aboard ship. Upon a dais, at one end of the room, a man was seated upon a large, ornately carved chair. It was The Cid, and as David's eyes fell upon him his mind suddenly grasped, for the first time, a significant suggestion in the title of the ruler of the Korsars.

Previously the name had been only a name to David. He had not considered it as a title; nor had it by association awakened any particular train of thought, but now, coupled with the Moorish palace and the carved throne, it did.

The Cid! Rodrigo Diaz de Bivar—El Campeador—a national hero of eleventh century Spain. What did it mean? His thoughts reverted to the ships of the Korsars—their motley crews with harquebuses and cutlasses—and he recalled the thrilling stories he had read as a boy of the pirates of the Spanish Main. Could it be merely coincidence? Could a nation of people have grown up within the inner world, who so closely resembled the buccaneers of the seventeenth century, or had their forebears in truth found their way hither from the outer crust? David Innes did not know. He was frankly puzzled. But now he was being led to the foot of The Cid's throne and there was no further opportunity for the delightful speculation that had absorbed his mind momentarily.

The cruel, cunning eyes of The Cid looked down upon the three prisoners from out his brutal face. "The Emperor of Pellucidar!" he sneered. "The King of Anoroc! The son of the King of Sari!" and then he laughed uproariously. He extended his hand, his fingers parted and curled in a clutching gesture. "Emperor! King! Prince!" he sneered again, "and yet here you all are in the clutches of The Cid. Emperor—bah! I, The Cid, am the Emperor of all Pellucidar! You and your naked savages!" He turned on David. "Who are you to take the title of Emperor? I could crush you all," and he closed his fingers in a gesture of rough cruelty. "But I shall not. The Cid is generous and he is grateful, too. You shall have your freedom for a small price that you may easily pay." He paused as though he expected them to question him, but no one of the three spoke. Suddenly he turned upon David. "Where did you get your firearms and your powder? Who made them for you?"

"We made them ourselves," replied David.

"Who taught you to make them?" insisted The Cid. "But never mind; it is enough that you know and we would know. You may win your liberty by teaching us."

David could make gunpowder, but whether he could make any better gunpowder than the Korsars he did not know. He had left that to Perry and his apprentices in The Empire, and he knew perfectly well that he could not reconstruct a modern rifle such as was being turned out in the arsenals at Sari, for he had neither the drawings to make the rifles, nor the machinery, nor the drawings to make the machinery, nor the shops in which to make steel. But nevertheless here was one opportunity for possible freedom that might pave the way to escape and he could not throw it away, either for himself or his companions, by admitting their inability to manufacture modern firearms or improve the powder of the Korsars.

"Well," demanded The Cid, impatiently, "what is your answer?"

"We cannot make powder and rifles while a man eats," replied David; "nor can we make them from the air or from conversation. We must have materials; we must have factories; we must have trained men. You will sleep many times before we are able to accomplish all this. Are you willing to wait?"

"How many times shall we sleep before you have taught our people to make these things?" demanded The Cid.

David shrugged. "I do not know," he said. "In the first place I must find the proper materials."

"We have all the materials," said The Cid. "We have iron and we have the ingredients for making powder. All that you have to do is to put them together in a better way than we have been able to."

"You may have the materials, but it is possible that they are not of sufficiently good quality to make the things that will alone satisfy the subjects of the Emperor of Pellucidar. Perhaps your niter is low grade; there may be impurities in your sulphur; or even the charcoal may not be properly prepared; and there are even more important matters to consider in the selection of material and its manufacture into steel suitable for making the firearms of the Pellucidarians."

˙ "You shall not be hurried," said The Cid. He turned to a man standing near him. "See that an officer accompanies these men always," he said. "Let them go where they please and do what they please in the prosecution of my orders. Furnish them with laborers if they desire them, but do not

let them delay and do not let them escape, upon
pain of death." And thus ended their interview
with The Cid of Korsar.

As it chanced, the man to be detailed to watch
them was Fitt, the fellow whom David had chosen
to accompany him and Ja in their pursuit of the
Korsar fleet, and Fitt, having become well acquainted with David and Ja and having experienced
nothing but considerate treatment from them, was
far from unfriendly, though, like the majority of
all other Korsars, he was inclined to be savage and
cruel.

As they were passing out of the palace they
caught a glimpse of a girl in a chamber that opened
onto the corridor in which they were. Fitt, big
with the importance of his new position and feeling
somewhat like a showman revealing and explaining
his wonders to the ignorant and uninitiated, had
been describing the various objects of interest that
they had passed as well as the personages of importance, and now he nodded in the direction of the
room in which they had seen the girl, although they
had gone along the corridor so far by this time that
they could no longer see her. "That," he said, "is
The Cid's daughter." Tanar stopped in his tracks
and turned to Fitt.

"May I speak to her?" he asked.

"You!" cried Fitt. "You speak to the daughter
of The Cid!"

"I know her," said Tanar. "We two were left
alone on the abandoned ship when it was deserted
by its officers and crew. Go and ask her if she will
speak to me."

Fitt hesitated. "The Cid might not approve," he said.

"He gave you no orders other than to accompany us," said David. "How are we to carry on our work if we are to be prevented from speaking to anyone whom we choose? At least you will be safe in leading us to The Cid's daughter. If she wishes to speak to Tanar the responsibility will not be yours."

"Perhaps you are right," said Fitt. "I will ask her." He stepped to the doorway of the apartment in which were Stellara and Gura, and now, for the first time, he saw that a man was with them. It was Bulf. The three looked up as he entered.

"There is one here who wishes to speak to The Cid's daughter," he said, addressing Stellara.

"Who is he?" demanded Bulf.

"He is Tanar, a prisoner of war from Sari."

"Tell him," said Stellara, "that The Cid's daughter does not recall him and cannot grant him an interview."

As Fitt turned and quit the chamber, Gura's ordinarily sad eyes flashed a look of angry surprise at Stellara.

Chapter Fourteen

Two Suns

DAVID, Ja, and Tanar were quartered in barracks inside the palace wall and immediately set to work to carry out a plan that David had suggested and which included an inspection, not only of the Korsars' powder factory and the arsenals in which their firearms were manufactured, but also visits to the niter beds, sulphur deposits, charcoal pits and iron mines.

These various excursions for the purpose of inspecting the sources of supply and the methods of obtaining it aroused no suspicion in the mind of the Korsar, though their true purpose was anything other than it appeared to be.

In the first place David had not the slightest intention of teaching the Korsars how to improve their powder, thereby transforming them into a far greater menace to the peace of his empire than they could ever become while handicapped by an inferior grade of gunpowder that failed to explode quite as often as it exploded. These tours of inspection, however, which often took them considerable distances from the city of Korsar, afforded an excuse for delaying the lesson in powder making, while David and his companions sought to concoct some plan of escape that might contain at least the seed of success. Also they gave the three men a better knowledge of the surrounding country, familiarized them with the various trails and acquainted them with the manners and customs of the primitive tribes that carried on the agriculture of Korsar and all of the labor of the mines, niter beds and charcoal burning.

It was not long before they had learned that all the Korsars lived in the city of Korsar and that they numbered about five hundred thousand souls, and, as all labor was performed by slaves, every male Korsar above the age of fifteen was free for military service, while those between ten and fifteen were virtually so since this included the period of their training, during which time they learned all that could be taught them of seamanship and the art of piracy and raiding. David soon came to realize that the ferocity of the Korsars, rather than their number, rendered them a menace to the peace of Pellucidar, but he was positive that with an equal number of ships and men he could overcome them and he was glad that he had taken upon himself this dangerous mission, for the longer the three reconnoitered the environs of Korsar the more convinced they became that escape was possible.

The primitive savages from whom the Korsars had wrested their country and whom they had forced into virtual slavery were of such a low order of intelligence that David felt confident that they could never be successfully utilized as soldiers or fighting men by the Korsars, whom they outnumbered ten to one; their villages, according to his Korsar informant, stretching away into the vast hinterland, to the farthest extremities of which no man had ever penetrated.

The natives themselves spoke of a cold country to the north, in the barren and desolate wastes of which no man could live, and of mountains and forests and plains stretching away into the east and southeast to, as they put it, "the very shores of Molop Az"—the flaming sea of Pellucidarian legend upon which the land of Pellucidar floats.

This belief of the natives of the uninterrupted extent of the land mass to the south and southeast corroborated David's belief that Korsar lay upon the same continent as Sari, and this belief was further carried out by the distinct sense of perfect orientation which the three men experienced the moment they set foot upon the shores of Korsar; or rather which the born Pellucidarians, Ja and Tanar, experienced, since David did not possess this inborn homing instinct. Had there been an ocean of any considerable extent separating them from the land of their birth, the two Pellucidarians felt confident that they could not have been so certain as to the direction of Sari as they now were.

As their excursions to various points outside the city of Korsar increased in number the watchfulness of Fitt relaxed, so that the three men occasionally found themselves alone together in some remote part of the back country.

Tanar, wounded by the repeated rebuffs of Stellara, sought to convince himself that he did not love her. He tried to make himself believe that she was cruel and hard and unfaithful, but all that he succeeded in accomplishing was to make himself more unhappy, though he hid this from his companions and devoted himself as assiduously as they to planning their escape. It filled his heart with agony to think of going away forever from the vicinity of the woman he loved, even though there was little or no hope that he might see her should he remain, for gossip of the approaching nuptials of Stellara and Bulf was current in the barracks where he was quartered.

The window of the room to which he had been assigned overlooked a portion of the garden of The Cid—a spot of great natural beauty in which trees and flowers and shrubs bordered gravelled pathways and a miniature lake and streamlet sparkled in the sunlight.

Tanar was seldom in his apartment and when he was he ordinarily gave no more than casual attention to the garden beyond the wall, but upon one occasion, after returning from an inspection of an iron mine, he had been left alone with his own sad thoughts, and, seating himself upon the sill of the window, he was gazing down upon the lovely scene below when his attention was attracted by the figure of a girl as she came into view almost directly before him along one of the gravelled paths. She was looking up toward his window and their eyes met simultaneously. It was Gura.

Placing her finger to her lips, cautioning him to silence, she came quickly forward until she reached a point as close to his window as it was possible for her to come.

"There is a gate in the garden wall at the far end of your barracks," she said in a low whisper attuned to reach his ears. "Come to it at once."

Tanar stopped to ask no questions. The girl's tone had been peremptory. Her whole manner bespoke urgency. Descending the stairway to the ground floor Tanar left the building and walked slowly toward its far end. Korsars were all about him, but they had been accustomed to seeing him, and now he held himself to a slow and careless pace that aroused no suspicion. Just beyond the end of the barracks he came to a small, heavily planked door set in the garden wall and as he arrived opposite this, it swung open and he stepped quickly within the garden, Gura instantly closing the gate behind him.

"At last I have succeeded," cried the girl, "but I thought that I never should. I have tried so hard to see you ever since Fitt took you from The Cid's palace. I learned from one of the slaves where your quarters were in the barracks and whenever I have been free I have been always beneath your window. Twice before I saw you, but I could not attract your attention and now that I have succeeded, perhaps it is too late."

"Too late! What do you mean? Too late for what?" demanded Tanar.

"Too late to save Stellara," said the girl.

"She is in danger?" asked Tanar.

"The preparations for her marriage to Bulf are complete. She cannot delay it much longer."

"Why should she wish to delay it?" demanded

the Sarian. "Is she not content with the man she has chosen?"

"Like all men, you are a fool in matters pertaining to a woman's heart," cried Gura.

"I know what she told me," said Tanar.

"After all that you had been through together; after all that she had been to you, how could you have believed that she loved another?" demanded Gura.

"You mean that she does not love Bulf?" asked Tanar.

"Of course she does not love him. He is a horrid beast."

"And she still loves me?"

"She has never loved anyone else," replied the girl.

"Then why did she treat me as she did? Why did she say the things that she said?"

"She was jealous."

"Jealous! Jealous of whom?"

"Of me," said Gura, dropping her eyes.

The Sarian stood looking dumbly at the dark-haired Himean girl standing before him. He noted her slim body, her drooping shoulders, her attitude of dejection. "Gura," he asked, "did I ever speak words of love to you? Did I ever give Stellara or another the right to believe that I loved you?"

She shook her head. "No," she said, "and I told Stellara that when I found out what she thought. I told her that you did not love me and finally she was convinced and asked me to find you and tell you that she still loves you. But I have another message for you from myself. I know you, Sarian. I know that you are not planning to remain here contentedly a prisoner of the Korsars. I know that you will try to escape and I have come to beg you to take Stellara with you, for she will kill herself before she will become the mate of Bulf."

"Escape," mused Tanar. "How may it be accomplished from the heart of The Cid's palace?"

"That is the man's work," said Gura. "It is for you to plan the way."

"And you?" asked Tanar. "You wish to come away with us?"

"Do not think of me," said Gura. "If you and Stellara can escape, I do not matter."

"But you do matter," said the man, "and I am sure that you do not wish to stay in Korsar."

"No, I do not wish to remain in Korsar," replied the girl, "and particularly so now that The Cid seems to have taken a fancy to me."

"You wish to return to Hime?" asked Tanar.

"After the brief taste of happiness I have had," replied the girl, "I could not return to the quarrels, the hatred and the constant unhappiness that constitute life within the cave of Scurv and which would be but continued in some other cave were I to take a mate in Hime."

"Then come with us," said the Sarian.

"Oh, if I only might!" exclaimed Gura.

"Then that is settled," exclaimed Tanar. "You shall come with us and if we reach Sari I know that you can find peace and happiness for yourself always."

"It sounds like a dream," said the girl, wistfully,

"from which I shall awaken in the cave of Scurv."

"We shall make the dream come true," said the Sarian, "and now let us plan on how best we can get you and Stellara out of the palace of The Cid."

"That will not be so easy," said Gura.

"No, it is the most difficult part of our escape," agreed the Sarian; "but it must be done and I believe that the bolder the plan the greater its assurance of success."

"And it must be done at once," said Gura, "for the wedding arrangements are completed and Bulf is impatient for his mate."

For a moment Tanar stood in thought, seeking to formulate some plan that might contain at least a semblance of feasibility. "Can you bring Stellara to this gate at once?" he asked Gura.

"If she is alone, yes," replied the girl.

"Then go and fetch her and wait here with her until I return. My signal will be a low whistle. When you hear it, unlatch the gate."

"I shall return as quickly as possible," said Gura, and, as Tanar stepped through the doorway into the barrack yards, he closed and latched the gate behind him.

The Sarian looked about him and was delighted to note that apparently no one had seen him emerge from the garden. Instead of returning along the front of the barracks the way he had come, he turned in the opposite direction and made his way directly to one of the main gates of the palace. And this strategy was prompted also by another motive—he wished to ascertain if he could pass the guard at the main gate without being challenged.

Tanar had not adopted the garments of his captors and was still conspicuous by the scant attire and simple ornaments of a savage warrior and already his comings and goings had made him a familiar figure around the palace yard and in the Korsar streets beyond. But he had never passed through a palace gate alone before; nor without the ever present Fitt.

As he neared the gate he neither hastened nor loitered, but maintained a steady pace and an unconcerned demeanor. Others were passing in and out and as the former naturally received much closer scrutiny by the guards than the latter, Tanar soon found himself in a Korsar street outside the palace of The Cid.

Before him were the usual sights now grown familiar—the narrow, dusty street, the small open shops or bazaars lining the opposite side, the swaggering Korsars in their brilliant kerchiefs and sashes, and the slaves bearing great burdens to and fro—garden truck and the fruits of the chase coming in from the back country, while bales of tanned hides, salt and other commodities, craved by the simple tastes of the aborigines, were being borne out of the city toward the interior. Some of the bales were of considerable size and weight, requiring the services of four carriers, and were supported on two long poles, the ends of which rested on the shoulders of the men.

There were lines of slaves carrying provisions and ammunition to a fleet of ships that was outfitting for a new raid, and another line bearing plunder from the hold of another ship that had but recently come to anchor in the river before the city.

All this activity presented a scene of apparent confusion, which was increased by the voices of the merchants hawking their wares and the shrill bickering of prospective purchasers.

Through the motley throng the Sarian shouldered his way back toward another gate that gave entrance to the palace ground close to the far end of the long, rambling barracks. As this was the gate through which he passed most often he was accorded no more than a glance as he passed through, and once within he hastened immediately to the quarters assigned to David. Here he found both David and Ja, to whom he immediately unfolded a plan that he had been perfecting since he left the garden of The Cid.

"And now," he said, "before you have agreed to my plan, let me make it plain that I do not expect you to accompany me if you feel that the chances of success are too slight. It is my duty, as well as my desire, to save Stellara and Gura. But I cannot ask you to place your plans for escape in jeopardy."

"Your plan is a good one," replied David, "and even if it were not it is the best that has been suggested yet. And as for our deserting either you or Stellara or Gura, that, of course, is not even a question for discussion. We shall go with you and I know that I speak for Ja as well as myself."

"I knew that you would say that," said the Sarian, "and now let us start at once to put the plan to test."

"Good," said David. "You make your purchases and return to the garden and Ja and I will proceed at once to carry out our part."

The three proceeded at once toward the palace gate at the far end of the barracks, and as they were passing through the Korsar in charge stopped them.

"Where now?" he demanded.

"We are going into the city to make purchases for a long expedition that we are about to make in search of new iron deposits in the back country, further than we have ever been before."

"And where is Fitt?" demanded the captain of the gate.

"The Cid sent for him, and while he is gone we are making the necessary preparations."

"All right," said the man, apparently satisfied. "You may pass."

"We shall return presently with porters," said David, "for some of our personal belongings and then go out again to collect the balance of our outfit. Will you leave word that we are to be passed in the event that you are not here?"

"I shall be here," said the man. "But what are you going to carry into the back country?"

"We expect that we may have to travel even beyond the furthest boundaries of Korsar, where the natives know little or nothing of The Cid and his authority, and for this reason it is necessary for us to carry provisions and articles of trade that we may barter with them for what we want, since we shall not have sufficient numbers in our party to take these things by force."

"I see," said the man; "but it seems funny that The Cid does not send muskets and pistols to take what he wants rather than spoil these savages by trading with them."

"Yes," said David, "it does seem strange," and the three passed out into the street of Korsar.

Beyond the gate David and Ja turned to the right toward the market place, while Tanar crossed immediately to one of the shops on the opposite side of the street. Here he purchased two large bags, made of well tanned hide, with which he returned immediately to the palace grounds and presently he was before the garden gate where he voiced a low whistle that was to be the signal by which the girls were to know that he arrived.

Almost immediately the gate swung open and Tanar stepped quickly within. As Gura closed the gate behind him, Tanar found himself standing face to face with Stellara. Her eyes were moist with tears, her lips were trembling with suppressed emotion as the Sarian opened his arms and pressed her to him.

The market place of the city of Korsar is a large, open square where the natives from the interior barter their agricultural produce, raw hides and the flesh of the animals they have taken in the chase, for the simple necessities which they wish to take back to their homes with them.

The farmers bring in their vegetables in large hampers made of reed bound together with grasses. These hampers are ordinarily about four feet in each dimension and are borne on a single pole by two men if lightly loaded, or upon two poles and by four carriers if the load is heavy.

David and Ja approached a group of men whose hampers were empty and who were evidently preparing to depart from the market, and after questioning several of the group they found two who were returning to the same village, which lay at a considerable distance almost due north of Korsar.

By the order of The Cid, Fitt had furnished his three prisoners with ample funds in the money of Korsar that they might make necessary purchases in the prosecution of their investigations and their experiments.

The money, which consisted of gold coins of various sizes and weights, was crudely stamped upon one side with what purported to be a likeness of The Cid, and upon the other with a Korsar ship. For so long a time had gold coin been the medium of exchange in Korsar and the surrounding country that it was accepted by the natives of even remote villages and tribes, so that David had little difficulty in engaging the services of eight carriers and their two hampers to carry equipment at least as far as their village, which in reality was much further than David had any intention of utilizing the services of the natives.

Having concluded his arrangements with the men, David and Ja led the way back to the palace gate, where the officer passed them through with a nod.

As they proceeded along the front of the barracks toward its opposite end their only fear was that Fitt might have returned from his interview with

The Cid. If he had and if he saw and questioned them, all was lost. They scarcely breathed as they approached the entrance to their quarters, which were also the quarters of Fitt. But they saw nothing of him as they passed the doorway and hastened on to the door in the garden wall. Here they halted, directing the bearers to place the baskets close to the doorway. David Innes whistled. The door swung in, and at a word from Tanar the eight carriers entered, picked up two bundles just inside the gate and deposited one of them in each of the hampers waiting beyond the wall. The lids were closed. The slaves resumed their burden, and the party turned about to retrace its steps to the palace gate through which the carriers had just entered with their empty hampers.

Once again apprehension had chilled the heart of David Innes for fear that Fitt might have returned, but they passed the barracks and reached the gate without seeing him, and here they were halted by the Korsar in charge.

"It did not take you long," he said. "What have you in the hampers?" and he raised the cover of one of them.

"Only our personal belongings," said David. "When we return again we shall have our full equipment. Would you like to inspect it all at the same time?"

The Korsar, looking down at the skin bag lying at the bottom of the hamper, hesitated for a moment before replying. "Very well," he said, "I will do it all at the same time," and he let the cover drop back into place.

The hearts of the three men had stood still, but David Innes's voice betrayed no unwonted emotion as he addressed the captain of the gate. "When Fitt returns," he said, "tell him that I am anxious to see him and ask him if he will wait in our quarters until we return."

The Korsar nodded a surly assent and motioned for them to pass on through the gate.

Turning to the right, David led the party down the narrow street toward the market place. There he turned abruptly to the left, through a winding alleyway and double-backed to the north upon another street that paralleled that upon which the palace fronted. Here were poorer shops and less traffic and the carriers were able to make good time until presently the party passed out of the city of Korsar into the open country beyond. And then, by dint of threats and promises of additional pieces of gold, the three men urged the carriers to accelerate their speed to a swinging trot, which they maintained until they were forced to stop from exhaustion. A brief rest with food and they were off again; nor did they slacken their pace until they reached the rolling, wooded country at the foothills of the mountains, far north of Korsar.

Here, well within the shelter of the woods, the carriers set down their burdens and threw themselves upon the ground to rest, while Tanar and David swung back the covers of the hampers and untying the stout thongs that closed the mouths of the bags revealed their contents. Half smothered and almost unable to move their cramped limbs,

Stellara and Gura were lifted from the baskets and revealed to the gaze of the astounded carriers.

Tanar turned upon the men. "Do you know who this woman is?" he demanded.

"No," said one of their number.

"It is Stellara, the daughter of The Cid," said the Sarian. "You have helped to steal her from the palace of her father. Do you know what that will mean if you are caught?"

The men trembled in evident terror. "We did not know she was in the basket," said one of them. "We had nothing to do with it. It is you who stole her."

"Will the Korsars believe you when we tell them of the great quantities of gold we paid you if we are captured?" asked Tanar. "No, they will not believe you and I do not have to tell you what your fate will be. But there is safety for you if you will do what I tell you to do."

"What is that?" demanded one of the natives.

"Take up your hampers and hasten on to your village and tell no one, as long as you live, what you have done, not even your mates. If you do not tell, no one will know for we shall not tell."

"We will never tell," cried the men in chorus.

"Do not even talk about it among yourselves," cautioned David, "for even the trees have ears, and if the Korsars come to your village and question you tell them that you saw three men and two women traveling toward the east just beyond the borders of the city of Korsar. Tell them that they were too far away for you to recognize them, but that they may have been The Cid's daughter and her companion with the three men who abducted them."

"We will do as you say," replied the carriers.

"Then be gone," demanded David, and the eight men hurriedly gathered up their hampers and disappeared into the forest toward the north.

When the two girls were sufficiently revived and rested to continue the journey, the party set out again, making their way to the east for a short distance and then turning north again, for it had been Tanar's plan to throw the Korsars off the trail by traveling north, rather than east or south. Later they would turn to the east, far north of the area which the Korsars might be expected to comb in search of them, and then again, after many marches, they would change their direction once more to the south. It was a circuitous route, but it seemed the safest.

The forest changed to pine and cedar and there were windswept wastes dotted with gnarled and stunted trees. The air was cooler than they had ever known it in their native land, and when the wind blew from the north they shivered around roaring camp fires. The animals they met were scarcer and bore heavier fur, and nowhere was there sign of man.

Upon one occasion when they stopped to camp Tanar pointed at the ground before him. "Look!" he cried to David. "My shadow is no longer beneath me," and then, looking up, "the sun is not above us."

"I have noticed that," replied David, "and I am

trying to understand the reason for it, and perhaps I shall with the aid of the legends of the Korsars."

As they proceeded their shadows grew longer and longer and the light and heat of the sun diminished until they traveled in a semi-twilight that was always cold.

Long since they had been forced to fashion warmer garments from the pelts of the beasts they had killed. Tanar and Ja wanted to turn back toward the southeast, for their strange homing instinct drew them in that direction toward their own country, but David asked them to accompany him yet a little further for his mind had evolved a strange and wonderful theory and he wished to press on yet a little further to obtain still stronger proof of its correctness.

When they slept they rested beside roaring fires and once, when they awoke, they were covered by a light mantle of a cold, white substance that frightened the Pellucidarians, but that David knew was snow. And the air was full of whirling particles and the wind bit those portions of their faces that were exposed, for now they wore fur caps and hoods and their hands were covered with warm mittens.

"We cannot go much further in this direction," said Ja, "or we shall all perish."

"Perhaps you are right," said David. "You four turn back to the southeast and I will go yet a little further to the north and overtake you when I have satisfied myself that a thing that I believe is true."

"No," cried Tanar, "we shall remain together. Where you go we shall go."

"Yes," said Ja, "we shall not abandon you."

"Just a little further north, then," said David, "and I shall be ready to turn back with you," and so they forged ahead over snow covered ground into the deepening gloom that filled the souls of the Pellucidarians with terror. But after a while the wind changed and blew from the south and the snow melted and the air became balmy again, and still further on the twilight slowly lifted and the light increased, though the midday sun of Pellucidar was now scarcely visible behind them.

"I cannot understand it," said Ja. "Why should it become lighter again, although the sun is ever further away behind us?"

"I do not know," said Tanar. "Ask David."

"I can only guess," said David, "and my guess seems so preposterous that I dare not voice it."

"Look!" cried Stellara, pointing ahead. "It is the sea."

"Yes," said Gura, "a gray sea; it does not look like water."

"And what is that?" cried Tanar. "There is a great fire upon the sea.

"And the sea does not curve upward in the distance," cried Stellara. "Everything is wrong in this country and I am afraid."

David had stopped in his tracks and was staring at the deep red glow ahead. The others gathered around him and watched it, too. "What is it?" demanded Ja.

"As there is a God in heaven it can be but one

thing," replied David; "and yet I know that it cannot be that thing. The very idea is ridiculous. It is impossible and outlandish."

"But what might it be?" demanded Stellara.

"The sun," replied David.

"But the sun is almost out of sight behind us," Gura reminded him.

"I do not mean the sun of Pellucidar," replied David; "but the sun of the outer world, the world from which I came."

The others stood in silent awe, watching the edge of a blood red disc that seemed to be floating upon a gray ocean across whose reddened surface a brilliant pathway of red and gold led from the shoreline to the blazing orb, where the sea and sky seemed to meet.

Chapter Fifteen

MADNESS

"NOW," said Stellara, "we can go no further;" nor indeed could they for east and west and north stretched a great, sullen sea and along the shore-line at their feet great ice cakes rose and fell with sullen roars and loud reports as the sea ground the churning mass.

For a long time David Innes, Emperor of Pellucidar, stood staring out across that vast and desolate waste of water. "What lies beyond?" he murmured to himself, and then, shaking his head, he turned away. "Come," he said, "let us strike back for Sari."

His companions received his words with shouts of joy. Smiles replaced the half troubled expressions that had marked their drawn faces since the moment that they had discovered that their beloved noonday sun was being left behind them.

With light steps, with laughter and joking, they faced the long, arduous journey that lay ahead of them.

During the second march, after they had turned back from the northern sea, Gura discovered a strange object to the left of their line of march.

"It looks as though it might be some queer sort of native hut," she said.

"We shall have to investigate it," said David, and the five made their way to the side of the strange object.

It was a large, heavy, wicker basket that lay inverted upon the barren ground. All about it were the rotted remnants of cordage.

At David's suggestion the men turned the basket over upon its side. Beneath it they found well preserved remnants of oiled silk and a network of fine cord.

"What is it?" asked Stellara.

"It is the basket and all that remains of the gas bag of a balloon," said David.

"What is a balloon," asked the girl, "and how did it get here?"

"I can explain what a balloon is," said David; "but if I were positive that I was correct in my conjecture as to how it came here, I would hold the answer to a thousand questions that have puzzled the men of the outer crust for ages." For a long time he stood silently contemplating the weather-worn basket. His mind submerged in thought was oblivious to all else. "If I only knew," he mused. "If I only knew, and yet how else could it have come here? What else could that red disc upon the horizon of the sea have been other than the midnight sun of the arctic regions."

"What in the world are you talking about?" demanded Gura.

"The poor devils," mused David, apparently oblivious of the girl's presence. "They made a greater discovery than they could have hoped for in their wildest dreams. I wonder if they lived to realize it." Slowly he removed his fur cap and stood facing the basket with bowed head, and for some unaccountable reason, which they could not explain, his companions bared their heads and followed his example. And after they had resumed their journey it was a long time before David Innes could shake off the effects of that desolate reminder of one of the world's most pathetic tragedies.

So anxious were the members of the party to reach the cheering warmth of the beloved Pellucidar that they knew, that they pressed on toward the south with the briefest of rests; nor were they wholly content until once more their shadows lay directly beneath them.

Sari, lying slightly east of south, their return from the north took them over a different route from that which they had followed up from Korsar. Of course the Pellucidarians did not know these points of compass as north or south, and even David Innes carried them in his mind more in accordance with the Pellucidarian scheme than that with which he had been familiar upon the outer crust.

Naturally, with the sun always at zenith and with no stars and no moon and no planets, the Pellucidarians have been compelled to evolve a different system of indicating direction than that with which we are familiar. By instinct they know the direction in which their own country lies and each Pellucidarian reckons all directions from this base line, and he indicates other directions in a simple and ingenious manner.

Suppose you were from Sari and were traveling from the ice girt sea above Korsar to any point upon Pellucidar, you would set and maintain your course in this manner. Extend the fingers of your right hand and hold it in a horizontal position, palm down, directly in front of your body, your little finger pointing in the direction of Sari—a direction which you know by instinct—and your thumb pointing to the left directly at right angles to the line in which your little finger is pointing. Now spread your left hand in the same way and lower it on top of your right hand, so that the little finger of your left hand exactly covers the little finger of your right hand.

You will now see the fingers and thumbs of your two hands cover an arc of one hundred and eighty degrees.

Sari lies southeast of Korsar, while The Land of Awful Shadow lies due south. Therefore a Sarian pointing in the direction toward The Land of Awful Shadow would say that he was traveling two left fingers from Sari, since the middle finger of the left hand would be pointing about due south toward The Land of Awful Shadow. If he were going in the opposite direction, or north, he would merely add the word "back," saying that he was traveling two left fingers back from Sari, so that by this plan every point of compass is roughly covered, and with sufficient accuracy for all the requirements of the primitive Pellucidarians. The fact that when one is traveling to the right of his established base line and indicates it by mentioning the fingers of his left hand might, at first, be deemed confusing, but, of course, having followed this system for ages, it is perfectly intelligible to the Pellucidarians.

When they reached a point at which the city of Korsar lay three right fingers back from Sari, they were, in reality, due east of the Korsar city. They were now in fertile, semi-tropical land teeming with animal life. The men were armed with pistols as well as spears, bows and arrows and knives; while Stellara and Gura carried light spears and knives, and seldom was there a march that did not witness an encounter with one or more of the savage beasts of the primeval forests, verdure clad hills or rolling plains across which their journey led them.

They long since had abandoned any apprehension of pursuit or capture by the Korsars and while they had skirted the distant hinterland claimed by Korsar and had encountered some of the natives upon one or two occasions, they had seen no member of the ruling class with the result that for the first time since they had fallen into the clutches of the enemy they felt a sense of unquestioned freedom. And though the other dangers that beset their way might appear appalling to one of the outer world, they had no such effect upon any one of the five, whose experiences of life had tended to make them wholly self-reliant, and, while constantly alert and watchful, unoppressed by the possibility of future calamity. When danger suddenly confronted them, they were ready to meet it. After it had passed they did not depress their spirits by anticipating the next encounter.

Ja and David were anxious to return to their mates, but Tanar and Stellara were supremely happy because they were together, and Gura was content merely to be near Tanar. Sometimes she recalled Balal, her brother, for he had been kind to her, but Scurv and Sloo and Dhung she tried to forget.

Thus they were proceeding, a happy and contented party, when, with the suddenness and unexpectedness of lightning out of a clear sky, disaster overwhelmed them.

They had been passing through a range of low, rocky hills and were descending a narrow gorge on the Sari side of the range when, turning the shoulder of a hill, they came face to face with a large party of Korsars, fully a hundred strong. The leaders saw and recognized them instantly and a shout of savage triumph that broke from their lips was taken up by all their fellows.

David, who was in the lead, saw that resistance would be futile and in the instant his plan was formed. "We must separate," he said. "Tanar, you and Stellara go together. Ja, take Gura with you, and I shall go in a different direction, for we must not all be captured. One, at least, must escape to return to Sari. If it is not I, then let the one who wins through take this message to Ghak and Perry. Tell Perry that I am positive that I have discovered that there is a polar opening in the outer crust leading into Pellucidar and that if he ever gets in radio communication with the outer world, he must inform them of this fact. Tell Ghak to rush his forces by sea on Korsar, as well as by land. And now, good-bye, and each for himself."

Turning in their tracks the five fled up the gorge

and being far more active and agile than the Korsars, they outdistanced them, and though the rattle of musketry followed them and bits of iron and stone fell about them, or whizzed past them, no one was struck.

Tanar and Stellara found and followed a steep ravine that led upward to the right, and almost at the same time Ja and Gura diverged to the left up the course of a dry waterway, while David continued on back up the main gorge.

Almost at the summit and within the reach of safety, Tanar and Stellara found their way blocked by a sheer cliff, which, while not more than fifteen feet in height, was absolutely unscalable; nor could they find footing upon the steep ravine sides to the right or left, and as they stood there in this cul-de-sac, their backs to the wall, a party of twenty or thirty Korsars, toiling laboriously up the ravine, cut off their retreat; nor was there any place in which they might hide, but instead were compelled to stand there in full view of the first of the enemy that came within sight of them, and thus with freedom already within their grasp they fell again into the hands of the Korsars. And Tanar had been compelled to surrender without resistance because he did not dare risk Stellara's life by drawing the fire of the enemy.

Many of the Korsars were for dispatching Tanar immediately, but the officer in command forbade them for it was The Cid's orders that any of the prisoners that might be recaptured were to be returned alive. "And furthermore," he added,

"Bulf is particularly anxious to get this Sarian back alive."

During the long march back to Korsar, Tanar and Stellara learned that this was one of several parties that The Cid had dispatched in search of them with orders never to return until they had rescued his daughter and captured her abductors. They also had impressed upon them the fact that the only reason for The Cid's insistence that the prisoners be returned alive was because he and Bulf desired to mete out to them a death commensurate with their crime.

During the long march back to Korsar, Tanar and Stellara were kept apart as a rule, though on several occasions they were able to exchange a few words.

"My poor Sarian," said Stellara upon one of these. "I wish to God that you had never met me for only sorrow and pain and death can come of it."

"I do not care," replied Tanar, "if I die tomorrow, or if they torture me forever, for no price is too high to pay for the happiness that I have had with you, Stellara."

"Ah, but they will torture you—that is what wrings my heart," cried the girl. "Take your life yourself, Tanar. Do not let them get you. I know them and I know their methods and I would rather kill you with my own hands than see you fall into their clutches. The Cid is a beast, and Bulf is worse than Bohar the Bloody. I shall never be his mate; of that you may be sure, and if you die by your own hand I shall follow you shortly. And if there is a life after this, as the ancestors of the Korsars taught them, then we shall meet again where all is peace and beauty and love."

The Sarian shook his head. "I know what is here in this life," he said, "and I do not know what is there in the other. I shall cling to this, and you must cling to it until some other hand than ours takes it from us."

"But they will torture you so horribly," she moaned.

"No torture can kill the happiness of our love, Stellara," said the man, and then guards separated them and they plodded on across the weary, interminable miles. How different the country looked through eyes of despair and sorrow from the sunlit paradise that they had seen when they journeyed through it, hand in hand with freedom and love.

But at last the long, cruel journey was over, a fitting prelude to its cruel ending, for at the palace gate Stellara and Tanar were separated. She was escorted to her quarters by female attendants whom she recognized as being virtually her guards and keepers, while Tanar was conducted directly into the presence of The Cid.

As he entered the room he saw the glowering face of the Korsar chieftain, and standing below the dais, just in front of him, was Bulf, whom he had seen but once before, but whose face no man could ever forget. But there was another there whose presence brought a look of greater horror to Tanar's face than did the brutal countenances of The Cid or Bulf, for standing directly before the dais, toward which he was being led, the Sarian saw

David I, Emperor of Pellucidar. Of all the calamities that could have befallen, this was the worst.

As the Sarian was led to David's side he tried to speak to him, but was roughly silenced by the Korsar guards; nor were they ever again to be allowed to communicate with one another.

The Cid eyed them savagely, as did Bulf. "For you, who betrayed my confidence and abducted my daughter, there is no punishment that can fit your crime; there is no death so terrible that its dying will expiate your sin. It is not within me to conceive of any form of torture the infliction of which upon you would give me adequate pleasure. I shall have to look for suggestions outside of my own mind," and his eyes ran questioningly among his officers surrounding him.

"Let me have that one," roared Bulf, pointing at Tanar, "and I can promise you that you will witness such tortures as the eyes of man never before beheld; nor the body of man ever before endured."

"Will it result in death?" asked a tall Korsar with cadaverous face.

"Of course," said Bulf, "but not too soon."

"Death is a welcome and longed for deliverance from torture," continued the other. "Would you give either one of these the satisfaction and pleasure of enjoying even death?"

"But what else is there?" demanded The Cid.

"There is a living death that is worse than death," said the cadaverous one.

"And if you can name a torture worse than that which I had in mind," exclaimed Bulf, "I shall gladly relinquish all my claims upon this Sarian."

"Explain," commanded The Cid.

"It is this," said the cadaverous one. "These men are accustomed to sunlight, to freedom, to cleanliness, to fresh air, to companionship. There are beneath this palace dark, damp dungeons into which no ray of light ever filters, whose thick walls are impervious to sound. The denizens of these horrid places, as you know, would have an effect opposite to that of human companionship and the only danger, the only weak spot in my plan, lies in the fact that their constant presence might deprive these criminals of their reason and thus defeat the very purpose to which I conceive their presence necessary. A lifetime of hideous loneliness and torture in silence and in darkness! What death, what torture, what punishment can you mete out to these men that would compare in hideousness with that which I have suggested?"

After he had ceased speaking the others remained in silent contemplation of his proposition for some time. It was The Cid who broke the silence.

"Bulf," he said, "I believe that he is right, for I know that as much as I love life I would rather die than be left alone in one of the palace dungeons."

Bulf nodded his head slowly. "I hate to give up my plan," he said, "for I should like to inflict that torture upon this Sarian myself: But," and he turned to the cadaverous one, "you are right. You have named a torture infinitely worse than any that I could conceive."

"Thus is it ordered," said The Cid, "to separate palace dungeons for life."

In utter silence, unbroken by the Korsar assemblage, Tanar and David were blindfolded; Tanar felt himself being stripped of all his ornaments and of what meager raiment it was his custom to wear, with the exception of his loin cloth. Then he was pushed and dragged roughly along, first this way and then that. He knew when they were passing through narrow corridors by the muffled echoes and there was a different reverberation of the footsteps of his guards as they crossed large apartments. He was hustled down flights of stone steps and through other corridors and at last he felt himself lowered into an opening, a guard seizing him under each arm. The air felt damp and it smelled of mold and must and of something else that was disgusting, but unrecognizable to his nostrils. And then they let go of him and he dropped a short distance and landed upon a stone flagging that felt damp and slippery to his bare feet. He heard a sound above his head—a grating sound as though a stone slab had been pushed across a stone floor to close the trap through which he had been lowered. Then Tanar snatched the bandage from his eyes, but he might as well have left it there for he found himself surrounded by utter darkness. He listened intently, but there was no sound, not even the sounds of the retreating footsteps of his guards— darkness and silence—they had chosen the most terrible torture that they could inflict upon a Sarian —silence, darkness and solitude.

For a long time he stood there motionless and then, slowly, he commenced to grope his way forward. Four steps he took before he touched the wall and this he followed two steps to the end, and there he turned and took six steps to cross before he reached the wall on the opposite side, and thus he made the circuit of his dungeon and found that it was four by six paces—perhaps not small for a dungeon, but narrower than the grave for Tanar of Pellucidar.

He tried to think—to think how he could occupy his time until death released him. Death! Could he not hasten it? But how? Six paces was the length of his prison cell. Could he not dash at full speed from one end to the other, crushing his brains out by the impact? And then he recalled his promise to Stellara, even in the face of her appeal to him to take his own life—"I shall not die of my own hand."

Again he made the circuit of his dungeon. He wondered how they would feed him, for he knew that they would feed him because they wished him to live as long as possible, as only thus might they encompass his torture. He thought of the bright sun shining down upon the table-lands of Sari. He thought of the young men and the maidens there free and happy. He thought of Stellara, so close, up there above him somewhere, and yet so infinitely far away. If he were dead, they would be closer. "Not by my own hand," he muttered.

He tried to plan for the future—the blank, dark, silent future—the eternity of loneliness that confronted him, and he found that through the despair of utter hopelessness his own unconquerable spirit could still discern hope, for no matter what his plans they all looked forward to a day of freedom and he realized that nothing short of death ever could rob him of this solace, and so his plan finally developed.

He must in some way keep his mind from dwelling constantly upon the present. He must erase from it all consideration of the darkness, the silence and the solitude that surrounded him. And he must keep fit, mentally and physically, for the moment of release or escape. And so he planned to walk and to exercise his arms and the other muscles of his body systematically to the end that he might keep in good condition and at the same time induce sufficient fatigue to enable him to sleep as much as possible, and when he rested preparatory to sleep he concentrated his mind entirely upon pleasant memories. And when he put the plan into practice he found that it was all that he had hoped that it would be. He exercised until he was thoroughly fatigued and then he lay down to pleasant day dreams until sleep claimed him. Being accustomed from childhood to sleeping upon hard ground, the stone flagging gave him no particular discomfort and he was asleep in the midst of pleasant memories of happy hours with Stellara.

But his awakening! As consciousness slowly returned it was accompanied by a sense of horror, the cause of which gradually filtered to his awakening sensibilities. A cold, slimy body was crawling across his chest. Instinctively his hand seized it to thrust it away and his fingers closed upon a scaly thing that wriggled and writhed and struggled.

Tanar leaped to his feet, cold sweat bursting from every pore. He could feel the hairs upon his head rising in horror. He stepped back and his foot touched another of those horrid things. He slipped and fell, and, falling, his body encountered others— cold, clammy, wriggling. Scrambling to his feet he retreated to the opposite end of his dungeon, but everywhere the floor was covered with writhing, scaly bodies. And now the silence became a pandemonium of seething sounds, a black caldron of venomous hisses.

Long bodies curled themselves about his legs and writhed and wriggled upward toward his face. No sooner did he tear one from him and hurl it aside than another took its place.

This was no dream as he had at first hoped, but stark, horrible reality. These hideous serpents that filled his cell were but a part of his torture, but they would defeat their purpose. They would drive him mad. Already he felt his mind tottering and then into it crept the cunning scheme of a madman. With their own weapons he would defeat their ends. He would rob them quickly of the power to torture him further, and he burst into a shrill, mirthless laugh as he tore a snake from around his body and held it before him.

The reptile writhed and struggled and very slowly Tanar of Pellucidar worked his hand upward to its throat. It was not a large snake for Pellucidar, measuring perhaps five feet in length with a body about six inches in diameter.

Grasping the reptile about a foot below its head with one hand, Tanar slapped it repeatedly in the face with the other and then held it close to his breast. Laughing and screaming, he struck and struck again, and at last the snake struck back, burying its fangs deep in the flesh of the Sarian.

With a cry of triumph Tanar hurled the thing from him, and then slowly sank to the floor upon the writhing, wriggling forms that carpeted it.

"With your own weapons I have robbed you of your revenge," he shrieked, and then he lapsed into unconsciousness.

Who may say how long he lay thus in the darkness and silence of that buried dungeon in a timeless world. But at length he stirred; slowly his eyes opened and as consciousness returned he felt about him. The stone flagging was bare. He sat up. He was not dead and to his surprise he discovered that he had suffered neither pain nor swelling from the strike of the serpent.

He arose and moved cautiously about the dungeon. The snakes were gone. Sleep had restored his mental equilibrium, but he shuddered as he realized how close he had been to madness, and he smiled somewhat shamefacedly, as he reflected upon the futility of his needless terror. For the first time in his life Tanar of Pellucidar had understood the meaning of the word fear.

As he paced slowly around his dungeon one foot came in contact with something lying on the floor in a corner—something which had not been there before the snakes came. He stooped and felt cautiously with his hand and found an iron bowl fitted with a heavy cover. He lifted the cover. Here was food and without questioning what it was or whence it came, he ate.

Chapter Sixteen

THE DARKNESS BEYOND

THE deadly monotony of his incarceration dragged on. He exercised; he ate; he slept. He never knew how the food was brought to his cell, nor when, and after a while he ceased to care.

The snakes came usually while he slept, but since that first experience they no longer filled him with horror. And after a dozen repetitions of their visit they not only ceased to annoy him, but he came to look forward to their coming as a break in the deadly monotony of his solitude. He found that by stroking them and talking to them in low tones he could quiet their restless writhing. And after repeated recurrences of their visits he was confident that one of them had become almost a pet.

Of course in the darkness he could not differentiate one snake from another, but always he was awakened by the nose of one pounding gently upon his chest, and when he took it in his hands and stroked it, it made no effort to escape; nor ever again did one of them strike him with its fangs after that first orgy of madness, during which he had thought and hoped that the reptiles were venomous.

It took him a long time to find the opening

through which the reptiles found ingress to his cell, but at length, after diligent search, he discovered an aperture about eight inches in diameter, some three feet above the floor. Its sides were worn smooth by the countless passings of scaly bodies. He inserted his hand in the opening and feeling around discovered that the wall at this point was about a foot in thickness, and when he inserted his arm to the shoulder he could feel nothing in any direction beyond the wall. Perhaps there was another chamber there—another cell like his—or possibly the aperture opened into a deep pit that was filled with snakes. He thought of many explanations and the more he thought the more anxious he became to solve the riddle of the mysterious space beyond his cell. Thus did his mind occupy itself with trivial things, and the loneliness and the darkness and the silence exaggerated the importance of the matter beyond all reason until it became an obsession with him. During all his waking hours he thought about that hole in the wall and what lay beyond in the Stygian darkness which his eyes could not penetrate. He questioned the snake that rapped upon his chest, but it did not answer him and then he went to the hole in the wall and asked the hole. And he was on the point of becoming angry when it did not reply when his mind suddenly caught itself, and with a shudder he turned away, realizing that this way led to madness and that he must, above all else, remain master of his mind.

But still he did not abandon his speculation; only now he conducted it with reason and sanity, and at last he hit upon a shrewd plan.

When next his food was brought and he had devoured it he took the iron cover from the iron pot,
which had contained it, and hurled it to the stone
flagging of his cell, where it broke into several
pieces. One of these was long and slender and had
a sharp point, which was what he had hoped he
would find in the débris of the broken cover. This
piece he kept; the others he put back into the pot
and then he went to the aperture in the wall and
commenced to scratch, slowly, slowly, slowly at the
hard mortar in which the stones around the hole
were set.

He ate and slept many times before his labor
was rewarded by the loosening of a single stone
next to the hole. And again he ate and slept many
times before a second stone was removed.

How long he worked at this he did not know, but
the time passed more quickly now and his mind was
so engrossed with his labors that he was almost
happy.

During this time he did not neglect his exercising,
but he slept less often. When the snakes came he
had to stop his work, for they were continually passing in and out through the hole.

He wished that he knew how the food was
brought to his cell, that he might know if there was
danger that those who brought it could hear him
scraping at the mortar in the wall, but as he never
heard the food brought he hoped that those who
brought it could not hear him and he was quite
sure that they could not see him.

And so he worked on unceasingly until at last he
had scratched away an opening large enough to ad-

mit his body, and then for a long time he sat before it, waiting, seeking to assure himself that he was master of his mind, for in this eternal night of solitude that had been his existence for how long he could not even guess, he realized that this adventure which he was facing had assumed such momentous proportions that once more he felt himself upon the brink of madness. And now he wanted to make sure that no matter what lay beyond that aperture he could meet it with calm nerves and a serene and sane mind, for he could not help but realize that keen disappointment might be lying in wait for him, since during all the long periods of his scratching and scraping since he had discovered the hole through which the snakes came into his cell he had realized that a hope of escape was the foundation of the desire that prompted him to prosecute the work. And though he expected to be disappointed he knew how cruel would be the blow when it fell.

With a touch that was almost a caress he let his fingers run slowly over the rough edges of the enlarged aperture. He inserted his head and shoulders into it and reached far out upon the other side, groping with a hand that found nothing, searching with eyes that saw nothing, and then he drew himself back into his dungeon and walked to its far end and sat down upon the floor and leaned back against the wall and waited—waited because he did not dare to pass that aperture to face some new discouragement.

It took him a long time to master himself, and then he waited again. But this time, after reasoned consideration of the matter that filled his mind.

He would wait until they brought his food and had taken away the empty receptacle—that he might be given a longer interval before possible discovery of his absence, in the event he did not return to his cell. And though he went often to the corner where the food was ordinarily deposited, it seemed an eternity before he found it there. And after he had eaten it, another eternity before the receptacle was taken away; but at last it was removed. And once again he crossed his cell and stood before the opening that led he knew not where.

This time he did not hesitate. He was master of his mind and nerves.

One after the other he put his feet through the aperture until he sat with his legs both upon the far side of the wall. Then, turning on his stomach, he started to lower himself, because he did not know where the floor might be, but he found it immediately, on the same level as his own. And an instant later he stood erect and if not free, at least no longer a prisoner within his own cell.

Cautiously he groped about him in the darkness, feeling his way a few inches at a time. This cell, he discovered, was much narrower than his own, but it was very long. By extending his hands in both directions he could touch both walls, and thus he advanced, placing a foot cautiously to feel each step before he took it.

He had brought with him from his cell the iron sliver that he had broken from the cover of the pot and with which he had scratched himself thus far toward freedom. And the possession of this bit of iron imparted to him a certain sense of security, since it meant that he was not entirely unarmed.

Presently, as he advanced, he became convinced that he was in a long corridor. One foot came in contact with a rough substance directly in the center of the tunnel. He took his hands from the walls and groped in front of him.

It was a rough-coated cylinder about eight inches in diameter that rose directly upward from the center of the tunnel, and his fingers quickly told him that it was the trunk of a tree with the bark still on, though worn off in patches.

Passing this column, which he guessed to be a support for a weak section of the roof of the tunnel, he continued on, but he had taken but a couple of steps when he came to a blank wall—the tunnel had come to an abrupt end.

Tanar's heart sank within him. His hopes had been rising with each forward step and now they were suddenly dashed to despair. Again and again his fingers ran over the cold wall that had halted his advance toward hoped for freedom, but there was no sign of break or crevice, and slowly he turned back toward his cell, passing the wooden column and retracing his steps in utter dejection. But as he moved sadly along he mustered all his spiritual forces, determined not to let this expected disappointment crush him. He would go back to his cell, but he would still continue to use the tunnel. It would be a respite from the monotony of his own four walls. It would extend the distance that he might walk and after all he would make it worth the effort that had been necessary to gain ingress to it.

Back in his own cell again he lay down to sleep, for he had denied himself sleep a great deal of late that he might prosecute the work upon which he had been engaged. When he awoke the snakes were with him again and his friend was tapping gently on his chest, and once again he took up the dull monotony of his existence, altered only by regular excursions into his new found domain, the black interior of which he came to know as well as he did his own cell, so that he walked briskly from the hole he had made to the wooden column at the far end of the tunnel, passed around it and walked back again at a brisk gait and with as much assurance as though he could see plainly, for he had counted the paces from one end to the other so many times that he knew to an instant when he had covered the distance from one extremity to the other.

He ate; he slept; he exercised; he played with his slimy, reptilian companion; and he paced the narrow tunnel of his discovery. And often when he passed around the wooden column at its far end, he speculated upon the real purpose of it.

Once he went to sleep in his own cell thinking about it, and when he awoke to the gentle tapping of the snake's snout upon his breast he sat up so suddenly that the reptile fell hissing to the flagging, for clear and sharp upon the threshold of his awakening mind stood an idea—a wonderful idea —why had he not thought of it before?

Excitedly he hastened to the opening leading into

the tunnel. Snakes were passing through it, but he fought for precedence with the reptilian horde and tumbled through head first upon a bed of hissing snakes. Scrambling to his feet he almost ran the length of the corridor until his outstretched hands came in contact with the rough bole of the tree. There he stood quite some time, trembling like a leaf, and then, encircling the column with his arms and legs, he started to climb slowly and deliberately aloft. This was the idea that had seized him in its compelling grip upon his awakening.

Upward through the darkness he went, and pausing now and then to grope about with his hands, he found that the tree trunk ran up the center of a narrow, circular shaft.

He climbed slowly upward and at a distance of about thirty feet above the floor of the tunnel, his head struck stone. Feeling upward with one hand he discovered that the tree was set in mortar in the ceiling above him.

This could not be the end! What reason could there be for a tunnel and a shaft that led nowhere? He groped through the darkness in all directions with his hand and he was rewarded by finding an opening in the side of the shaft about six feet below the ceiling. Quitting the bole of the tree he climbed into the opening in the wall of the shaft, and here he found himself in another tunnel, lower and narrower than that at the base of the shaft. It was still dark, so that he was compelled to advance as slowly and with as great caution as he had upon that occasion when he first explored his tunnel below.

He advanced but a short distance when the tunnel turned abruptly to the right, and ahead of him, beyond the turn, he saw a ray of light!

A condemned man snatched from the jaws of death could not have greeted salvation with more joyousness than Tanar of Pellucidar greeted this first slender ray of daylight that he had seen for a seeming eternity. It shone dimly through a tiny crevice, but it was light, the light of heaven that he had never expected to again behold.

Enraptured, he walked slowly toward it, and as he reached it his hand came in contact with rough, unpainted boards that blocked his way. It was through a tiny crack between two of these boards that the light was filtering.

As dim as the light was it hurt his eyes, so long unaccustomed to light of any kind. But by turning them away so that the light did not shine directly into them, he finally became accustomed to it, and when he did he discovered that as small as the aperture was through which the light came it let in sufficient to dispel the utter darkness of the interior of the tunnel and he also discovered that he could discern objects. He could see the stone walls on either side of the tunnel, and by looking closely he could see the boards that formed the obstacle that barred his further progress. And as he examined them he discovered that at one side there was something that resembled a latch, an invention of which he had been entirely ignorant before he had come aboard the Korsar ship upon which he had been made prisoner, for in Sari there are no locks nor latches.

But he knew the thing for what it was and it told him that the boards before him formed a door, which opened into light and toward liberty, but what lay immediately beyond?

He clinched his ear to the door and listened, but he heard no sound. Then very carefully he examined the latch, experimenting with it until he discovered how to operate it. Steadying his nerves, he pushed gently upon the rough planks. As they swung away from him slowly a flood of light rushed into the first narrow crack, and Tanar covered his eyes with his hands and turned away, realizing that he must become accustomed to this light slowly and gradually, or he might be permanently blinded.

With closed eyes he listened at the crack, but could hear nothing. And then with utmost care he started to accustom his eyes to the light, but it was long before he could stand the full glare that came through even this tiny crack.

When he could stand the light without pain he opened the door a little further and looked out. Just beyond the door lay a fairly large room, in which wicker hampers, iron and earthen receptacles and bundles sewed up in hides littered the floor and were piled high against the walls. Everything seemed covered with dust and cobwebs and there was no sign of a human being about.

Pushing the door open still further Tanar stepped from the tunnel into the apartment and looked about him. Everywhere the room was a litter of bundles and packages with articles of clothing strewn about, together with various fittings for ships, bales of hide and numerous weapons.

The thick coating of dust upon everything suggested to the Sarian that the room had not been visited lately.

For a moment he stood with his hand still on the open door and as he started to step into the room his hand stuck for an instant where he had grasped the rough boards. Looking at his fingers to ascertain the cause he discovered that they were covered with sticky pitch. It was his left hand and when he tried to rub the pitch from it he found that it was almost impossible to do so.

As he moved around the room examining the contents everything that he touched with his left hand stuck to it—it was annoying, but unavoidable.

An inspection of the room revealed several windows along one side and a door at one end.

The door was equipped with a latch similar to that through which he had just passed and which was made to open from the outside with a key, but which could be operated by hand from the inside. It was a very crude and simple affair, and for that Tanar would have been grateful had he known how intricate locks may be made.

Lifting the catch Tanar pushed the door slightly ajar and before him he saw a long corridor, lighted by windows upon one side and with doors opening from it upon the other. As he looked a Korsar came from one of the doorways and, turning, walked down the corridor away from him and a moment later a woman emerged from another doorway, and then he saw other people at the far end of the corridor. Quickly Tanar of Pellucidar closed and latched the door.

Here was no avenue of escape. Were he back in his dark cell he could not have been cut off more effectually from the outer world than he was in this apartment at the far end of a corridor constantly used by Korsars; for with his smooth face and his naked body, he would be recognized and seized the instant that he stepped from the room. But Tanar was far from being overwhelmed by discouragement. Already he had come much further on the road to escape than he had previously dreamed could be possible and not only this thought heartened him, but even more the effect of daylight, which had for so long been denied him. He had felt his spirit and his courage expand beneath the beneficent influence of the light of the noonday sun, so that he felt ready for any emergency that might confront him.

Turning back once more into the room he searched it carefully for some other avenue of escape. He went to the windows and found that they overlooked the garden of The Cid, but there were many people there, too, in that part of the garden close to the palace. The trees cut off his view of the far end from which he had helped Stellara and Gura to escape, but he guessed that there were few, if any, people there, though to reach it would be a difficult procedure from the windows of this storeroom.

To his left, near the opposite side of the garden, he could see that the trees grew closely together and extended thus apparently the full length of the enclosure.

If those trees had been upon this side of the

garden he guessed that he might have found a way to escape; at least as far as the gate in the garden wall close to the barracks, but they were not and so he must abandon thought of them.

There seemed, therefore, no other avenue of escape than the corridor into which he had just looked; nor could he remain indefinitely in this chamber where there was neither food nor water and with a steadily increasing danger that his absence from the dungeon would be discovered when they found that he did not consume the food they brought him.

Seating himself upon a bale of hide Tanar gave himself over to contemplation of his predicament and as he studied the matter his eyes fell upon some of the loose clothing strewn about the room. There he saw the shorts and shirts of Korsar, the gay sashes and head handkerchiefs, the wide topped boots, and with a half smile upon his lips he gathered such of them as he required, shook the dust from them and clothed himself after the manner of a Korsar. He needed no mirror though to know that his smooth face would betray him.

He selected pistols, a dirk and a cutlass, but he could find neither powder nor balls for his firearms.

Thus arrayed and armed he surveyed himself as best he might without a mirror. "If I could keep my back toward all Korsar," he mused, "I might escape with ease for I warrant I look as much a Korsar as any of them from the rear, but unless I can grow bushy whiskers I shall not deceive anyone."

As he sat musing thus he became aware suddenly

of voices raised in altercation just outside the door of the storeroom. One was a man's voice; the other a woman's.

"And if you won't have me," growled the man, "I'll take you."

Tanar could not hear the woman's reply, though he heard her speak and knew from her voice that it was a woman.

"What do I care for The Cid?" cried the man. "I am as powerful in Korsar as he. I could take the throne and be Cid myself, if I chose."

Again Tanar heard the woman speak.

"If you do I'll choke the wind out of you," threatened the man. "Come in here where we can talk better. Then you can yell all you want for no one can hear you."

Tanar heard the man insert a key in the lock and as he did so the Pellucidarian sought a hiding place behind a pile of wicker hampers.

"And after you get out of this room," continued the man, "there will be nothing left for you to yell about."

"I have told you right along," said the woman, "that I would rather kill myself than mate with you, but if you take me by force I shall still kill myself, but I shall kill you first."

The heart of Tanar of Pellucidar leaped in his breast when he heard that voice. His fingers closed upon the hilt of the cutlass at his side, and as Bulf voiced a sneering laugh in answer to the girl's threat, the Sarian leaped from his concealment, a naked blade shining in his right hand.

At the sound behind him Bulf wheeled about and

for an instant he did not recognize the Sarian in the Korsar garb, but Stellara did and she voiced a cry of mingled surprise and joy.

"Tanar!" she cried. "My Tanar!"

As the Sarian rushed him Bulf fell back, drawing his cutlass as he retreated. Tanar saw that he was making for the door leading into the corridor and he rushed at the man to engage him before he could escape, so that Bulf was forced to stand and defend himself.

"Stand back," cried Bulf, "or you shall die for this," but Tanar of Pellucidar only laughed in his face, as he swung a wicked blow at the man's head, which Bulf but barely parried, and then they were at one another like two wild beasts.

Tanar drew first blood from a slight gash in Bulf's shoulder and then the fellow yelled for help.

"You said that no one could hear Stellara's cries for help from this apartment," taunted Tanar, "so why do you think that they can hear yours?"

"Let me out of here," cried Bulf. "Let me out and I will give you your freedom." But Tanar rushed him into a corner and the sharp edge of his cutlass sheared an ear from Bulf's head.

"Help!" shrieked the Korsar. "Help! It is Bulf. The Sarian is killing me."

Fearful that his loud cries might reach the corridor beyond and attract attention, Tanar increased the fury of his assault. He beat down the Korsar's guard. He swung his cutlass in one terrible circle that clove Bulf's ugly skull to the bridge of his nose, and with a gurgling gasp the great brute lunged forward upon his face. And Tanar of Pellucidar turned and took Stellara in his arms.

"Thank God," he said, "that I was in time."

"It must have been God Himself who led you to this room," said the girl. "I thought you dead. They told me that you were dead."

"No," said Tanar. "They put me in a dark dungeon beneath the palace, where I was condemned to remain for life."

"And you have been so near me all this time," said Stellara, "and I thought that you were dead."

"For a long time I thought that I was worse than dead," replied the man. "Darkness, solitude and silence—God! That is worse than death."

"And yet you escaped!" The girl's voice was filled with awe.

"It was because of you that I escaped," said Tanar. "Thoughts of you kept me from going mad—thought and hope urged me on to seek some avenue of escape. Never again as long as life is in me shall I feel that there can be any situation that is entirely hopeless after what I have passed through."

Stellara shook her head. "Your hope will have to be strong, dear heart, against the discouragement that you must face in seeking a way out of the palace of The Cid and the city of Korsar."

"I have come this far," replied Tanar. "Already have I achieved the impossible. Why should I doubt my ability to wrest freedom for you and for me from whatever fate holds in store for us?"

"You cannot pass them with that smooth face,

Tanar," said the girl, sadly. "Ah, if you only had Bulf's whiskers," and she glanced down at the corpse of the fallen man.

Tanar turned, too, and looked down at Bulf, where he lay in a pool of blood upon the floor. And then quickly he faced Stellara. "Why not?" he cried. "Why not?"

Chapter Seventeen

DOWN TO THE SEA

WHAT do you mean?" demanded Stellara.
"Wait and you shall see," replied Tanar,
and drawing his dirk he stooped and turned Bulf
over upon his back. Then with the razor-sharp
blade of his weapon he commenced to hack off the
bushy, black beard of the dead Korsar, while Stellara looked on in questioning wonder.

Spreading Bulf's headcloth flat upon the floor,
Tanar deposited upon it the hair that he cut from
the man's face, and when he had completed his
grewsome tonsorial effort he folded the hair into
the handkerchief, and, rising, motioned for Stellara
to follow him.

Going to the door that led into the tunnel through
which he had escaped from the dungeon, Tanar
opened it, and, smearing his fingers with the pitch
that exuded from the boards upon the inside of
the door, he smeared some of it upon the side of
his face and then turned to Stellara.

"Put this hair upon my face in as natural a way
as you can. You have lived among them all your
life, so you should know well how a Korsar's beard
should look."

Horrible as the plan seemed and though she

shrank from touching the hair of the dead man, Stellara steeled herself and did as Tanar bid. Little by little, patch by patch, Tanar applied pitch to his face and Stellara placed the hair upon it until presently only the eyes and nose of the Sarian remained exposed. The expression of the former were altered by increasing the size and bushiness of the eyebrows with shreds of Bulf's beard that had been left over, and then Tanar smeared his nose with some of Bulf's blood, for many of the Korsars had large, red noses. Then Stellara stood away and surveyed him critically. "Your own mother would not know you," she said.

"Do you think I can pass as a Korsar?" he asked.

"No one will suspect, unless they question you closely as you leave the palace."

"We are going together," said Tanar.

"But how?" asked Stellara.

"I have been thinking of another plan," he said. "I noticed when I was living in the barracks that sailors going toward the river had no difficulty in passing through the gate leaving the palace. In fact, it is always much easier to leave the palace than to enter it. On many occasions I have heard them say merely that they were going to their ships. We can do the same."

"Do I look like a Korsar sailor?" demanded Stellara.

"You will when I get through with you," said Tanar, with a grin.

"What do you mean?"

"There is Korsar clothing here," said Tanar;

"enough to outfit a dozen and there is still plenty of hair on Bulf's head."

The girl drew back with a shudder. "Oh, Tanar! You cannot mean that."

"What other way is there?" he demanded. "If we can escape together is it not worth any price that we might have to pay?"

"You are right," she said. "I will do it."

When Tanar completed his work upon her, Stellara had been transformed into a bearded Korsar, but the best that he could do in the way of disguise failed to entirely hide the contours of her hips and breasts.

"I am afraid they will suspect," he said. "Your figure is too feminine for shorts and a shirt to hide it."

"Wait," exclaimed Stellara. "Sometimes the sailors, when they are going on long voyages, wear cloaks, which they use to sleep in if the nights are cool. Let us see if we can find such a one here."

"Yes, I saw one," replied Tanar, and crossing the room he returned with a cloak made of wide striped goods. "That will give you greater height," he said. But when they draped it about her, her hips were still too much in evidence.

"Build out my shoulders," suggested Stellara, and with scarfs and handkerchiefs the Sarian built the girl's shoulders out so that the cloak hung straight and she resembled a short, stocky man, more than a slender, well-formed girl.

"Now we are ready," said the Sarian. Stellara pointed to the body of Bulf.

"We cannot leave that lying there," she said. "Someone may come to this room and discover it and when they do every man in the palace—yes, even in the entire city—will be arrested and questioned."

Tanar looked about the room and then he seized the corpse of Bulf and dragged it into a far corner, after which he piled bundles of hides and baskets upon it until it was entirely concealed, and over the blood stains upon the floor he dragged other bales and baskets until all signs of the duel had been erased or hidden.

"And now," he said, "is as good a time as another to put our disguises to the test." Together they approached the door. "You know the least frequented passages to the garden," said Tanar. "Let us make our way from the palace through the garden to the gate that gave us escape before."

"Then follow me," replied Stellara, as Tanar opened the door and the two stepped out into the corridor beyond. It was empty. Tanar closed the door behind him, and Stellara led the way down the passage.

They had proceeded but a short distance when they heard a man's voice in an apartment to the left.

"Where is she?" he demanded.

"I do not know," replied a woman's voice. "She was here but a moment ago and Bulf was with her."

"Find them and lose no time about it," commanded the man, sternly. And he stepped from the apartment just as Tanar and Stellara were approaching.

It was The Cid. Stellara's heart stopped beating as the Korsar ruler looked into the faces of Tanar and herself.

"Who are you?" demanded The Cid.

"We are sailors," said Tanar, quickly, before Stellara could reply.

"What are you doing here in my palace?" demanded the Korsar ruler.

"We were sent here with packages to the storeroom," replied Tanar, "and we are but now returning to our ship."

"Well, be quick about it. I do not like your looks," growled The Cid as he stamped off down the corridor ahead of them.

Tanar saw Stellara sway and he stepped to her side and supported her, but she quickly gained possession of herself, and an instant later turned to the right and led Tanar through a doorway into the garden.

"God!" whispered the man, as they walked side by side after quitting the building. "If The Cid did not know you, then your disguise must be perfect."

Stellara shook her head for even as yet she could not control her voice to speak, following the terror induced by her encounter with The Cid.

There were a number of men and women in the garden close to the palace. Some of these scrutinized them casually, but they passed by in safety and a moment later the gravel walk they were following wound through dense shrubbery that hid them from view and then they were at the doorway in the garden wall.

Again fortune favored them here and they passed out into the barracks yards without being noticed.

Electing to try the main gate because of the greater number of people who passed to and fro through it, Tanar turned to the right, passed along the full length of the barracks past a dozen men and approached the gate with Stellara at his side.

They were almost through when a stupid looking Korsar soldier stopped them. "Who are you," he demanded, "and what business takes you from the palace?"

"We are sailors," replied Tanar. "We are going to our ship."

"What were you doing in the palace?" demanded the man.

"We took packages there from the captain of the ship to The Cid's storeroom," explained the Sarian.

"I do not like the looks of you," said the man. "I have never seen either one of you before."

"We have been away upon a long cruise," replied Tanar.

"Wait here until the captain of the gate returns," said the man. "He will wish to question you."

The Sarian's heart sank. "If we are late in returning to our ship, we shall be punished," said he.

"That is nothing to me," replied the soldier.

Stellara reached inside her cloak and beneath the man's shorts that covered her own apparel and searched until she found a pouch that was attached to her girdle. From this she drew something which she slipped into Tanar's hands. He understood immediately, and stepping close to the soldier he pressed two pieces of gold into the fellow's palm. "It will go very hard with us if we are late," he said.

The man felt the cool gold within his palm. "Very well," he said, gruffly, "go on about your business, and be quick about it."

Without waiting for a second invitation Tanar and Stellara merged with the crowd upon the Korsar street. Nor did either speak, and it is possible that Stellara did not even breathe until they had left the palace gate well behind.

"And where now?" she asked at last.

"We are going to sea," replied the man.

"In a Korsar ship?" she demanded.

"In a Korsar boat," he replied. "We are going fishing."

Along the banks of the river were moored many craft, but when Tanar saw how many men were on or around them he realized that the plan he had chosen, which contemplated stealing a fishing boat, most probably would end disastrously, and he explained his doubts to Stellara.

"We could never do it," she said. "Stealing a boat is considered the most heinous crime that one can commit in Korsar, and if the owner of a boat is not aboard it you may rest assured that some of his friends are watching it for him, even though there is little likelihood that anyone will attempt to steal it since the penalty is death."

Tanar shook his head. "Then we shall have to risk passing through the entire city of Korsar," he said, "and going out into the open country without any reasonable excuse in the event that we are questioned."

"We might buy a boat," suggested Stellara.

"I have no money," said Tanar.

"I have," replied the girl. "The Cid has always kept me well supplied with gold." Once more she reached into her pouch and drew forth a handful of gold pieces. "Here," she said, "take these. If they are not enough you can ask me for more, but I think that you can buy a boat for half that sum."

Questioning the first man that he approached at the river side, Tanar learned that there was a small fishing boat for sale a short way down the river, and it was not long before they had found its owner and consummated the purchase.

As they pushed off into the current and floated down stream, Tanar became conscious of a sudden conviction that his escape from Korsar had been effected too easily; that there must be something wrong, that either he was dreaming or else disaster and recapture lay just ahead.

Borne down toward the sea by the slow current of the river, Tanar wielded a single oar, paddlewise from the stern, to keep the boat out in the channel and its bow in the right direction, for he did not wish to make sail under the eyes of Korsar sailors and fishermen, as he was well aware that he could not do so without attracting attention by his bungling to his evident inexperience and thus casting suspicion upon them.

Slowly the boat drew away from the city and from the Korsar raiders anchored in mid-stream and then, at last, he felt that it would be safe to hoist the sail and take advantage of the land breeze that was blowing.

With Stellara's assistance the canvas was spread and as it bellied to the wind the craft bore forward with accelerated speed, and then behind them they heard shouts and, turning, saw three boats speeding toward them.

Across the waters came commands for them to lay to.

The pursuing boats, which had set out under sail and had already acquired considerable momentum, appeared to be rapidly overhauling the smaller craft. But presently, as the speed of the latter increased, the distance between them seemed not to vary.

The shouts of the pursuers had attracted the attention of the sailors on board the anchored raiders, and presently Tanar and Stellara heard the deep boom of a cannon and a heavy shot struck the water just off their starboard bow.

Tanar shook his head. "That is too close," he said. "I had better come about."

"Why?" demanded Stellara.

"I do not mind risking capture," he said, "because in that event no harm will befall you when they discover your identity, but I cannot risk the cannon shots for if one of them strikes us, you will be killed."

"Do not come about," cried the girl. "I would rather die here with you than be captured, for capture would mean death for you and then I should not care to live. Keep on, Tanar, we may outdistance them yet. And as for their cannon shots, a small, moving boat like this is a difficult target and their marksmanship is none too good."

Again the cannon boomed and this time the ball passed over them and struck the water just beyond.

"They are getting our range," said Tanar.

The girl moved close to his side, where he sat by the tiller. "Put your arm around me, Tanar," she said. "If we must die, let us die together."

The Sarian encircled her with his free arm and drew her close to him, and an instant later there was a terrific explosion from the direction of the raider that had been firing on them. Turning quickly toward the ship, they saw what had happened—an overcharged cannon had exploded.

"They were too anxious," said Tanar.

It was some time before another shot was fired and this one fell far astern, but the pursuing boats were clinging tenaciously to their wake.

"They are not gaining," said Stellara.

"No," said Tanar, "and neither are we."

"But I think we shall after we reach the open sea," said the girl. "We shall get more wind there and this boat is lighter and speedier than theirs. Fate smiled upon us when it led us to this boat rather than to a larger one."

As they approached the sea their pursuers, evidently fearing precisely what Stellara had suggested, opened fire upon them with harquebuses and pistols. Occasionally a missile would come dangerously close, but the range was just a little too great for their primitive weapons and poor powder.

On they sailed out into the open Korsar Az,

which stretched onward and upward into the concealing mist of the distance. Upon their left the sea ran inward forming a great bay, while almost directly ahead of them, though at so great a distance that it was barely discernible, rose the dim outlines of a headland, and toward this Tanar held his course.

The chase had settled down into a dogged test of endurance. It was evident that the Korsars had no intention of giving up their prey even though the pursuit led to the opposite shore of the Korsar Az, and it was equally evident that Tanar entertained no thought of surrender.

On and on they sped, the pursued and the pursuers. Slowly the headland took shape before them, and later a great forest was visible to the left of it —a forest that ran down almost to the sea.

"You are making for land?" asked Stellara.

"Yes," replied the Sarian. "We have neither food nor water and if we had I am not sufficiently a sailor to risk navigating this craft across the Korsar Az."

"But if we take to the land, they will be able to trail us," said the girl.

"You forget the trees, Stellara," the man reminded her.

"Yes, the trees," she cried. "I had forgotten. If we can reach the trees I believe that we shall be safe."

As they approached the shore inside the headland, they saw great combing rollers breaking among the rocks and the angry, sullen boom of the sea came back to their ears.

"No boat can live in that," said Stellara.

Tanar glanced up and down the shore-line as far as he could see and then he turned and let his eyes rest sadly upon his companion.

"It looks hopeless," he said. "If we had time to make the search we might find a safer landing place, but within sight of us one place seems to be as good as another."

"Or as bad," said Stellara.

"It cannot be helped," said the Sarian. "To beat back now around that promontory in an attempt to gain the open sea again, would so delay us that we should be overtaken and captured. We must take our chances in the surf, or turn about and give up."

Behind them their pursuers had come about and were waiting, rising and falling upon the great billows.

"They think that they have us," said Stellara. "They believe that we shall tack here and make a run for the open sea around the end of that promontory, and they are ready to head us off."

Tanar held the boat's nose straight for the shore-line. Beyond the angry surf he could see a sandy beach, but between lay a barrier of rock upon which the waves broke, hurling their spume far into the air.

"Look!" exclaimed Stellara, as the boat raced toward the smother of boiling water. "Look! There! Right ahead! There may be a way yet!"

"I have been watching that place," said Tanar. "I have been holding her straight for it, and if it is a break in the rocky wall we shall soon know it, and if it is not——"

The Sarian glanced back in the direction of the Korsars' boats and saw that they were again in pursuit, for by this time it must have become evident to them that their quarry was throwing itself upon the rocky shore-line in desperation rather than to risk capture by turning again toward the open sea.

Every inch of sail was spread upon the little craft and the taut, bellowing canvas strained upon the cordage until it hummed, as the boat sped straight for the rocks dead ahead.

Tanar and Stellara crouched in the stern, the man's left arm pressing the girl protectingly to his side. With grim fascination they watched the bowsprit rise and fall as it rushed straight toward what seemed must be inevitable disaster.

They were there! The sea lifted them high in the air and launched them forward upon the rocks. To the right a jagged finger of granite broke through the smother of spume. To the left the sleek, water-worn side of a huge boulder revealed itself for an instant as they sped past. The boat grated and rasped upon a sunken rock, slid over and raced toward the sandy beach.

Tanar whipped out his dirk and slashed the halyards, bringing the sail down as the boat's keel touched the sand. Then, seizing Stellara in his arms, he leaped into the shallow water and hastened up the shore.

Pausing, they looked back toward the pursuing Korsars and to their astonishment saw that all three boats were making swiftly toward the rocky shore.

"They dare not go back without us," said Stellara, "or they would never risk that surf."

"The Cid must have guessed our identity, then, when a search failed to reveal you," said Tanar.

"It may also be that they discovered your absence from the dungeon, and coupling this with the fact that I, too, was missing, someone guessed the identity of the two sailors who sought to pass through the gate and who paid gold for a small boat at the river," suggested Stellara.

"There goes one of them on the rocks," cried Tanar, as the leading boat disappeared in a smother of water.

The second boat shared the same fate as its predecessor, but the third rode through the same opening that had carried Tanar and Stellara to the safety of the beach and as it did the two fugitives turned and ran toward the forest.

Behind them raced a dozen Korsars and amidst the crack of pistols and harquebuses Tanar and Stellara disappeared within the dark shadows of the primeval forest.

The story of their long and arduous journey through unknown lands to the kingdom of Sari would be replete with interest, excitement and adventure, but it is no part of this story.

It is enough to say that they arrived at Sari shortly before Ja and Gura made their appearance, the latter having been delayed by adventures that had almost cost them their lives.

The people of Sari welcomed the Amiocapian mate that the son of Ghak had brought back to his own country. And Gura they accepted, too, because she had befriended Tanar, though the young men accepted her for herself and many were the trophies that were laid before the hut of the beautiful Himean maiden. But she repulsed them all for in her heart she held a secret love that she had never divulged, but which, perhaps, Stellara had guessed and which may have accounted for the tender solicitude which the Amiocapian maid revealed for her Himean sister.

CONCLUSION

As Perry neared the end of the story of Tanar of Pellucidar, the sending became weaker and weaker until it died out entirely, and Jason Gridley could hear no more.

He turned to me. "I think Perry had something more to say," he said. "He was trying to tell us something. He was trying to ask something."

"Jason," I said, reproachfully, "didn't you tell me that the story of the inner world is perfectly ridiculous; that there could be no such place peopled by strange reptiles and men of the stone age? Didn't you insist that there is no Emperor of Pellucidar?"

"Tut-tut," he said. "I apologize. I am sorry. But that is past. The question now is what can we do."

"About what?" I asked.

"Do you not realize that David Innes lies a prisoner in a dark dungeon beneath the palace of

The Cid of Korsar?" he demanded with more excitement than I have ever known Jason Gridley to exhibit.

"Well, what of it?" I demanded. "I am sorry, of course; but what in the world can we do to help him?"

"We can do a lot," said Jason Gridley, determinedly.

I must confess that as I looked at him I felt considerable solicitude for the state of his mind for he was evidently laboring under great excitement.

"Think of it!" he cried. "Think of that poor devil buried there in utter darkness, silence, solitude —and with those snakes! God!" he shuddered. "Snakes crawling all over him, winding about his arms and his legs and his body, creeping across his face as he sleeps, and nothing else to break the monotony—no human voice, the song of no bird, no ray of sunlight. Something must be done. He must be saved."

"But who is going to do it?" I asked.

"I am!" replied Jason Gridley.

The End

In the Bison Frontiers of Imagination series

University of Nebraska Press

Also of Interest by Edgar Rice Burroughs:

AT THE EARTH'S CORE
Introduction by Gregory A. Benford
Afterword by Phillip R. Burger

Five hundred miles beneath the earth's surface lies a timeless world of eternal daylight, prehistoric beasts, and primeval peoples—Pellucidar. David Innes and Abner Perry break through into this fantastic world, and their ensuing struggle to unite the human communities and overthrow the Mahars is a thrilling tale of conquest, deceit, and wonder.

ISBN: 0-8032-6174-8; 978-0-8032-6174-7 (paper)

PELLUCIDAR
Illustrated by J. Allen St. John
Introduction by Jack McDevitt
Afterword by Phillip R. Burger

When American explorer David Innes first discovered Pellucidar, he fell under the spell of the strange world, earning the respect of many, the hatred of a few, and the love of the beautiful Dian. Torn from her arms by trickery, Innes vows revenge and returns to the Inner World to seek his lost love.

ISBN: 0-8032-6204-3; 978-0-8032-6204-1 (paper)

THE ETERNAL SAVAGE
Nu of the Neocene
Introduction by Tom Deitz
Illustrated by Thomas L. Floyd

Time travel, a millennium-spanning romance, and rousing action in modern African jungles and the prehistoric wilderness ignite this classic adventure tale. Set in both a terrifyingly dangerous primeval setting and the beloved world of Tarzan, *The Eternal Savage* reveals whether eternal love is strong enough to triumph over undying adversity.

ISBN: 0-8032-6216-7; 978-0-8032-6216-4 (paper)

Order online at www.nebraskapress.unl.edu or call 1-800-755-1105.
Mention the code "BOFOX" to receive a 20% discount.